The Netherworlds

Curse of Fate

The Netherworlds

Curse of Fate

Kaylin R Boyd

Boyd's
Books

The Netherworlds: Curse of Fate
Copyright © 2022 by Kaylin R. Boyd. All rights reserved.

Published by Boyd's Books, LLC.
First Printing, 2022
Cover and illustration designed by Josh Spellman

Boyd's Books, LLC.
7389 E. IN-46
Bloomington, IN 47401

979-8-9880716-0-0 Ebook
979-8-9880716-1-7 Paperback
979-8-9880716-2-4 Hardback

This book is dedicated to
my sister, Raven, and all the voices in my head.
I would not be here without you guys.

1

Once upon a time...

Sekhmet, goddess of war and fertility, coupled with Death and became heavy with child. She kept her future son a secret from all, including Death himself, fearing the worst of what the gods could do with such a babe.

The Fates, however, saw the result of this union and foretold what would become of her son. Just as she feared, he would become the most powerful god in existence.

They told her she must rid herself of the unborn child, so she pleaded and threatened with the might and mane of a mother lion to keep her son. They permitted her to keep the child as long as she did not raise him as a god, but as a nameless servant in her temple. For if she gave him a name or told him of his true identity, he would be forced to endure the hellish prison known as Tartarus. To this she agreed, and when he was born, her loyal priests pried him from her grasp as she had requested.

She watched with hatred and envy as her loyal servants and worshipers swaddled and breastfed him. The son of Death and Sekhmet was brought up amongst the other worshipers. He was schooled along with the sons and daughters of the priests and priestesses, and was educated to become a priest himself.

Each day, he grew more and more beautiful, and she told him that he was her favorite kitten, but it must be a secret. She could not tell him the truth in fear of what the Fates would do.

In secret, she worshiped him and treated him to the delicacies, oils, and scented smokes meant only for the gods. Upon entering manhood, he confessed to her a love that ran deeper than his priestly devotion - true love.

Sekhmet's heart broke, and she banished him from the temple, and from the city itself, hoping that would keep her son safe.

Alone, the young, nameless priest wandered the desert.

He was dying of thirst and exhaustion, but he trudged on across the sand. The desert was a sea of rolling dunes for as far as the eye could see. The sky was an omnipresent blue, caging down around him. There was no end to this valley of the shadow of death. He walked without comfort, without water. Exiled from the protection of the goddess, he was in the presence of unknown enemies. He feared no evil, only because he did not know that it was there.

After a time, he lifted his eyes up from his blistered feet and saw a mirage in the scorching haze.

Inside the mirage there was green grass and shady palms. There was a lagoon of still, crystalline water. A woman dancing inside the mirage. She moved with the ripples of the heatwaves and twisted like a cobra being charmed.

Upon seeing him, the dancing woman immediately hid from view behind a palm tree.

"How have you come to be here?" she asked.

The young priest stumbled into the mirage. "I walked. I've been wandering the desert-"

He approached the trunk of the palm and looked around it to see her, but she disappeared around to the other side, "-for what has felt like-"

Again, he moved around the trunk to see her, and she moved away, "-forever."

He reached around the palm and grabbed her arm. Spinning her like a ballerina, she fell into him.

He asked impatiently, "Can I please have a drink of water from your lagoon?"

"It is not my water to give. It is my master's." She coyly walked away.

He smiled, relieved. "Then I shall drink at my own peril."

Crouching on the bank of the lagoon, he splashed his face with the cool, clear water. "Is he fierce, your master?"

he asked.

"It is not *he* you should fear, but what he'll have *me* do to *you*... should he find you."

He barked out a laugh, and she glared.

"What makes you so mighty?" He took a drink of the water cupped in his hands.

With her chin held erect, she said, "I'm a Jinni."

He choked on the water.

"Do you still not believe me mighty?"

"N-no!" He stammered and hopped to his feet. "I have heard many tales of Jinni. Enough to know I should leave this place and should have never entered."

He hastened across the grass to exit the mirage, knowing he'd be safer in the heat of the desert rather than trapped in a mirage with a deceptive Jinni.

"A traveler of the desert could use the help of someone like me," she cooed.

He slowed to a stop, grinding his teeth at the truth she told.

Her voice was dripping with seduction. "The desert is cruel. Crueler to you than my master is to me."

"I..." He looked back at her, determined to turn down the proposal. "I have spent my life in the desert cities-"

"The cities are nothing compared to these dunes. You won't survive." She blinked her dark eyes as she sauntered up to him, beguiling him with her charm.

He pressed his lips together, then pursed them in

tantalizing thought.

"Save me from my bore of a master, and I will make you a king." She glided her hand up his chest.

He accidentally laughed aloud and said, "I have no desire to be a king."

She glared for a brief second. She hesitated. Stumbling upon her next move, her voice lost some of its silk. "Then I will make you... *comfortable*, and I shall tell you tales of my life and the mysteries of my land. I will be your companion."

The thought of food and water was a tempting offer, but from a Jinni it was a dangerous one. However, the romantic tales of a Jinni and magickal far away lands were enticing. Danger can be seductive, and he wanted to get away from what he had left behind.

"Okay," he said, to which the Jinni shrugged in disbelief.

She had started to worry this was going to be a harder sell.

He put his hand upon his hip. "So... How do I save you from your master without *him* turning you on *me*?"

"I will resist him if it comes to that," she pointed her tiny chin proudly in the air, "but, you must be quick and light of foot. He sleeps just over there." She pointed to an elaborate tent, which had not been there before. Its fabric flapped in the non-existent desert breeze.

"He keeps my prison on his finger as a ring. Take it from him, and I will be yours," she breathed.

"Only for a time," he looked down at her, "and then you shall be free."

With the heroics of youth, he slipped into the tent.

The Jinni let out a tense breath and rolled her eyes, then she sat down in the shade of a palm and happily waited for his defeat.

He walked into the tent to find not a man, but something nearly a beast. It was covered in scars, and tattoos, and piercings. The beast looked more like the legendary description of Jinn than the beautiful girl outside.

The floor of the tent was covered with gold, and armor, and bones. Thus, the very first step the nameless priest took sent a bronze helmet clattering into a gladiator shield. The priest froze, but the metallic clanking awoke the beast.

With a groan and a flat voice, the beast said, "Not this shit again." The towering creature stood.

The young priest gulped as the monster cracked his neck and knuckles. The beast mumbled and complained under his breath, and our young hero turned an ear to listen.

He asked the grumbling thing before him, "What's that now?"

The monster gave him an exhausted look. "That damn Jinni!" He pointed to the tent flaps, beyond which, she waited. "Dude, I wished to be an unbeatable champion... but I meant, like, in my video games, like Prince of Persia. But, she keeps sending warriors after me for fun, man! I was a good looking guy once. It's her fault I got all

6

these scars and why I look like this! That's why we're hiding in the desert! To keep me away from dudes like *you*! Eager to prove themselves in battle. Let's just get this over with." He picked up a double-edged axe.

The young hero put up his hands and backed away. "I'm not eager to prove myself in a battle I can't win. If a Jinni made you *unbeatable* then it is no mere title. It is truth, and I am no fool."

"To be determined..." The creature shrugged.

"Fine. But, instead of battling to death, perhaps you and I could come to terms instead?"

The beast raised an eyebrow. "You wish to make a deal?" He dropped his battle-axe.

"Let us not use that word, but yes. I *want* to make a deal. I am no warrior, nor do I have a deathwi-... death want... death desire? I have no desire to die!"

It was dangerous to make wishes when a Jinni was nearby and could be listening.

The beast smiled and stood up, straight and tall. He spoke in a suddenly ceremonial voice. "Then come, my dude! Let us sit-eth, and smoke-eth, and make-merry on common ground!"

***

The Jinni waited impatiently for the sounds of battle that never came. After some time, she paced the sand outside the tent, waiting for her master to emerge.

When her master trampled out, her lips pulled tight into a thin smile. When the tent flaps opened again, the young hero emerged alive and well. Her jaw fell agape.

"Well, this is truly a miracle. I-" she began.

Her master tried to look displeased, but his voice was hardly intimidating, sounding more like a whimper than anything else, "You are a curse, Sephora!"

"Well, I-"

"This er... dude is going to take you in his possession," he decreed.

She stepped up to her master. "Oh, will he now?"

"Yes, he will!" The unbeatable champion folded his arms. "I'm sick of you treating me like a *loser*, even when I've proven myself to you over and over and over."

"Psht. You know that was my magic and not *you*... and if you're just going to pass me off like property, then I can finally say it... *You are a loser!*" She made the shape of an L with her hand and pressed it to her forehead.

"Be gone, you wicked Delilah! Go hang out with the cool, ripped hunk from the freaking *Arabian Nights*! I don't care!"

"Fine! I will!" She folded her arms, and stamped her foot.

"But one last wish?" he simpered.

She looked down her nose at him, as if he were a slug. "What is it?"

"Change me back? Put me back to normal. In my world. In my time. Please, for old time's sake?"

Her lower lip stuck out a little. "Fine. Say the words."

"I wish…" was all he said.

And the giant beast shrank into a small man with a Def Leppard t-shirt. He slipped off the ring.

"I guess this is goodbye." Looking a bit dejected, she said, "It was going to happen no matter what, so…"

"Hey." The little man lifted her pointed chin. "Don't frown because it's over. Smile because it happened."

"Don't you… forget about me?"

He reached up and touched his thumb to her lips. "Here's looking at you, kid."

Our hero stood there confused, his mind circling around references he was too far away, in both time and space, to ever grasp.

"Okay." The little man handed the ring to the bewildered young hero. "Here."

He stretched out his hand, and a silver ring tumbled into his palm. It had a large ruby-red gemstone, around which was stamped *NHS Lions 1987*.

"Just say *I wish,* and she'll fill in the rest," the once unbeatable champion said.

"Er…" He knew better than to leave a wish in the hands of the Jinni.

Jinn, or when they are not imprisoned, *Djinn*, are notoriously tricky, even when a wish is explicitly worded.

There was no turning back, so he did it anyway. He thought of the strange, little man's last request, and without knowing the details of when or where the Jinni's former master called home, he said aloud, "I wish…"

And the little man was gone.

The Jinni, Sephora, turned away, trying to secretly wipe a tear from her eye.

"If you cared for him… why did you..?" He gestured vaguely.

"It's complicated," she snapped. "The Jinni curse - it only allows the vessel to stay with someone so long before it gets lost or stolen anyway. It was better this way than if he had gotten stuck here in this world, in this time."

Our hero only nodded. "So, you *are* a curse?"

Her back to him, she took a deep breath to calm her tears. Then, she turned to face him with an unconvincing smile. "When is a woman anything other than a curse to a man?"

Remembering the goddess, he said, "I wish I knew."

Her smile became taunting, and she tutted at him.

His brow furrowed in confusion for a second, then he waved his arms wildly. "No. No. No. I didn't mean it!"

She put a hand on his shoulder. "Do not worry. I've had enough practice to control the wish reflex when it's a small mistake. Try not to make big mistakes though. Those compulsions are not as easily redirected."

He nodded, and she walked him to the tent, which he wished clean of all the armored corpses of slain warriors. Then, he wished for comforts like bread, fruits, and wine, and nothing else.

She told him fantastic tales from her world, the

world of Djinn. The Djinn were a pious and serious race. No magick was allowed inside the citadel of their land. Each Djinn had phenomenal powers to forge wills and bend reality; powers which needed to be *contained*. When a young Djinn came of age - which, due to their nearly immortal life spans, took several hundred years - they entered the rite of Holy Servitude. The rite was developed to send the adolescents out into the universe as *Jinni*, and made them agents to the whims of Fate and Desire. The Holy Servitude was a religious quest to learn of the dangers and temptations of the infinite powers inherent to the Djinn. The lesson was a torment to learn, but had enchanting side benefits.

She told him tales of other worlds and different times - like the time her last master was from called "the 80's." She spoke to him of ancient and future wars. The kindness of strangers and the cruelties of friends. Her stories taught him more than he had ever learned inside the walls of the temple.

He told her of his short life as a priest and its troubles.

She offered to fix the past for him, no tricks, as a favor from a stranger. He thanked her, but no, he didn't think that would be right, and he was too heartsick to return.

She told him of the injustices which had befallen her, the evils people wished for. Her retellings made her shiver, made her cry, and she told him those were the tales easiest to tell. There were worse, far worse memories she couldn't bear to utter.

She was shackled to this fate until an unknowable time. The universe would decide when she was ready to return home, having fully learned the dogmatic lessons of her people. But, if she was wished free, that would mean another must take her place, and then she would never be permitted to return to the land of her people. For, to sacrifice another to save oneself was the ultimate sin of the Jinn.

He held her. They kissed. They made love, and he wished her free of course, but not before having a long conversation about it.

"You'll have to take my place," she cautioned.

"I know," he said.

"You'll become a Jinni."

"I know."

"You might be doomed for thousands of years before you find freedom again. You will face horrors that you must, in turn, pass to another if they wish to take your place."

He grabbed her hand, "I understand."

He had no idea.

Our hero had learned too young, and too passionately, how to devote his life to a cause, to a person, with complete undying loyalty. The exile and betrayal were not enough to undo all that learning. He had devoted himself to this girl like she was his new religion, and she knew it. Though she didn't think this was exactly how it would happen, she had planned on this being the end result. This was the deal she had made- her freedom for his. But she was starting to regret her bargain. She had started to wonder if there was a way out of it.

But the more she protested, the more sincere became his proclamations.

Until she held his hand and asked, "Are you really going to do this?"

"Yes."

"Are you sure?"

"Yes," he nodded.

She gripped his hands tighter and tears of shame, and love, and freedom filled her eyes.

"Thank you." The words barely came out as a whisper.

Hand in hand, he tried to look her in her eyes as he said the words, "I wish you free." Her knees buckled as he said it, and the tears ripped through her in piercing, soul-tearing sobs.

She was free. She had betrayed her religion and her people. And this man - this stupid, sweet, naive, beautiful boy had just damned himself to save her wretched life.

"Take it back!" She heaved and sobbed as her fingers slipped from his. "Take it all back! Take the wish back."

But magick was warping around him like a sand storm. It roared, and whipped, and stung. The magick became so thick, his hands were disappearing through the opaque cloud of dust.

He could barely make out Sephora crumpled in her garments and bangles in the sand.

He called to her and reached out, but there was only

black...

After the magick faded and she could breathe through the sobs, Sephora looked up. Wet sand clung to her face where it had mixed with the snot, and the drool, and the tears, from where her heart had ripped her open.

She saw the ring a short distance away in the sand. Sensing no time to stand, she crawled and dug her way toward it, but it was too late. A gray hand swept across it like a shadow. Sephora lifted her reddened eyes to the three old crones before her.

"Let me undo it! Please..."

The three sisters named Fate towered above her like three gray obelisks. Their eyeless sockets bore down at her with fearsome finality. Their shrouds pooled heavily onto the sand. The thinnest sister pulled out a string from her shroud, and three echoing voices in unison said, *"This is the only peace you will meet in the freedom which you seek."*

The eldest sister pulled a pair of metal shears out from her sleeve.

Sephora released one last quivering sob. She shook her head, and grasped for comfort that was not there. The sand slipped through her fingers.

"We are grateful for your aid. By this snip our debt to you is paid."

Then, came the sound of grinding, rusted metal. The severed string drifted to the desert floor, and the girl lay her head down in the sand. She was free.

***

Cupid sat at the bar, looking deep into the bottom of his ambrosia as he swirled the glass. The gods who sat at the bar during any of Death's solstice parties were always inherent social outcasts. Not that he had always sat at the bar, but maybe he should have. He had never enjoyed any of these *soirees*. They were obscene family reunions. Not parties.

All of the family was there. The Greco-Romans, the Pantheon of Greater Egypt, and the Celts were all old friends. The Norse, who only had ties to Cupid's family through the Fates, were also there causing their usual ruckus, much to the disdain of everyone else.

Thor was trying to pick a thunderstorm fight with Zeus. Pan and Cernunnos were both eyeing Freyja. The Fates crocheted and knitted in a corner while gossiping in riddles about The Morrigan, who pretended, though scowling, they had no idea they were being talked about. Loki was down at the other end of the bar with Hypnos, provoking a drinking contest between Dionysus and Heimdall. Sober Heimdall hated Loki very much, and drunk Heimdall was even more intolerant.

There was some banter and a crash, then Loki came strolling away from the now-fighting mob with a streak of blood sliding down his forehead and along the side of his nose.

Loki was muscular like a Viking. Being half-giant, he

was taller and leaner than Odin and Thor and the whole Norse lot. People called him the red-headed step-child of the Norse family, but he was really more of a strawberry-blond. He had agile, crafty hands and a constant, curious twinkle in his gaze.

Cupid watched the mob of sparring gods in unamused entertainment, though the fighting gods seemed to be having a great time. He made the mistake of making eye contact with Loki as the god passed.

Cupid gave a small disapproving head shake, which was all Loki needed to change course and sit a barstool away from him.

"Well," Loki said, pulling a small shard of glass from his bloodied face, "I suppose my work here is done."

He was mocking himself in a maudlin sort of way, and in interest, Cupid shot another glance at him.

"It is what you do. And you're adept at it. That-" Cupid gestured to the brawl, which had already devolved back into a drinking contest, "-is the natural order of your Chaos... So, what's your problem?"

Loki tried to hide a smirk spreading across his face, but he couldn't stop it from creeping into his eyes.

Cupid rolled his amber eyes. He had fallen into a Loki-trap, or rather walked right into it.

"Well, that's the rub, isn't it? I must always fulfill the universe's expectations of me. To cause a ruckus, to make a scene. I am what I am. I cannot deviate from that path, nor amend what I was *fated* to be." He shot a glance at the Fates.

The trickster continued, "We mustn't err from the role we are required to play on their Cosmic stage." He sighed dramatically, "The universe is a cruel mistress... but, you know that better than anyone right now, don't you, *Eros*? How are you liking the Netherworlds?"

Loki turned to him with an irritatingly fake, sympathetic smirk. A scarred smirk. His lips were covered with little dots and scratches of scar tissue. His legendary scars were from the time when Odin had given two dwarves permission to sew Loki's mouth shut, but that's what blood brothers were for... gods will be gods.

Cupid merely sighed. He just wanted to drink in peace without someone reminding him of how far he had fallen. "Are you quite finished?"

Loki's faux concern turned seamlessly into pure amusement. "Oh, no. I've only just gotten started. You see, I'm quite curious about your *punishment*. It seems the sentencing of your co-conspirators, your aunt and uncle, Strife and Charon-"

Cupid went rigid. "Niece and Nephew. *Niece* and *Nephew*," he corrected with a snarl. Not even a snarl could mar the beauty of the Desire god's face.

"My apologies." He waved his hand and bowed his head, "But you Greco- Romans... Each of you have ten different names, and trying to understand your family lineage is the same level of torture as sitting through an entire season of Jerry Springer. Loud people throwing dishes, vengeful, conniving mothers-in-law, and at the end you still don't know who the father is."

"Like the Norse are any better?" Cupid smirked a little, and took a sip of his ambrosia. "...And by the way, the father is usually Zeus."

Loki materialized a horn of mead. "So, back to your punishment, then..."

The god of Desire chuckled and shook his head. Here came the punchline.

"Your *niece and nephew* were sent to Tartarus for help-ing your boss, Clermiel, to - what was it? Take over the Mor-talworld? While you, yourself, *Eros*, were merely extradited here."

Loki smiled. He knew all the answers to his ques-tions. He was just looking for validation.

He continued. "And given that you said they are your *niece* and *nephew*, not *aunt* or *uncle* ... why, that would make you *far* older than them, and Venus not really your mother at all which means the rumors are true. The reason you got off so easy is... you *are* actually a Primordial deity?"

Exasperated, the god of Desire pressed his lips to-gether and did his best to ignore the comment, hoping in vain Loki would take the silence as a win and go away to brag about it.

He didn't.

"How is it that the myths came to know you as Ve-nus's babe then? When you are, instead, one of the first gods in existence?" The giant smirked.

The response came quick. "How is it you kept *your*

truth from the Norsemen for so long, *Angel*?"

"Well, to be fair, I couldn't hide it for that long. I did have giant Angel wings once, and in the end, I was still punished for hiding my origins, as you will be too."

"Loki Laufey, are you threatening me?"

"Me? Threaten a *Primordial*? Fruitless. I'm offering a helping hand."

With an abrupt laugh, Eros looked down at Loki's outstretched hand. "I've damned myself enough, thanks."

"Of course... You're better off remaining as *Cupid*, staying under Venus's wings rather than attempting to spread your own, you cherub." He stood and straightened his suit. "Just look where your rebellion got you. The universe put you right back in your cage, little bird, and it will time and time again."

"The Cosmos is out to get us, is it?" He shot the irritating trickster a condescending look.

"It is," Loki said.

Eros stood, "It *isn't*. And I'm *not* in a cage, and I'm *not* in the market for your unsolicited *help*, as you call it."

Loki was hardly taken aback by his curt reply. He seemed to enjoy it. "Ah. I see. I've scared you, haven't I?"

Eros was appalled. A retort formed behind his lips, but was cut short as Loki continued, "You drank *their* Kool Aid, didn't you?"

"Whose Kool Aid?" Eros sneered.

"The Fates."

They both dared a glance in that direction. The three

sisters were still crocheting and knitting, unaware they were being talked about, or at least pretending not to know.

"No." Eros shook his head.

"You did. You drank their poison, and you took your punishment like a good little boy. That's another reason why they let you off so quickly and easily, eh? Parole for good behavior?"

Eros clenched his jaw, which Loki only laughed at.

"Oh, gods! If looks could kill. So, I'm right? Who am I kidding? Of course I'm right. I'm always right. And you know who else was right?" Loki took a dramatic pause to lean in closer, "Clermeil. Clermeil was right. Crazy and fanatic, taking over the Mortalworld and all, but right. And you knew it then, the same as you know it now. Deep down. Actually, not that deep down. I can see it bubbling just under your surface. The Fates are, as they always have been, *using* us deities. Like puppets."

"That is the way of things," Eros justified.

"It doesn't have to be," Loki said quietly.

"Your hubris knows no bounds."

Loki scoffed, indignant. "Says the humility of a lesson well learned." He took his horn of mead from the bar. "Come find me if you ever wise up. There are far better ways to make a stand than what you did in the Mortalworld. Trust me."

Loki smiled and glided back into the party like he hadn't missed a beat. He walked straight up to Thanatos, Angel of Death, Grim Reaper, *Mr. Tall-Blond-and-Terrifying,* who nodded to him with casual expectation.

Loki whispered into his ear, and Death listened before whispering back, the way businessmen do at social functions when they don't want to be caught working. But businessmen like them were always working. They never made eye contact with each other, as if eye contact would give them up and get them caught. Their eyes always looked past one another, scanning the crowd, looking for... Eros didn't know what.

He fell back into his brooding silence, where he continued punishing himself. No matter what he did, he couldn't get a hold of the situation he was in. As always, he felt like he fit into the Cosmos around him like a soggy puzzle piece placed in its proper spot, perfectly cut to complete the puzzle, but limp and without any conviction.

The Cosmos just wanted him to drink himself into lethargy, and for him to sit around like a pretty, useless ornament, all the while blowing heart-shaped smoke rings.

Even when he had the chance to do something meaningful, he let Clermeil do all the work. He was a good little boy, did as he was told, and he lied around blowing smoke rings. Maybe, if he actually acquired the gumption, he could alter everything.

Eros finished off his ambrosia and switched to scotch... right as his *mother* approached. She was the epitome of beauty itself, of fertility, of sexuality, and she made all the goddesses of the same vein just a touch jealous.

"Cupid, my love, my darling boy," she put her hand

on his forearm, "this shadowy disposition of yours is starting to make people talk."

He rolled his eyes. "My disposition isn't what is making them talk, Venus. My disposition hasn't changed in aeons. They are talking because they haven't anything better to do besides talk, especially about things they don't understand."

"I wish you'd call me *Mother*," she soothed.

His head dropped. "Venus-"

"When I adopted you, I vowed to love you and cherish you as my own. Have I not done that?"

"No. You have, just-"

"Am I not protecting you and your reputation like a fierce Ursa Major?"

"I'm sure you are, but-"

"But, then, how is it you're suddenly too - too - what? *Cool*? For me to be your mother?"

"Oh my goddess!"

"Have you been talking to that Psyche again? I've told you that girl is -"

"Mother, stop!"

Her cheeks flushed and her eyes glistened. She kissed him on the cheek.

His shoulders sank when he realized why she was gleaming. He had inadvertently called her *Mother*.

"See?" She said proudly, "What kind of mother would I be if I couldn't embarrass my son?" She pressed her fingertip against his nose before floating away.

Eros was frozen in shock for a minute, blinking rapidly before he growled, got up from the bar, and headed for the door.

In the frigid night air, he stopped and pulled out a lighter and a cigarette. The Netherworlds' air tasted stagnant despite the light breeze. This world was a tomb, after all. The breeze was more like the draft of a vacant and haunted manor, being that it came from nowhere and was heavy with dread.

He headed home through the streets of New Bedlam. It was the cleanest city in the Cosmos on the outside to disguise the flaws just under the surface. Like a corpse at the viewing, it was all makeup and formaldehyde. Under the streets were veins of sewers, rank with putrid blood and discarded bones from the nightclubs and luxury apartment buildings.

Eros could feel the bloodlust pouring out of every doorway he passed, and he buttoned up his peacoat and quickened his pace. The desiderium of the city both tempted and disgusted him. *Desire* was his true nature.

It was once true, and perhaps still was, that he was feared by all the gods. The things he could drive them to do- *anything*. The horrors he could make them yearn for. The disgraced fools he could crumple *all* of them, *any* of them into with the power of Desire. The sheer possibility of his power created an anxiety that spread like a contagion. Nevermind his sense of propriety. Nevermind his innocent love for his fellows. The Fates had decided. They downgraded him.

Instead of a Primordial god born of Chaos, he became the son of Love and War, as an Erotes. They fashioned a new position for him as an agent of Desire, rather than its very essence, rather than its very own personification.

At the time, at the height of Olympus, he had been eager to be a part of his family again and desperate to quell their phobias of him. Naively pining for their trust and acceptance to return, he quickly and earnestly agreed to the degradation without thinking of the consequences. His own desire had bested him, which the Fates knew would happen. They knew everything. And, for what he had done in the Mortalworld, they degraded him again, trapping him in the Netherworlds after spending thousands of years amongst mortals. He was with his own kind once again, and he hated them as much as they hated him. He found humans much more tolerable.

He stepped into his flat, the enormous windows overlooking New Bedlam. The design was sharp, sleek, and clean, and he took great care to keep it minimal and colorless. He had become afraid of his own nature. The Fates had instilled irrational fears about him inside his own pantheon, and the fears had even crept into his own being. A fear that if he had done more, the Fates would have destroyed him somehow. He shouldn't have gone to the Mortalworld on that ridiculous crusade, because in his *rebellion,* he did as he had always done, *nothing*. Everything he could have been was at arm's length, and he had left it all alone.

As he stood in front of the windows and gazed out at the Netherworlds' purple night sky, dripping with falling stars and glitter, he assured himself those fears were real.

He'd pity himself if he saw any use to it, but he didn't. It wouldn't change anything.

His desires would always get the better of him, as they do anyone. Though, being the perfect archetype of desire itself, they got to him most of all. Eros knew better than anyone that passions always have a way of biting you in the ass.

He had wished for Psyche to love him for who he was as a man, not as a godly essence, and she had betrayed him. She had gazed upon his godly form, which no mortal could bear witness to without falling maddeningly in love. Though he had saved her from the jealous hands of his *mother,* and they had been happy for a time, she was not in love with *him* any longer. She had been transfixed by the force of his ensnaring power, the power the other gods feared. This led to fights and sleepless nights, and her reminding him quite often that it was he who started this whole mess by accidentally pricking himself, instead of her, with an arrow of Desire. And after many fables and songs were written about their pure, immortal love… they divorced.

During his first year in the Netherworlds, he had lived with five boyfriends, all of whom he had used for money and companionship, and all of whom kicked him out onto the streets on his ass. When he was finally able to save up enough demonics, around δ14,000 for his flat, he swore off men for good.

He knew this was the end of the line. There was nothing beyond this horizon, and he must be resigned to this *Amor Fati.*

Eros took off his coat and tossed it to the back of the sofa. With dexterous fingers, he removed his cufflinks on the way to his home bar. He left the two anatomical heart cufflinks on the black marble countertop, and rolled up his sleeves before pouring himself a scotch and making his way back to the sofa to drink and smoke himself into a stupor.

Desire turned into despair so quickly. He wondered how Strife was getting on with her punishment. Her and Charon, and several other gods and goddesses, had been dealt worse punishments than he. With Eros, Fate's best course of action had always been to lull him off into lotus dreams and deep self-loathing. Strife, though, was probably subject to whatever soup of the day Tartarus was serving.

Tartarus was a god, himself... itself. The Netherworlds was partly an aspect of the Underworld, The Dream World, The Subconscious, but Tartarus was the coal engine that fueled it all. It was a distinct, desolate abyss, somewhere even further down the roots of the World Tree than the Underworld itself. Perhaps, where the roots of the tree trailed off.

It had been an endless amount of aeons since Eros had last seen his brother, Tartarus. He wouldn't know what Tartarus looked like, let alone where it might be, or what fresh hell it was concocting and subjecting its inhabitants to.

Perhaps, even Tartarus wasn't fond of the role Fate had stuck it with. Maybe, even Tartarus was condemned to its own hell of being Hell.

Laying on his sofa in a drunken and dreamy state, his hand lofting a cigarette just before his lips, Eros recalled Loki's words. *The universe is a cruel mistress… but you know that better than anyone right now…*

Eros rolled his eyes and snorted at a Loki who wasn't there.

"Plenty have it worse than I," he said to the scarred-lipped trickster god in his imagination.

Says the humility of a lesson well learned.

Eros snuffed out his cigarette in the ashtray on the coffee table and sat up drunkenly on the sofa.

Wise up.

Eros scoffed. He took a last sip of his scotch, and made for bed.

2

*E*ros stood before the townhome on the old side of New Bedlam. The new end of the city, with its office buildings and high-end shops, was paved with concrete so clean it was nearly white. The buildings were glass and stainless steel. On *this* end, the old end, they were brick and wrought iron, and the cobblestone sidewalks were cracked with an aged charm. It still looked staged like everything in the city, but this side of the city was at least staged to be a bit cozy.

He stared at the door for a long minute, weighing the options, wondering if the Fates knew he was there. If they had led him there. He wondered if Loki was an innocent bystander, a cog in their scheme, or if he was their willing agent. There was no way to tell with that god. He had always been a double agent in his tales and in truth. Sometimes, the myth was greater than the man. In this case, Eros thought, the myth was probably the more palatable of the two, given the company Loki kept, or rather, the people who kept Loki as company.

Eros rolled his eyes at himself for being there in the first place, but also for having stood there for so long in petrified inaction.

He remembered the Catholic tales of the Inferno, of the humans who couldn't decide if they believed in God one way or the other and spent eternity going in circles getting stung by hornets.

Eros set his jaw and ascended the steps to the cherry door of the townhome. He knocked and immediately felt his insides shiver. He really must be a glutton for punishment. At this rate, he and his sibling Tartarus would be reunited soon enough.

But, the way Eros saw it, there were two options. The first option being to fight - win or lose. The second, was to do nothing and deal, which meant he must keep his mouth shut... for forever and ever and ever. He rapped his knuckles on the door.

A sleepy and hungover Loki opened the door.

"Oh," was all Loki said when he recognized Eros through the slits of his lids.

Eros cleared his throat and clenched his fists in the pockets of his peacoat. "I thought... perhaps, I should apologize for my rudeness last night at the party..." Eros's brow furrowed as he recognized Loki was wearing the same slacks and dress shirt as last night, "...which you probably just got home from."

"Nonsense. The party ended in the wee hours of the morning," Loki said. "I just got home from the after-party business meeting." He rested his head against the doorframe.

Eros closed his eyes for a moment and thought of running off the stoop. "My apologies."

"No need for that." Loki changed his demeanor, and made a slight hand gesture, "Come in."

Loki stayed in the entrance to close the door behind the Greek god as he walked in. Eros had to squeeze uncomfortably close to the giant to gain entry.

Loki was towering. Eros was tall and athletic, but his head only reached the man's shoulders. Loki was undoubtedly sturdy enough to swing around an axe all day long, like it was a mere wiffle-ball bat, and he smelled of expensive cologne and pipe tobacco.

But, Eros didn't make it very far into the front sitting room. Though it was adorned with ornate Edwardian furniture, it was littered with books and loose notes, knick-knacks and weapons. They covered *every* surface.

Loki stepped around him. "Ah! The mess." Loki explained, "I don't know how it happened. It sort of wandered out of my office, down the stairs, and into the other rooms of the house." He began bundling the random newspaper clippings and assorted daggers from a sofa into his arms and set the load down into another armchair by the fireplace. "It has a mind of its own. What can you do?"

Two sofas faced one another, framing the fireplace, with a coffee table between them. Eros took off his coat and folded it in his lap as he sat in the spot Loki had just cleared. Loki collapsed on the only clean spot on the second of the two sofas.

"Your home is…" Eros swallowed, "…lovely."

Loki tried to hide his smile and failed miserably, and the laugh he restrained came out as a snort. "No need to stand on ceremony and bullshit. I know what my house must look like to you."

Eros's attention was on the magick protection symbols, some he recognized, others he didn't, scrawled in red paint all across the 19th-century wallpaper. "Fine. It looks like a mad man lives here," he deadpanned.

"We're all mad here," Loki quipped back. He waved a hand over the coffee table, and a silver tray and china cups appeared. "Tea?"

Eros took a breath, "Why not?" He added a spot of cream to his tea, as he watched Loki put in lump after lump of sugar, to the point it seemed he'd never stop.

Eros blinked as he raised the china to his lips, and found the trickster god still depositing endless sugar cubes into the dainty cup.

"*What* are you doing?"

"Illustrating your point." Loki stirred the no-longer tea, and tapped his spoon on the rim. He took a sip. "And mine. I am indeed a mad man, which is what spikes my curiosity. I know that *you know* that I am a mad man, yet *you're* the one who showed up at my door impossibly early in the afternoon to apologize for being rude to *me*, a mad man, last night at the party, supposedly. We both know why you're here, and apologizing is merely the gateway to what you want, a step towards it."

"Well, yes-"

"What if I don't accept your apology?" Loki smiled humorlessly. "Then what would you do?"

Eros let out a tense breath at Loki's strange jab at social conversational structures, and said, "I'd tell you to get over it, because we have more important things to discuss!"

"Well, I don't accept your apology." Loki shrugged and sipped his not-tea.

Eros let out a bitter laugh, "Fine!"

"Because, I didn't think you were being *rude* last night. You haven't a thing to apologize for, and you didn't even mean the apology."

Sitting tense and wide-eyed on the sofa, Eros shrugged, "...Okay, then.

"The trickster smiled, "You need to lighten up, Cupid. I have to fuck with you a bit. To be honest, I didn't think you'd wisen up this quickly, if at all. You threw me off guard."

Eros scowled. "So, you threw me off guard in return?"

"Eh. An eye for an eye. And it was just so much fun.

You're easily worked up."

Eros's eyes narrowed.

Loki continued, "You need to let go of all that rage, or at least put it to good use... which is why you're here?"

"Again, yes." Eros blinked furiously, "Unless, this is a complete waste of time? Given that you're obviously *mad*."

"You're mad too. You're *angry* too. It's good- anger, the fever. But how long can you stay angry?" Loki squinted at him with a devilish grin.

"*What*?"

"This is a long-run game, to conspire against Fate, and often you don't win, and you might lose more than you know you have. Is it worth it? Can you stay angry through all of that?"

Eros quipped, "Sounds like the very nature of it would make anyone angry."

"It also makes one tired, sad, defeated, resigned, which you have already been for the greater part of existence." Loki leaned back on the sofa, arms outstretched, "Why should I think this rebellious streak of yours won't waver?"

Eros set down his tea, and he too leaned back on the sofa, folding his arms. "You tell me?"

Loki gave him a small headshake, as if to tell him the question was a cop-out.

"No." Eros corrected, "You came to me. You initiated this conversation *with me* for a reason. I'm a Primordial.

With something so nefarious, you wouldn't go blurting it out so carelessly."

Loki quirked his eyebrow.

Even as Eros said it, he realized he misjudged. "Okay," Eros tightened his jaw, "maybe you would."

Eros remembered hearing about the last trick Loki had played on the Norsemen- the secret devising of the death of Baldr.

The Norsemen were told by the Norns, aka the Fates, Baldr would die. Baldr's mother, Frigg, made every living thing vow to never hurt him in an attempt to evade this fate; however, the mistletoe vine refused. Despite this, the gods threw a party celebrating his *immortality*- a throwing party. They threw dangerous things at Baldr to prove his invincibility.

From the tales Eros was told, the Norns had prophesied that Loki's monstrous children would cause Ragnarok, the end of the world. The Norse gods then banished his children and made him their scapegoat, and Loki wanted to get even.

He dressed an arrow tip in the juice of the mistletoe. In disguise, he gave the arrow to Hoder, Baldr's *blind* brother. Hoder, not realizing he had been tricked, fired the lethal arrow at Baldr, the invincible and beloved god, who was not so invincible after all.

Baldr died as a result, and Loki, who otherwise might have gotten away with it, bragged drunkenly at a party of his nefarious deed. He also blabbed out *all* of the gods' and goddess's secrets... *very loudly.* It was this outburst that caused Odin, Baldr's father and Loki's blood brother, to condemn him to a cave, where Loki was chained down by his own son's intestines, so that a viper would drip acidic venom on his bare body day and night.

Eros realized Loki indeed had no issue blabbing out sensitive information.

"I cannot escape my nature," Loki smiled.

Eros reconsidered Loki's concern. How long could he stay angry? He still knew his own point was valid. There was a reason Loki had come to him the night before, even if Eros didn't know the exact reasoning himself yet, but he still had to convince Loki that his sudden change of heart was not capricious.

Unsure of himself, Eros began, "Once a desire is lit, you can't blow it out like a match. It lives. Forever in your soul, that seed, however small, grows roots like Hydras grow heads, and the more you try to weed it out the deeper the roots penetrate. They will ensnare your heart and your brain, and those roots of desire feel no empathy for the host. They aren't afraid to kill you."

"Hm...," Loki smirked. "Like mistletoe."

Eros gave a small nod. "Like invasive, strangling mistletoe... This nagging, hollow ache in my soul won't go away, won't get blown out. It's too late. It's rooted."

Loki's eyes were burning, alight with thought, as he took in the Greek god. He studied him for so long that Eros had to pull his own eyes away and sip his tea, but the trickster still gazed on.

"Well," Loki finally said, standing, "set down your coat. Anywhere is fine. Make yourself at home. I wasn't really prepared for this sort of thing. Honestly, last night I was just trying to ruffle your feathers a bit. My mouth likes to run, and oftentimes I have no idea where the devil it's running off to. It will be there one minute and gone the next."

"Ruffle my… Wait, this isn't all a practical joke, is it?"

"A joke? No, don't be daft. Of course it's not a *joke*. Any god with half a brain knows the Fates are fucking us all, twisting and turning us like spindled yarn. And mind you, I don't plan on anyone turning me into an afghan." There was a darkness in Loki's eyes for a second.

Eros smiled, reassured, and the tension let up. He had questions and concerns, but knowing for certain that he and Loki were on the same side, he knew his anxieties would be eased in time. There was only one he felt needed to be addressed right away.

Eros said, "Okay, good, but… aren't you worried? The Fates, well, they know everything. They've mapped out every twist and turn to existence. The fact that you spoke to me at the bar could be fate. The fact that I got up the gumption to knock on your door could be fate. This whole conversation could have been devised by them."

"And, so what?"

Eros blinked, "Well, then, we've played right into their hands, and we think we are plotting against them, but really, they are just looking at us as children playing make believe, like it's cute!"

"Trust me when I say plenty of morons might look at you as if you're a child, but *no one* has ever looked at *me* that way, and they would sorely regret it if they did. If we're playing right into their hands, so be it! There will come a day when fate is in *our* hands."

Eros took his coat off his lap and set it on the wooden box on the sofa next to him. "Well, that's a relief," he said, not quite convinced.

"Come on upstairs. I want to show you something."

Eros stood and stepped around the clutter to head for the stairs in the entryway.

"What exactly is all this rubbish?"

"It's not rubbish." Loki justified, "It's my work. My collection."

Loki took the steps two at a time with ease, while Eros had to hop and navigate around the picture frames and stacks of books, leaning hither and thither, in the stairway.

"Collection of *what* exactly?" Eros snarled, as he nearly fell.

Loki reached the top of the stairs. "Ancient and magickal artifacts, and relics, and books."

"Have you considered an index system?" Eros glared up at him.

"No reason. I know where almost everything is at..." He waved a hand, which faltered as he grimaced at the blatant lie he had just told.

A smirk crept across Eros's face as he made it safely to the second story. "Except your mouth, which runs away from you?"

"And my slippers!" His eyes scanned the hall, "I can never seem to find those sodding things. They keep running away without my feet... Anyway, my office is this way."

Loki led Eros into a room that was an even bigger disaster than the rest of the house. It was quickly apparent that the office was the epicenter of the mess. This was mostly due to the fact that the office was enchanted to be even bigger than the townhome itself, which meant there was more room inside it for more chaos.

"Bleeding hell! This is ludicrous! Use magick to organize this shit."

"Well, I can't do that for two reasons, I'm afraid. One, being that it's against my nature…" He smiled with false guilt, "I really would have no idea where to start, and secondly, these are all incredibly expensive relics and the like. Using any magick on them whatsoever, that is not of the item's intended use, depreciates the value tenfold. Using the wrong kind of magick on a magickal artifact often destroys the object itself. It's a failsafe, to protect them from unworthy hands."

He was flipping up the lids to the crates in the center of the room, which looked to Eros like it was meant to be a library. Shelves lined the walls, but they were spaced to allow for more height than that of most bookshelves, and they were deeper. Perhaps, they were once meant to hold all of his collection, but Loki didn't bother using them. He had instead decided to scatter his *precious* collection around helter-skelter, in no particular sequence.

This mode of organization might prevent thieves from finding an object if they were looking to steal a particular one, but that was the only good the bloody mess served. Loki's only attempt at organizing his office was the heap of leather-bound books leaning in the mouth of the upstairs fireplace. The sofas, no longer usable as chairs, were used instead to cushion the most fragile items of the collection.

"No. That's not it," Loki mumbled to himself. "It's around here somewhere!"

Eros tore his amazed and wandering eyes to attention, "What are you looking for? Can I help you find-"

"Here she is!" Loki dipped his hands into a box of aspen wood wool and pulled out a bowl. The ribbed bowl looked like it was made of tanned human skin and bone. In all likelihood, it probably was.

Eros did not recognize this significant, sacred object at first. It was meant to be elevated on an elaborate marble pedestal, surrounded by blinded virgin priestesses, dancing tantrically in the twisting firelight of a secret cave, hidden somewhere between Hades and Mount Olympus. It was meant to be given offerings of blood, and placenta, and tears that had been shed by nymphs. Instead, it was in this place of dust and cluttered chaos, packaged away in one of the many unmarked pine boxes.

There was a lag in Eros's mind as he tried to place it.

Compared to those times of yore, when what that mighty bowl represented was menacing and ominous, it now looked awkward and fragile in the hands of Loki Laufey.

"That's the Bowl of Fate," Eros cautioned forward.

"Yes," Loki gazed upon it with the admiration of an objective historian, "it is."

Eros blinked, appalled at the lack of reverence, and his lungs tightened. "Put that down," he ordered the giant, who only squinted back at him. "You can't just have *that*," Eros gestured towards it, "lying around in this heap of mess! Have you no sanctity at all? Any sort of idea what kind of *thing* that is? And you just have it boxed up like, like cheap china or something!"

"China's not cheap." Loki looked mildly amused.

"Exactly! Still! *That*," Eros pointed at it again, "is something you lock into a curse box, encased in iron, sealed in concrete, and dropped into a merciless ocean inside an eternal black abyss, is what *that* thing is!"

"And you know what it does then?" Loki set it carefully back into the crate.

"Of course I know what that insidious thing can do! It practically has the power to change..." Eros trailed off, remembering the ancient tales of that bowl. He remembered seeing it for the first time, the way it breathed like it was the mouth of the universe, ready to swallow existence up whole. But, it didn't breathe like that now, while Loki was holding it, while it sat lifelessly in that crate.

"Yes?" Loki urged, looking less amused and more

wickedly excited. "Go on, what does it have the power to do?"

Eros's eyes were drifting across the mess, "...to change Fate."

"To change Fate! Exactly! And you know who probably wove those tales to make the gods fear this foul punch bowl? Probably the same hags who made them fear *you*. It is a thing powerful enough to destroy them, so they demonized it, saying something so powerful should not exist."

"How did you come by it?" Eros asked.

Both of them were standing over the box, looking at the cold and innocent bowl.

"The shadow market. Damn thing is useless now. Somehow they must've turned it off, and I can't seem to find the on-switch."

"I highly doubt it's a switch," Eros deadpanned and peered up at him.

"No." He chewed on the side of his scarred lip. "Probably an incredibly elaborate ritual devised by the Fates that one can only ever hope to perform if one happened to be the Fates, so..."

"So... we're still fucked."

"Essentially. But, it's *cool*, right?" Loki stuck his hands in the pockets of his trousers and stood tall. "All of my collection is that way. These old artifacts have to be paired up with proper rituals, incantations, and ingredients. They're like puzzles, and I happen to like puzzles."

"Again, I ask, have you considered an index system?"

Loki grimaced.

***

Eros opened each crate and one by one took out the artifacts to be labeled and shelved.

The index system couldn't be quite as alphabetical as he would have liked, given many of the objects' names were in different languages. They couldn't be organized by category because relics of war should never be next to each other, given their nature. They would repel each other like magnets or destroy their neighbors with excessive force. They had to be neutralized by more calming and peacefully-auraed artifacts. They couldn't be organized quite by origination date, due to some of them existing outside of space and time. The placement of a timeless object next to another timeless object would create a world-melting paradox.

Eros did his best to chronologically alphabetize them by category, from left to right when possible, on the newly numbered shelves, and he created a corresponding rolodex in the same order.

And due to this dizzying non-ordered order, Loki was pleased. Beyond pleased. He loved the organizational structure like it was his favorite joke. Sure, he liked the way he had it before, in absolute chaos, but he thought this way was even better. He said it was over-organized the way taxes and corporations are, to the extent that it becomes a convoluted mess.

"It's all cyclical." He lazed on the sofa, ankles crossed, and his heavy eyes glittered. "Chaos eventually coagulates into some form of order, which people overwork in their hands like clay until it devolves back into utter unmanageable chaos, and somehow they still think they've got it under control. Like the cartoon of that dog in the burning house saying, '*this is fine*'… I think you might have made my day! When this is all said and done and you've *organized* everything, and I have company over, I'll get the chance to explain how the *system* works, and their heads will go round!"

Loki chuckled an amused and maniacal laugh at the thought.

Eros sat at a desk with cold tea and a hand cramp from writing out countless index cards. He shook his head and glared at the amused trickster. "You know, you could help?"

Loki grimaced and tapped his finger against the arm of the sofa. "This is more your thing."

"Actually, all of this is *your* thing, *your* collection and- why am I helping?" Eros dropped the pen onto the desk.

"Because you're being appreciated, and that is the forever-temptation of the gods, to be needed and appreciated. It's our driving force."

"Yes. True. But it's asinine."

"You're asinine." Loki stretched and yawned, and in a different reality there was an earthquake due to it. "If that's our driving force, or desire, then that's on you. You're asinine."

Eros dramatically dropped his head to the desk. "This room isn't even half-way finished yet!"

"Well, I suppose you'll just have to come back tomorrow, won't you?"

Eros raised his chin an inch to look at the giant creature, who had a wicked smile gracing his lips. He was very attractive with that smile. Despite his scars, tattoos, the bags under his eyes, and the fact that he was still wearing the same wrinkled shirt from the night before. As long as he wore that smile, he was cunningly charming.

"You're a monster. You did this," Eros snapped, his mental exhaustion wearing him down.

"I have yet to run into a problem that wasn't somehow my fault." His smile twisted into a joker-like grin, "This is fine!"

Eros laughed, shook his head, and rubbed the stinging out of his eyes.

He made his way to the foot of Loki's couch and asked, "Is this what fighting Fate looks like, then?"

"It's a long-run game." Loki tilted his head to the side. "You just spent all day, doing whatever you wanted, thinking whatever you wanted, under your own free will. Those hours will add up, trust me. It may not look like it now, but free will is something you actually get better at."

Eros only nodded, his mind in no shape to think deeply on the matter. "Don't bother getting up. I'll show myself out. Are you going to bed or is that completely covered in junk as well?"

"I'm far too knackered to move from this spot, even if the bed wasn't currently being used as a table for my collection of spears."

"You're a hoarder. Goodnight."

Loki only nodded and closed his lids.

***

Eros nearly forgot his coat on the way out the door, and he slipped through the streets like in a dream. His head grew heavier and heavier as he walked.

The cool night air was not as refreshing as he hoped it would be. It was stale. He lit the first cigarette he had smoked in hours, but it did nothing for his clarity either. He wondered if the Fates were watching, listening to his thoughts, even though there weren't many wracking around in his brain. All that was in there was a suddenly overwhelming sense of paranoia.

He daren't think about how far the omnipotence nor the omnipresence of the Fates went, lest the fear draw him back into the realm of inaction. Not that organizing Loki's collection was *doing* much...

Unless Loki was right, and free will was actually something one got *better* at. Tantalizing as that thought was, Eros didn't have the mental capacity to ponder it for very long, and he let his paranoia swallow the thought.

But, again... just what he had already seen of Loki's collection was overwhelming. The height and glory of a thousand forgotten temples and fallen kingdoms was kept safely tucked away inside a cramped townhouse on the old end of New Bedlam. It boggled the mind.

Eros had held in his hands, just today, boxes of cursed treasure, the petrified bones of prophets, and most of the lost books of Alexandria. Then, there would be whatever relics the following weeks would bring. Excalibur and the Holy Grail? The Apple of Discord and Pandora's Jar? The man even had the bleeding Bowl of Fate, for fuck's sake! Loki couldn't even remember whether or not the object on the desk was the Orb of Thesulah or just a fancy paperweight.

Eros stepped into his flat and immediately poured himself a nightcap before heading off to sleep.

3

Our nameless, young hero was suspended by two chains around his wrists in darkness for a thousand years and a thousand years more before a door opened in the pitch. The light of a dull fire illuminated the opening, and demons walked in with a metal rolling cart, housing ritual blades and metal instruments.

The two demons had faces of stone as they approached him. The broader one looked him over and spoke in a gruff monotone. "The choice is yours, kid. Do you want us to stay or go?"

The other one was emaciated and bent. This one prepared the instruments while laughing and conversing with himself.

"Where am I? Who are you?" our hero asked.

"Asking questions wasn't an option. I asked if you want us to stay or if you want us to leave. If we leave, we won't be back for a long while. If we stay, I might be able to answer some questions, but nothing's for free around here."

Our hero knew the cost. It was laid out next to him on the rolling cart.

"Stay," he said.

"Okay." The gruff demon took a knife from the tray and sniffed. "I'm going to cut out all of your teeth, and if you can still ask your questions after that, I'll try to answer them."

Our hero nodded.

In the background, the hunched and crooked demon laughed to himself.

"Alright," said the leader, "here we go." He adjusting the small angled knife in his hand. Without malice or passion, the demon began his work.

And our hero screamed.

***

The next day, Eros again found himself before the steps leading up to the townhome of Loki Laufey. He had a song stuck in his head by The Clash. If he left and never returned there would be trouble, but if he stayed there would be *double-double, toil and trouble.*

He gritted his teeth and forced his way up the steps to knock, the punk music in his head giving him an unjustified amount of courage.

Loki opened the door, looking refreshed and pressed. His tailored gray suit was crisp and fitted, and his facial scruff had been cleaned up. He leaned on the doorframe at an angle that blocked the whole entrance, and the stem of a pipe was fixed in his teeth. "You really are a glutton for punishment, aren't you?" A cloud of smoke tumbled over his lips.

Eros rolled his eyes and nimbly navigated around the giant. "Your collection can help us win this fight. Not in the state that it's in, *but* if it were operating efficiently, there would be enough power here to run the Cosmos... Not that that's what *I* want."

Eros had taken off his peacoat and thrown it on the sofa, only to find that the sitting room had been tidied up a bit. Much of the clutter was now piled into the front corner of the sitting room. He turned back to face Loki, who had closed the door and was now leaning against the stair rail, tamping his pipe.

"But," Eros continued, "I have to shake this feeling that everything I do is being watched, all my impulses and thoughts being downloaded and used by the Fates, and... They're impossible to escape! They're everywhere! Around every street corner and in every empty room."

Loki smirked, "Who do you think is worse? Zuckerberg or the Fates?"

"Very funny." Eros heaved a weighted breath. "I can't - and won't - be their puppet. I won't! So, we are going to get your shit together and start connecting dots until we have something nuclear to use. I'm in this, even if it means I have to tolerate your existence for the rest of mine."

Loki raised his eyebrows, "If I had known you were going to propose I would have worn a better suit."

"Must you joke about everything?"

"Why so serious?" His chest vibrated with silent laughter as he encircled himself with a halo of smoke.

Eros grunted and walked past him to ascend the stairs. "You're obnoxious."

Loki looked off after him with a raised eyebrow, and then followed behind, taking the steps two at a time. Immediately after entering the office, Eros began his work with a permanent pretentious scowl on his face, same as yesterday. Loki only shrugged to himself and collapsed on the sofa to enjoy his pipe, as had been his plan before Eros knocked. He wasn't about to change his plans and waste a perfectly packed pipe, not even for Eros and his permanent scowl, which Loki knew would soon turn in his direction to utter something condescending.

"I figured you'd actually help today," Eros shot from across the room. The god was undoubtedly beautiful, but that attitude… "but leave it to you to do the *unexpected…*" His tone was flippant and sarcastic.

Loki just laughed in pure enjoyment and puffed on his pipe. He could make out Eros's incredulous expression from the corner of his eye, which only made him laugh harder, and by the time he was done with his rolling hysterics, his pipe had gone cold and the ember had gone out. He puffed on it to no avail.

"Damn." Loki wiped a tear from the corner of his eye, his breast still tingling from his laughing fit. He stood and walked towards the desk where Eros sat. He dumped the cold ash and remaining bits of tobacco in the bin and set his pipe on the rack with the others on the desk.

"*What* was that?" Eros blinked, arms folded on the desk.

Loki sighed and shook his head, "I thought you knew well and good that I was a nutter?"

Eros turned out his hands and blinked, stunned at his behavior.

"Yes. Alright." Loki said, "I *was* planning on helping today, but can a man not enjoy his pipe for a moment - innuendo intended - before getting started?" He couldn't tell if the adorable and disgusted face Eros made was holding back laughter or a pure rage.

Eros put up his hands in surrender to the giant's chaos. "That's all you need to have said."

Loki noticed that Eros gestured when his mind was having trouble finding words. Loki, on the contrary, gestured with his hands at *all* times, even without the accompaniment of words. "Eh." Loki shrugged, "I have a quota on pestering you I must fulfill daily now. Plus, you actually work better when you're aggravated."

Eros's head tilted, "I do?"

"You do." Loki sat on the edge of the desk, "When

you're angry or annoyed, you focus. When you're happy, you daydream." He picked up the fancy paperweight that might have been the Orb of Thesulah. He tossed it and caught it in the air like it was a baseball. "See, I did something yesterday. I paid attention."

He only managed to catch the orb twice, when on the third toss, Eros's olive hand plucked it from the air. "Are we paying attention *now*?"

"Ugh. All work and no play makes... How are *you* Eros, god of *eroticism*? Eros, god of *fertility cults*? Eros, god of *orgies*?"

Desire's nostrils flared, "*Dionysus* was the god of orgies, actually."

Loki tossed this factoid away with his hand, "Oh, bollocks. You're at the root of it all. You're a *Primordial*!"

The truth of his former glory, constantly being rubbed in his face by Loki, stung. He had fallen so far from what he had once been. He had been debased, and it hurt.

"And *you're* an *Angel*!" Eros stood furiously, slamming his hands on the desk. The Orb of Thesulah, still clutched in his hand, immediately shattered and turned to dust under his palm as his chair rolled back and crashed into a box. "Not *really* a giant, or a trickster, not even a *god*, are you? You're a bleeding *Angel*!" He pointed a finger at Loki's chest. "Don't think that I have forgotten what you really are, and what I *really* am! The reason I haven't mentioned your wings is because it doesn't really matter, now does it? It was a *long* time ago. Just drop it already."

Loki was frozen, transfixed by the furnace illuminating Eros's eyes. Desire could stay mad alright, for a very, *very* long time. All of the doubts Loki held for the lofty, youthful god of Love were incinerated in the inferno of the god's gaze.

Eros composed himself with a shallow breath and said, "It's been countless aeons since I basked in the ecstasy of my temples, and it's been roughly the same amount of time since you were banished in an exodus of fire from the celestial kingdom. So long ago, in fact, that mentioning either is fruitless."

Loki never tore his gaze from Eros's wild eyes, a fact which startled Eros.

"Not fruitless." Loki gave a gentle shake of his head. "Out of all these relics and magickal artifacts, my favorites aren't even here. Well, nevermind, two are here."

"What are you talking about?"

"I'm talking about us, about gods and people, about our brains, and all that they're capable of. Our histories aren't lost to the sea of time. They are part of us, and we *must* remember that. We are the greatest weapons in this collection, you see?"

"You collect people?" Eros went to move his hand and felt the crunch of powdered glass beneath it.

"Gods collect people," Loki said, "for reasons many of us don't remember or care to admit- *power*. Minds and souls are like fucking solar-powered batteries. Keep them fed, happy, and healthy, and they have the energy to *tran-*

scend. Humans are not the only ones with this ability."

Eros began to brush the broken glass into the bin. "Then why do you keep your Angelic origin a secret?"

"Frankly, it's no one's business besides my own. Let them think what they will. I hid it from the Norsemen for so long, because, well, I don't know. I was embarrassed, ashamed, afraid?" Loki said, trying to remember. "There were a lot of Angels, abandoned by heaven and unclaimed by *hell*, and we all had to make do in the Mortalworld somehow. Odin, he, uh… took me in. At the time, I think, he was protecting me when he adopted me as his blood brother. He knew what I was from the start. But now, I see this puts me in a fantastic position to be on no one's side but my own, and I will leave no reserve untapped. Now… I showed you mine. You show me yours."

Eros gave him a laborious look.

"Do they have something over you? The Fates?" asked Loki.

"No. I don't know." Eros sighed. "I just grew used to hiding, repressing what I am. I accepted my new lot in life, especially after seeing the fate which befell others who didn't take the Fates seriously. Tartarus. Extinction. Exile. This was certainly the lesser of the evils."

"A gilded cage?"

"Yes. Better than the alternatives, or at least… it used to be better than the alternatives."

"What changed?" Loki asked.

Eros shrugged. "An overwhelming sense of discontent? Timing? And now it's too late. No amount of rationale will persuade me to continue hiding away."

"Because of the *other not-yet-mentioned* alternative?" Eros's eyes narrowed in interest.

Loki continued, "The *other* alternative being... we could win and save ourselves and be free."

"Yes. That." Eros disappeared into himself and sat back down at the desk.

Loki watched Eros's inferno dissipate and wondered why he extinguished himself. He wasn't sure what it was he had said, but he shelved the thought for later in a mind as cluttered as his house.

"Right." Loki got up from the corner of the desk he had been occupying and crouched next to Eros's chair. "Show me what I can do to help."

Eros never made eye contact with him, but a thousand and one micro-expressions crossed his face before he said, "Okay, well…"

Eros explained the ins and outs of the index system he had created, which the trickster tried to take seriously and understand thoroughly so that he might actually be of some use.

*****

When our hero was released from the Darkness, he was standing in the burning light of the Sahara next to a mirage he vaguely remembered. Before him was a man dressed in many layers of garments, and behind him was a small traveling caravan. The man held in his hand a ring. Around the red gemmed ring was stamped *NHS Lions 1987*, and it gleamed in the sunlight.

"You are a Jinni?" The man said in a shaking tone.

"So it would seem." He squinted to take in the blinding sun, trying to make sense of it all.

Many of the man's fellows dropped to their knees in the sand, and a beautiful young woman peeked out from behind the man holding the ring.

"You grant wishes?" asked the man, who was turning giddy with fantasies of wealth and power.

Our hero's mind pieced together fragments of memory. "From what I understand."

The man jumped in excitement and turned to his fellows. "Up. Up," he commanded, and they stood, though some were hesitant. "You can give us gold and food and power?"

Our hero remembered the young girl he had once saved from a warrior beast. "And travel through time and realities," he offered, unaware of the beast he, himself, had just created.

The man's fellows joined him now, admiring the ring, remarking on how strange it was. They all confided in each other and debated on what to wish for, while the man's daughter remained hidden and silent.

After speaking aloud dreams of women, luxury, and fertile land, the men had settled on a plan, and they composed themselves. "Jinni," The man with the ring cleared his throat, "I wish…"

When the wishes went well, he was offered his own palace of gold and a harem. He refused both. But, when the wishes didn't work in the man's favor, the Jinni was threatened with torture and was put back into the ring to be suspended in the eternal darkness. How the wishes worked out, the Jinni couldn't control. That was in the hands of fate.

Sometimes, the man wished for water and received a canteen, other times, he would receive a flood. Sometimes, he wished for priceless gems, and he would be granted an overflowing chest. Other times, he'd wish for gold and be granted a single coin. Then, he wished to be king and found he had no loyal subjects, because they all wanted his power which resided in his ring.

One night, the man's daughter entered the hero's modest and private room. Oftentimes, the hero thought he and she had shared empathetic looks with one another, glances and nods that said *I see you*.

When she had slipped into the room, he saw she had the ring stamped *NHS Lions 1987* pinched between her fingers. "Hello, Jinni."

His brows furrowed as she glanced at the ring. "What have you done?" he asked, envisioning her father's wrath once he discovered the ring was missing.

"I haven't done much, yet. But, imagine what you and I can do together. I am the one with the power now." She twirled the ring on her tiny index finger.

59

"That thing is a curse!" he spat. "Have you not seen what it has done to your father, the king?"

"What *you* have done to him, my friend." Her ringed hand was seated upon her hip.

"No." Our hero shook his head, pleadingly.

"Yes," she urged, "you have embarrassed him and foiled him at every turn, a fate he deserves. At times, your mistreatment of him has left me feeling envious. I wish… I've longed for the ability to diminish him as you have, even when I was a little girl. He is a monster."

Our hero explained in earnest, "He wasn't before he got the ring. Once, he was a hardworking tradesman, desiring what any other man desires, and now his pride and his lust have destroyed him, as yours will you."

"Together, you and I could rule this kingdom, which you made appear from sand and air. *If* you help me, rather than trick me like you do my father, I will make you king by my side."

"No. I have no desire to be a king."

"I will grant you your freedom. That is what Jinn desire most, is it not?"

Our hero thought on this. He remembered another girl he had saved from this fate. He thought of this tradesman's daughter, now a princess, taking *his* place in his suspended dark abyss with the demons. He took a ragged breath. "No."

"What can I persuade you with then?"

"Nothing." He said, "There is nothing you can do

that can change what is. The ring is cursed, and any good that comes from it is negated with wrongs. *Wish* at your own peril, but I can do nothing to save you from yourself."

A look of piercing malice slipped across her delicate face. "Fine. So be it. When I am sovereign you will rue this day. I will make you beg at my feet, and may you never dream, and may you be cursed all your days."

Our hero knew there was nothing he could do. His heart broke and cried out for understanding and mercy, but he swallowed it and bowed his head. "So be it then. What is your first wish?"

"I wish my father was dead." The king died in that moment while he slept.

"I wish to be crowned Queen as his rightful heir." She was crowned Queen the next day, and her father's enemies struck out and attacked the palace while it was in transition and weakened.

The Queen was awoken in the dead of night and dragged to the throne room. Though she cried out wish after wish, none of them were granted, for they had wisely removed the ring from her finger while she had still been asleep. It was, after all, far too big for her slim hands.

The leader of the rebellion was her father's brother, the man appointed to run the kingdom's military, and he slipped on the ring as they forced her to her knees before the throne. "Jinni?"

At this call, our hero was summoned into the throne room. This was a wish the former king had made, that the

Jinni should appear when he was called.

"Yes?" He swallowed as he took in the scene. He had known it would end this way. He had warned her.

"I wish the Queen, my niece, the daughter of my only brother, the girl who bows before us now... I wish she was dead."

She died before she could gasp.

The Jinni watched powerlessly, hopelessly, as she crumpled to the floor in her silk gown.

"Hm," was all her uncle said as his compatriots cheered. "This *wishing* thing is too ostentatious, and it reminds me of my brother. I prefer simplicity, less words. I *wish* you to do whatever it is the holder of the ring *commands* of you."

Something rearranged inside the Jinni's being.

"Granted," he affirmed to his new overlord.

"Good. I have no use for you now. Back to your ring."

"Good. I have no use for you now. Back to your ring." Magick enveloped him, and he was suspended in agonizing darkness, to be alone for a thousand years. He allowed his self-loathing to spread. It ripped open his soul, and he wept.

4

By the time Eros had gone for the day, Loki was emotionally exhausted enough to retire early and sleep for a thousand years, but there was a call he needed to make first. Not wanting to get up from his couch, he waved a hand over the coffee table before him, and a cordless rotary dial phone appeared. Loki chuckled to himself, as this was *his* version of a mobile phone.

Gods could manage communication without phones, but phones were easier than a summoning circle, classier than a bowl of blood, and more private than both. One could choose not to answer a phone. Magickal communication, however, went right into one's head, and an ignored call, rather than resulting in a voicemail, could result in nosebleed, headache, blurred-vision, dizziness, and other ailments best fit for a pharmaceutical commercial.

Loki dialed 4. The rotary wheel clicked as it unwound back to center and connected the lines.

The voice on the other end said, "We appreciate you choosing Grim Enterprises. This is Patrice. How may I direct your call?"

"Thanatos, please."

"Who, sir?"

Loki grunted. The man had a million names, and liked to change them frequently. "Death, Grim, Reaper, Malak al-Mawt, *your boss!*"

"And who may I say is calling?" She sounded bored.

This was the sort of excessive corporate order that Loki couldn't stand, and he let out a frustrated sigh. Maybe he should have called him the old-school way. "Loki. Just Loki."

"One moment please..." There was smooth jazz holding music, then, "He's out at the moment. I'll take a message and have him call you back. Would you like to leave your name and number?"

"No..." Loki rubbed his forehead, knowing damn good and well the bastard just didn't want to talk to him.

"Oh... Okay...," said Death's secretary, lifelessly. "Is there anything else I can help you with?"

He disappeared off his couch, and materialized himself in front of Patrice's desk.

She was still on the phone. "Hello? You still there?" she asked the silent phone.

"No." Loki buttoned his blazer. "I'm not there. I'm here, and you can tell the prick I'm going to show myself in."

In shock at his appearance she scrambled to page Death's office, but Loki's long legs were at the door before she connected. As he turned the stainless handle and stepped into Death's office, he could hear the intercom buzz.

"Loki's coming in, sir," came Patrice's voice from the speaker of Death's phone.

Death looked at Loki, then at his phone in steaming rage.

"God damn it, Patrice! What are you even good for?" Death growled. He picked up the receiver and slammed it back down on the cradle.

Death's office was white. The floors, the ceiling, and the walls were all glowing with radiant white light, and the god wore an all-white suit. Death was taller than even Loki. His hair was so blond, it too was nearly white, and his eyes were ice-cold. The left was green, the right blue, and they could burn you with their frigid intensity.

"Loki, please, come in and explain to me why you even bothered calling in the first place. Don't tell me it was because you *know* that I'm a very busy man, and that you wouldn't want to bother me if I was busy." Death's voice was always a low whispering hiss, like a winter wind.

"You're always busy," Loki retorted, sitting down in a white chair in front of the glass desk. "This is important."

"Everything I do is important, which is why I must

prioritize, which requires scheduling and delegation. What you *think* might be important, I have to work into my schedule of always-important matters, which is why I would have called you back at my earliest convenience."

"And when would that be? A literal eternity from now, when everything is dead in the universe except you?" Loki crossed his ankle over his knee, "No. I don't think so. I find it best to hound you mercilessly until you give in long enough to tell me to piss off."

"Very well then. *Piss off.*"

"Can't. This is important. This is about Cupid." Then he corrected, "Eros."

Death sat back down at his desk and made himself busy shuffling papers, "What about him?"

"He's in."

"In what?"

Loki's head fell back, "Will you pay attention? You're not as good at multitasking as you might think."

"Well, why would you think I have any interest in a pissant like Cupid?"

Loki found himself offended by this, and readjusted uncomfortably. "Because he's a Primordial."

"And? We already knew that." Death dialed Patrice's intercom. Before she could say anything, he said, "Reschedule tomorrow's appointment with Alec."

"There won't be an open date for another three months," she said without concern.

"What a shame." Death's tone was flat, but he smiled

66

and hung up. He looked back up at Loki, "What were you going on about?"

Loki's index finger tapped against the arm of the chair. "Eros. Primordial. Pissed. Fates. Helps our side. Organizing my collection. Good?"

"Fine, fine." Death waved a dismissive hand as he opened his laptop.

Irked to a precarious level, Loki stood and made for the door.

"Wait." Death's eyes snapped up from his screen. "What was it you just said?"

Loki spun on his heel to face Death. His lips were pressed tightly together to hold back profanities, and he inhaled sharply through his nose. "About... Eros?"

"No. Not just that." Death's brow was pulled together, then he snapped his fingers, "Your collection!"

Loki buried his feverish hands into his pockets. He tried to compress himself in every single way, but he was about to bust like a pierced pressurized canister. "This meeting had absolutely *nothing* to do with my collection."

"Yes. It did. Eros is organizing that catastrophe! He should be given a medal." And then, as an aside to himself, he said, "I'll send him a fruit basket. Are you paying him? Doesn't matter. Uh... good. I'll stop by to see it soon. I've always wanted to buy this or that from you, but I never wanted to step foot in that junkyard you call an *office*, and you never had a catalog. Is he making you a catalog? Because he should. It's impossible to do business without a catalog."

"Yes." Loki blinked, "He is *making* a catalog, and, more importantly, he's joining our free will campaign."

Death gave him a patronizing look. "Why do you keep mentioning that? You've already mentioned it five times."

"Making sure you heard me," Loki explained.

"That's why I'm sending him a fruit basket."

Loki tutted, "Uh. No. No, you said you were sending him a fruit basket for organizing my collection."

"Same thing. No one would organize that monstrosity unless there was something in it for them."

Loki's mouth opened to protest but couldn't find words, and Death was already paging Patrice. "Send Eros a fruit basket for joining our cause and for generously donating his time to help the... less-fortunate."

Loki's jaw snapped shut.

"There. Anything else?"

Loki forced a smile. "No. This has been such a *fruitful* meeting."

"Happy to help." Death was already back to his paperwork, and the fuming Loki showed himself out.

***

Eros stepped out of his flat the next morning to find a fruit basket on his doorstep. The vibrant purples, greens, and reds contrasted against the neutral colors of the hall. He placed the basket on the black countertop, and examined it and saw there was a bottle of champagne worth a thousand demonics nestled amid the figs and blackberries.

After deciding it was unlikely to be cursed, he reached out and took the card off the edge of the rim. He took in the rich texture of the cardstock and the eloquent gold foil design that said *In appreciation* on one side. On the other side it said, *For joining the team and for helping those less fortunate - Grim ENT.*

Getting a fruit basket from Death seemed like an omen, given that it was fruit from the garden that in one myth brought about Death's very existence.

Eros wasn't sure how true any of the myths were, given that no one could agree on any of the gods' origins. In Greek myth, Death was the son of Eros's sister, Nyx, and the twin brother to Hypnos. But this isn't *exactly* true. Though Hypnos and Thanatos were twins, they were also once the same being.

Time, myth, and truth are fluid concepts. Eros's memories of back then were tainted with the stories humans made of the lies gods often told. And Eros didn't really care what the truth was.

Hypnos, Sleep, Dream, was a suspicious character, whom all the gods brushed off as an inconvenience. He was a drunk, a druggie, a Cheshire-Cat, and Eros's oldest, occasional lover. Hypnos appeared at inopportune times to solicit riddled advice, offer backwards directions, and spout unwanted truths. The Dream King also looked identical to Death, the only difference being his eyes. Opposite of Death,

Hypnos's left eye was blue, and his right eye was green. He also wore a black, leather trench coat, as opposed to Death's all-white suit.

But therein was another Death origin story. He was the ArchAngel Death, Azrael, Malak al-Mawt of the Celestial Kingdom.

Personally, Eros imagined Death was something Primordial, more so than even himself. Humans and other mortal creatures are not the only things that die in the universe, after all. Gods die too. Eros had decided Death's existence wasn't dependent on any of them. Death was there at the beginning, and Death would be there at the end.

The way Eros figured it, the very moment the Cosmos came into being, Death stalked after it because anything born must die, even existence itself.

Destruction is in the very essence of creation.

But after everything in creation is gone, only Death would remain.

It was a grim enterprise, indeed.

Eros clenched his jaw, straightened his shoulders, and did not eat of the fruit basket.

He strode out the door to head off to *work.* It had been so long since he had a purpose outside of a holiday that didn't bear his name - Valentine's Day. Having something greater to do outside of himself was empowering, was meaningful, and that was dangerous - to *them.*

He met Loki in a little town called *Rose Noire* just south of Old New Bedlam. The town was brick and tudor, and the cafe where they met sat opposite a cemetery gated by an elaborate metal arch. The gate read *Black Rose* across the top in metal script. Loki had called Eros earlier that morning and asked him to join in on a sales call before heading to the townhome.

He saw Loki sitting in the cafe's outdoor seating area as he approached. The ice giant sat ankle over knee reading a newspaper, and he was chewing the corner of his scarred lower lip. Eros briefly pondered what it would be like to have your mouth sewn shut.

"Loki," Eros said, once he was within earshot.

Loki immediately released his lip. "Good morning. Have a seat. I already ordered for you. Coffee's still warm. Have you eaten?"

"Uh… No." Eros took off his coat and put it on the back of the chair before he sat. "I haven't. But, I'd just as soon not eat at all. I received a fruit basket from *Grim Enterprises*, and it rather put me off."

Loki snarled, "Don't remind me."

Eros raised his coffee cup. "Were *you* the *less-fortunate* the card was referring to?"

Loki groaned and folded his newspaper up more times than was necessary. "Anyway, I told him briefly about you, and that you were organizing the collection. It was a short disaster of a conversation, which resulted in your fruit basket."

Eros scoffed, "How impersonal."

"Death isn't personal," Loki deadpanned.

Eros gave him a small smile for his joke, and that was all.

Loki continued, "He said when you're... when *we're* through organizing the collection, he'll drop by to see it. He wants to buy bits and bobs off me... He wants a catalog."

"A catalog?"

"One cannot do business without a catalog," Loki said flippantly.

"I see. Fine... We can make a catalog, but in the business of fighting Fate, shouldn't these various artifact collections be communal?"

Loki laughed. "We're an army of islands."

"That's absurd." Eros slammed down his coffee cup, "Shouldn't this be obvious? You need to combine forces! This is the Fates we are talking about here!" He leaned into the table.

Then, he caught his anger and glanced around for the three gray women watching him. Even as he did it, he knew how ridiculous it was. They didn't need to be present to see. They didn't even have eyes.

"It is," Loki agreed, "but that's the way of it. We're all fighting our own predetermined path. Really, the whole thing is absurd, but we do it anyway for the dim chance of freedom."

Eros looked into his milky coffee and quoted, "Therefore he gives Man hope. In reality it is the worst of all evils, because it prolongs the torments of Man."

Loki made a dramatic face, "Nietzsche? *You're* a

Nihilist?"

"No," Eros said pointedly, "but I was there when Zeus made Pandora's jar and put Hope inside, and Nietzsche said it best. Zeus is a wanker."

"No, I think you said it best just now, and that seems to be the case with most *big* gods, don't you think? They're all big *wankers.*"

Eros's youthful face lit up in amusement for a brilliant second, and then it reflexively set like someone had closed the door on the sun. "When's our appointment?" Desire smoothed out a wrinkle in the linen tablecloth.

Loki noted Eros's recurring turnabouts, but chose not to comment, instead saying, "We can finish our coffee. There's no rush. The Vampire King, Victor Devereaux, is a lenient man. He likes to take his time and would appreciate us doing the same."

Eros went back to drinking his coffee.

"So, while we're still on the subject of philosophy," Loki began, "what do you think happened first, gods or man?"

"Gods. Obviously," Eros answered. "Why would you even ask something like that?"

Loki grimaced.

"What? You can't be serious!" Eros blurted. "You think *man* came first?"

"I think there's no way to tell, really. Chicken-egg metaphor."

"That's ridiculous. I was there. I remember when

Prometheus made his clay figurines and when Hephaestus molded Pandora. Gods came first. "

"*If* you're going in Chronological order. *Chronologic-*meaning Chronos, god of Time. But *we* know there are other ways to look at time. Time can be rewritten. You, for instance, are *no longer* considered Primordial. Your chronological order has been rewritten."

"Yes, but-"

"Magick can implant memories, not necessarily time itself. But, you could have been created yesterday, with your entire previous experience planted in your head to make you *think* it's been aeons, when it hasn't. You'd never be the wiser. Our relationship with these human beings-We're reliant on them, on their souls, on their belief in us. Our existence is hinged on their belief. That is why Fate is so strong and why Death isn't going anywhere. Did you know the humans made a movie about him where he was portrayed by Brad Pitt?"

"Really?" Eros hardly looked amused, his mind still reeling from Loki's creation theory.

He made an affirmative noise and added, "In the movie he had an unhealthy obsession with peanut butter..."

"There's a flaw to your argument," Eros said, "among the many that it possesses. I've been documented in human mythology since well before the common era."

Loki flailed his hands around, "When I said *yesterday* it was an exaggeration for illustration. But, the point still stands. Your memories of human creation could be false, implanted by human collective subconsciousness for their own mythological explanation."

"Well, if they made us, who made them?"

"Evolution? Chicken. Egg. Cosmic Egg."

"You're ridiculous." Eros deadpanned.

"Eh. Off to see the Vampire King?" Loki stood with a comic grin.

"Every word you say only illustrates my point. Your entire existence is ridiculous." Eros sighed and drained his coffee, and they headed off towards the mansion down the road.

5

Our hero hung in black loneliness for a thousand years each time his overlord put him in the ring. For the bearer of the ring, only a few hours or days might have passed, but to our hero it was always a quarter of an eternity in the darkness. The ring bounced from time to time and reality to reality. He could be put into the ring near the end of World War II, and reemerge in Snow White's kingdom a century after her second death.

The ring never stayed on one finger for long. It was cursed to be lost or stolen or pried off their cold dead hand by the mortician. Which is why it didn't remain a ring for long either. It was wished into different shapes by its possessors: Necklaces, bottles, jars, boxes.

Once, a teenage girl cleaned up her childhood

dollhouse and filled it with antique doll furniture and repurposed objects. This gave him a slight reprieve from his hellish other-dimensional prison, until her father sold the doll house during a school day to procure enough cash to pay the overdue gas bill. After that, he lived with a struggling interior designer in a downtown apartment who wished the *vessel,* as our hero began to call it, into the shape of an actual lamp with a shade and a lightbulb for irony's sake.

She moved him to California, where her career magickally sky-rocketed, and where she ended up in the hospital after wrecking in a three-car pile-up on the I-710. She died during surgery, and her boyfriend helped clean up and sell her belongings, and the lamp was sold to a struggling actor.

He unwittingly took the lamp home, plugged it in, and pulled the chain. A cloud of smoke and lightning whirled from the tungsten, and the young actor leapt to hide behind his couch. He tried to find something to arm himself against whatever *thing* was forming before him.

The man who emerged from the smoke was over six feet tall and had the musculature of an action movie stuntman. His skin was adorned with scars and strange tattoos like a Hell's Angel, but he was dressed like an Armani model.

"Who are you?" The actor's voice was fierce, despite the fact he was peeking up from behind the couch like a gopher.

The Jinni sighed at the vision of the new apartment before him. He had liked the last girl and her Norwegian-style decor. She had wished that he could materialize his own clothes and food. She had let him cook dinner from time to time. She had taken him shopping and sightseeing. She had even let him pick out his own name. It was sweet, but his name was whatever his new master wanted it to be. He considered her a friend, but he had known *this* would happen eventually.

Sardonically, he answered the man before him, "The Jinni of the Lamp…" He cast his eyes across the sea of pizza boxes in his new master's home, towards the lamp with its curved base and blue velvet shade.

"You're a *Jinni*?"

"So it would seem," our hero growled, exhausted with this repetitive Groundhog's-Day-Bill-Murray routine.

"You grant wishes?" asked the actor, who was cautiously rising to full height.

"From what I understand..." Our hero's eyes examined the apartment. He could tell from the beer cans, clothes, and DVDs on display exactly what this guy would wish for and when. The Jinni could predict what promises the actor would break and the stupid decisions he'd make.

"How many? Just three? Are there rules? *Or guidelines as it were*?" The actor laughed as he said this in his best pirate-voice.

The Jinni raised an eyebrow and lied, "Yeah… just three. And I've got plenty of advice, but no one ever listens."

The actor hopped back over the couch and grabbed a notepad and pen from the end table on which the lamp was sitting, surrounded by a stack of empty Chinese boxes.

"Sure! What's your advice? I'll listen, and on my third wish, I'll even wish you free." The actor beamed with naive innocence due to having watched too many Jinni movies growing up in the 90's.

Our hero laughed a dark and bitter laugh. "My first bit of advice... don't be a hero, and don't wish me free."

The struggling actor clicked his pen. "I have follow up questions."

"Sure. But, nothing's for free. You listen to me, and I might be able to answer some of your questions. Deal?"

The actor nodded.

"Okay," the Jinni said, pushing up his sleeves. "Here we go..."

***

Eros and Loki were greeted by the doorman at the entrance of the mansion. The man took their coats, and they were ushered through the Rococo corridors to the library, wherein Victor Devereaux, The Vampire King, waited.

Upon entrance, the gods bowed at the neck and stepped forward to shake the King's ringed hand. He was young in appearance with hollow cheeks, sunken eyes, and an anemic complexion. His black silken curls gently fell just above his green eyes. His choice in apparel was far more modern than the decor, but still quite dated.

"Welcome, Loki." Devereaux's voice was light and as smooth as his blue, velvet waistcoat.

"Your highness, this is Eros," Loki introduced, but Loki's eyes were scanning the walls of books.

"Eros, pleased to meet you. Loki mentioned you have been organizing his collection."

"Yes. I have."

"When he mentioned this, I knew I must speak with you. I have been hearing many tall tales of the artifacts he's procured, and I have been eager to see them. But he told me it was in no shape for visitors."

"It *really* wasn't." Eros smirked, "But, it will be soon, and we'd be happy to give you a tour once we're through."

"You see, the reason I called him over so early in the morning is that I have a matter of great importance which needs magickal remedy. Perhaps we might be able to do business today instead of a hazy future date?"

"Oh?" Loki prodded.

"Please, sit." The Vampire King gestured to the lavish seating arrangement in the center of the room.

They sat on one side and he on the other.

"May I offer you anything to drink?"

Loki didn't miss a beat. "I appreciate the offer, but unfortunately, I have to watch my red-blood-cell intake. The blood sugars do horrors for my cholesterol."

Eros gave him a slack-jawed, reproachful look for speaking to a King like that.

But Devereaux smiled like a child and laughed like an aristocrat. "Very well. I recently have taken in the progeny of my eldest, Alec, and-" The King's face grew intricately distressed. "Can I count on your utmost discretion?"

Both of them nodded.

"The girl is rabid. My contemptuous son suckled her on deadman's blood, which is the least of what he did to her... for sport." He rapped his rings against the wooden arm of his chair. "I need the antidote."

Eros leaned forward in interest and concern. "Which is?"

"Blood from the Fountain of Youth."

"A,." Said Loki. "I see. Well, I probably could have saved you a load of trouble had you asked me on the phone. I know for certain I don't have a giant fountain anywhere in my townhome."

"You do, actually," said Eros.

"I do?" Loki turned to him.

"Several. Metaphorical fountains, that is. Artifacts which give you immortality. The idea is the same as the Holy Grail, the Elixir of Life, the Philosopher's Stone-"

"You can't get blood from a stone. He said he needed blood," he whispered condescendingly from the corner of his mouth.

"Don't worry. I have this handled," Eros whispered sharply back.

In unison, Loki and Eros looked back at the King and gave him an apologetic smile.

"I'm sure I can find something in the rubble that can help," Eros assured him, and each man stood.

Devereaux shook Eros's hand. "I'd appreciate anything you could do. I've known Josanna since she was a young girl. Her mother was a friend of mine. Money is no object."

"Oh. No, no, no." Loki jumped in, "No money need be exchanged. You can write me out an I.O.U."

"I insist," Devereaux urged.

Loki's eyes turned dark and piercing. "No, *I* insist. I won't take *no* for an answer. You'll just *owe* me one... It's no skin off my back. Anything I can do to help a friend. Ciao." Loki about-faced and hastened towards the door, leaving Eros standing there stranded and confused.

"Er... We appreciate you," Eros tried to appear composed after Loki's abrupt departure, "your highness. We'll uh... show ourselves out... I suppose. I apologize... Lovely to meet you, sir..." He backed away slowly until he was out of the library door. Then, he slipped off after Loki.

When Eros entered the white and gold hall his accomplice was already halfway down it. Eros brisked up to him. "What in the bloody hell was that all about?"

"I'll explain outside." The giant didn't slow, and Eros was nearly jogging at his side.

The doorman, who seemed to be dozing off, was stunned awake by their approach. He stood at attention and retrieved their coats. He opened the door, and they exited the mansion. They walked down the cobbled path, past the garden, out the gate, and as soon as they were beyond the grounds, far enough away that the predatory hearing of the vampires was out of range, Loki stopped.

Eros took an aggravated breath.

"Again, I reiterate, what the *bloody hell* was that all about?"

"Remember what I said about my most favorite items in my collection, that they aren't *in* my collection."

"People?" Eros blurted out the answer to Loki's tired riddle.

"Yes. People. What people are capable of. What people can do. It's best to have them in your favor."

"You mean *owing* you a favor? You mean in your debt."

"Yes. That is exactly what I mean, and Devereaux is an *asset!*"

Eros rolled his eyes, but Loki pressed on.

"His power and legacy, his contacts, the legions at his command! He might not be in the same fight we're in, but he can damn sure help. Did you *see* that library?"

"Yes. I did," Eros said matter-of-factly.

"There could be countless grimoires in there, alchemical and necromantic, that relate to the items I have at home."

"I take it *you* didn't look closely enough at his library then."

"What do you mean?" Loki asked.

"His literary collection is not necromantic, but

romantic. He collects poetry. Love poetry, to be more precise. Mostly French and Italian, but some German as well. I didn't see a single occult book on the shelves."

"That's… that's unlikely." Loki's hands shied away into the pockets of his wool overcoat. "This is the Netherworlds!"

"Yes, well, the *Netherworlds* is bleak and dangerous and, most of all, it is a lonely world. Most of the time, when one has all the money in the world, one buys power. But sometimes, when one has any money at all, they buy something beautiful. Both think they are buying happiness, and sadly, both are wrong." Eros gave Loki a critical glance, and turned to walk away.

Loki looked off after him for a moment, then called, "Are you sure you're not a Nihilist?" before following after him.

"I'm sure," he called back.

Loki caught up to him quickly.

"Still," Eros conceded, "an asset is an asset. I don't really see how Devereaux can help, but… at least we can help the girl."

Loki squinted down at Eros. "What exactly is your philosophy? I'm a bit baffled at the fact I can't figure it out."

"What makes you think I subscribe to a particular philosophy?"

"Well, on the whole, most people tend to side with one philosophical stance or another."

"Well…" Eros thought of something clever and

smirked, "I happen to find myself in the wonderful position to be on no one's side but my own."

Loki smirked, unreasonably pleased that Eros was flippantly quoting *him.* He tried to restrain his smile as they walked silently, side by side, back to the townhome.

***

"Do you want us to stay or go?"

"Stay… please."

The demon tutted, "Okay. Your funeral… Well, you know. You get it," he said as he looked away to grab a sharp object off the rolling cart.

Our hero had said *no, he didn't want them to stay,* so many times after the first time. But, the empty darkness had turned out to pierce and cut apart his being in a far more tormenting way than any knife could ever manage. His wrists were bound by chains that had no end. He had managed once to climb all the way to *the top,* and had found that the chains weren't mounted to any cavern roof or prison ceiling by brackets or pulleys. He had felt around and discovered he was hung tight and firm from the air itself. No maneuvering or manipulation could free him. No amount of time would rust them away. He hung there perpetually in the darkness.

On his awkward descent back down the chains, his weak and tired hands had lost their grip, and he had fallen, his fingers tearing, trying to reclaim their grasp on the rough chain links. When he had run out of leash, his arms had been ripped above his head, and his wrists and elbows and shoulders had snapped, crackled, and popped.

His back had spasmed, and he had screamed in pain and frustration as he swung back and forth like a desolate pendulum.

In a sense, there was a freedom in knowing he was in an abyss. He could scream, and bellow, and cry, and break open and no one could hear him. The Darkness didn't judge him. It embraced him, and whispered back, *Yes, that's it. Let it all out. It's okay. I'm here for you. I'm here…*

He and the Darkness would have deep meaningful conversations about life, and suffering, and sacrifice, and he likened the Darkness to a narcissist from the way it talked. It liked to remind him how alone he was, and how no one really gave a damn about him, or anyone else for that matter. People were always out for themselves. And, really, none of that even mattered, because no one could ever understand what he, the hero, had gone through. No one would get it. Even if they did *care*, they would never understand or comprehend. The Darkness was the only one who understood him, who would listen to him cry and self-deprecate. No one else would want to be burdened with that shit, but the Darkness would bear all his burdens, and would never ever leave him...

The sound of the rattling wheel of the rolling cart severed him from his demented reverie. "Please… don't go," he said to the demons. They were leaving him now, and they were almost to the door.

"Got other rounds to make, kid... See you tomorrow." The demon waited for his response.

"*Tomorrow?*"

The gruff demon gave him a sympathetic smile as he wiped the hero's blood off his hands with a crusted rag. "Feels longer than that, don't it? Time's a real bitch."

The two left and closed the door, cutting off all the dim firelight, leaving him alone with his only friend...

The actor pulled the chain on his lamp. The incandescent bulb illuminated, and our hero reappeared in smoke and lightning in the small kitchen of the apartment.

"Hey, so, I'm heading to this audition tomorrow," the actor began, "for a role as an old, hardened criminal. I mean not *that old*. But like... been around the bend. So, I was wondering if maybe I could ask you some questions now? Because I think that- not that you're a criminal- but you're hardened, and uh... Can you help?" He gestured to the jar of peanut butter he had bought for bribery. It sat ceremoniously in the center of the kitchen table.

Our Hero had lived with this actor for three weeks, and the actor had yet to make a wish, a single one.

Instead, the actor was using him as a character study, and made notes on what he liked and what he didn't. He made a list of his idiosyncrasies, and together they had discovered the Jinni had a soft spot for extra crunchy Jif peanut butter.

The actor passed a plastic spork across the empty

space between them. "Please?"

The chair squeaked against the tile as our hero pulled it out to sit, and he opened the new jar of peanut butter. Still feeling disjointed and small, he reached out with unsteady fingers and took the spork between his index and thumb.

The actor bolted to the end table and grabbed his notebook and pen, which had been sitting next to the lamp. He sat down at the kitchen table and made ready his writing implement.

"Okay," the actor cleared his throat. "What is the motivation behind your stoicism?"

The warm peanut butter hit the Jinni's tongue as he plunged a spork-full into his mouth, and his nerves instantly mellowed.

He swallowed then raised his eyebrows, but he kept his eyes lowered into the depths of the Jif jar. "It's uh… choice. You can drive yourself insane fighting the way of things, or you can just accept it."

This wasn't the answer the actor was expecting, and he asked, "Why wouldn't you try to change things if you don't like the way things are?"

"Because… you can't change the way things are. The world is going to do what it's going to do. The only way to change the world is to change yourself. *'The mind is its own place, and in itself can make a heaven of hell, a hell of heaven.'*"

"There isn't one thing about the world *you'd* wish to change?"

"My wishes don't come true." He looked up from

stirring the Jif with the plastic utensil. "And even if they did… I'd know better."

The actor screwed his face up in concentration. Then, covering his mouth with his hand, he laughed and leaned back in the chair. He cleared his throat, and tried to do his best war-vet impression. "Is that scar on your arm from back in Nam?"

The Jinni looked down at a long j-shaped strip of discolored flesh going down his elbow. "No, that's when I was pitted against a wyvern for an Unseelie prince's entertainment."

The actor blinked, "Okay… What about that one?" He was pointing at the sigil burned into the hero's flesh, just peeking out from the collar of his t-shirt.

The Jinni pulled down his collar to reveal it fully. "That is a magick sigil burned into me for regeneration." He went back into his peanut butter snack.

"Regeneration?"

"Yeah… so that," he tried to find a way to explain, "they can pit me against a wyvern, which will eat me alive, and I won't die. Or tigers, or I don't know. So they can burn me, drown me, bury me, and I can still keep granting wishes. I don't know if I can die anyway, but it helps with their aim."

"Oh… People don't actually *do* that?" The actor looked horrified, so the Jinni lied with little conviction.

"No. Course they don't…"

The actor set down his pen and ran his fingers

through his hair. "Why don't they just wish for it instead of burning it into your flesh?"

"Sigils are pretty reliable. Wishes go wrong. I have trouble controlling their outcome."

"You control it?"

"It's not easy."

The actor leaned forward again, "And you can't be wished free?"

"I won't let anyone wish me free." The Jinni gave him a stoic frown.

And the actor replied, crossing his arms in indignation, "What if I just blurt it out?"

The Jinni's green eyes met his and threatened him without words. He just used the cold frigidity of his gaze.

"What?" The actor taunted, "Would you punch me in the face before I got the chance?"

The Jinni set down his spork and lifted the back of his shirt, and he twisted in his chair to show the actor a magickal scrawl in blue ink. "It's a magickal binding that means I cannot touch another person without permission from the owner of the vessel."

The actor's brows furrowed, "*Why*?"

The Jinni turned back and picked up his spork, "The guy who did it to me… I might have slept with his wife."

They made eye contact and began to giggle like boys.

"You did not!"

"I did! On my own free will too, and hers. *He* didn't like it much, though."

They laughed again.

"Well, uh," the actor swallowed, "I give you permission to punch me in the face if I need it."

"If you need it?" He gave the actor a raised eyebrow and a smirk.

"Yeah. Like or… you know, hand shakes, fist bumps… if you ever need to hug it out-"

"No." He turned him down hard.

The actor wrinkled his nose and played nonchalant. "Yeah I didn't peg you as that kind of guy." He wiggled his foot and slightly twisted side to side.

The kitchen fell silent, and the Jinni finally put the lid on the jar of peanut butter.

"You'd have to take my place. If you wished me free." He was looking down at the table top. "I wouldn't wish that on my worst enemy. Ever."

The actor only nodded.

"Did uh… any of this help for your audition tomorrow? Because you used up all the questions the peanut butter bought you."

"Yeah. No." The actor stood. "That helped. I'll uh… let you get out of here."

He walked to the lamp and nearly pulled the chain.

"No!" The Jinni stood, and feeling small and meek again said, "I mean… May I, please, sleep on the couch? W-with your permission? I uh-"

The actor nodded insistently. "Yeah, yeah of course! Do you not like it in there? If I had known-"

"It's not that I don't like it-," the Jinni tried to wave it away.

"Like, you have to communicate these things-"

"Really, it's not that bad…"

The young man threw out his hands. "If you don't tell me, then I don't know!"

"Well…" The eyes of the fierce Jinni were glued to the floor, and they both stood there for a second.

"Let me get you some blankets."

"No. I don't need it. Don't-" But, the actor was already heading towards the bedroom, "go to any trouble."

He came back and handed the Jinni the blankets. "It's no trouble."

The Jinni cleared his throat. "I appreciate it."

Instead of pulling the chain to turn off the lamp, the actor just ripped the cord from the wall with more force than was needed.

"I know I'm out of questions, but…" He gave the ominous lamp a look of pure hatred, "what's it like in there?"

The Jinni made himself small on the couch, feeling stupid and awkward for losing control of his *stoic* demeanor. His heart was racing. His palms were sweaty. He was wringing his hands as subtly as he could, and he couldn't breathe. He was thinking about the demons with the rolling cart, the loneliness, the Darkness.

He swallowed hard and tried to keep from rocking back and forth. He shrugged. "It's Hell."

The actor almost took the answer and walked back towards his room, but then asked, "Is that just a metaphor or..?"

"Yeah. Just a metaphor," the Jinni lied. "There isn't an audition, is there?"

The actor rubbed the back of his neck, "Oh, no. There is. Just, it's for a guy at a coffee shop. Unnamed. Four lines." He gave himself a sympathetic smile.

"You'll get there. I like to think hard and honest work pays off."

The actor laughed, "In my improv class last week, this guy, in a sketch about Ivanka Trump and P.T. Barnum at a dump- the sketch doesn't really matter, but he said, *nobody gets rich being honest,* but I like to think that too, what you said. It makes me think that the world could be fair."

"Nah. The world isn't fair, but it still pays off," he pointed at his head, "in here."

The actor shoved his hands into the pockets of his Levi's. "Okay. Well, goodnight. Make yourself at home, and er... help yourself to whatever. You have my permission, which is stupid that you need it, but uh... you got it."

The Jinni nodded and lay there in the dim living room once the actor disappeared into the hall. Light from the kitchen appliances made the darkness less oppressive than the pitch he was used to.

He took a breath and pinched the bridge of his nose. He should have given this guy a better chance from the start. If his eternal torment could be of any use, it ought to at least punish the shit-heads of the worlds and reward good-hearted nerds like this guy. But he had enough experience to know that good things happen to bad people, and bad things happen to good people. If he thought he could reward good behavior, he was missing the mark. It didn't work that way. Being rewarded quickly turns good people into entitled shit-heads.

He needed to release regrets and be content with the goodness of his present, to embrace the now, because this place was temporary. This would end, as all things do, and he would be consigned to darkness.

The Jinni awoke to a blinding California sun and the sound of an aggravated actor making a ruckus.

The Jinni got up and wandered to the sliding glass door in the kitchen, beyond which was a fenced-in patio and a spot of gravel not quite the size of the bathroom. The lamp and its velvet shade lay covered in gravel dust.

The actor caught his breath, hovering over the lamp. Laying by his feet was a small hammer. The kind that came in the small novice toolkits they sell around the holidays for renters and first-time home-buyers.

"What are you doing?" asked the Jinni.

Out of breath, the actor turned to him, "Trying to destroy it."

"Uh-huh." He leaned on the door frame, "and did you think that *maybe* if you did that, it would have destroyed me too? Or left me stranded in the hell dimension on the other side?"

"So *not* a metaphor. I knew it!"

The Jinni rolled his eyes.

"This thing is indestructible! The fabric isn't even torn! The fucking thing isn't even *scratched*!"

"I know. Look, I made a deal," he took a breath to let his next words sink in, "and I'm not getting out of it, and I'm okay with it."

"How? How are you okay with this?" He turned around to kick the thing, and it bounced off the wooden fence. Hurting his foot more than the lamp, the actor only grew more pissed off.

Resigned to his anger, he picked up the lamp and tried to pass it off to the Jinni, "Here."

The Jinni didn't flinch. "Yeah, I can't touch that thing… Like, physically cannot. It won't let me. I can't be my own master."

"*What?* Are you *kidding me?* Ugh! What kind of fucked up supernatural shit is this?" He groaned and lost all energy. His shoulders slumped, and he dragged himself inside. He set the lamp back on the end table with a bang, and he collapsed at the kitchen table.

The Jinni closed the sliding glass door and looked at him in mild amusement.

"Is there nothing I can do?" The actor looked up at the Jinni helplessly.

The Jinni nodded and sat at the kitchen table with him. "You're already doing it. You're being my friend."

"That's not enough."

"It has to be."

The actor squinted at him for a hard moment and said in a goofy voice, "'You know how you sound? Like a man who's trying to convince himself of something he doesn't even believe in his heart.'"

The Jinni said, "Isn't that from a movie?"

The actor groaned and said in a whimper, "Casablanca. You *liked* Casablanca."

"That's right!" He continued in his best Bogart impression. "Of all the *Jinn* joints, in all the towns, in all the worlds, you found mine." He gestured to the lamp.

"Quit flirting! I know you play for the other team."

"Huh?" The Jinni tilted his head.

"Ingrid Bergman?"

The Jinni's eyes went soft and dreamy, "Yeah, she's a babe- was. Alright, I'll quit flirting with you."

"Thank you."

"You're welcome."

The actor asked, "Why the fuck are you trying to make *me* feel better?"

"Because, I know what it feels like. To feel powerless. Helpless. To have no choice on the outcome."

"No choice? I don't believe that for a second!"

"Well…"

"No. Shut up and listen!"

The Jinni shut up and listened, as he was commanded by the owner of the table lamp.

"You have to keep fighting. You can't give up. No matter how dark it gets. You have to have *hope*. Even if it's not me who gets you out of this, someday, somehow, you'll find a way, but you have to believe there *is* a way!"

The Jinni felt something inside him change, and he nodded, knowing he had just been commanded by his only friend to endure the worst of all evils.

"Say something!"

"I couldn't. You commanded me not to."

The actor ripped his hands through his hair. "*That's a thing?*"

"That's a thing." His tone was flat. "That's why I love peanut butter. You said, '*You can't not love peanut butter.*' So, I now love peanut butter."

"Magick sucks!"

"Yeah. Pretty much. If I could have one wish- just one, it would be to be human, and to have died that way a long time ago. And Djinn magick can do that, go back in time and undo things like that- for *other* people. Not for Jinn though. That curse on that *lamp* is unbreakable. It's the most intricate ritual I've ever seen. Other *good* people before you have tried, and failed, but we'll find a way."

"Okay," he nodded and quipped in his own best Bogart, "'I think this is the beginning of a beautiful friendship.'"

They gave each other sympathetic looks.

Two weeks later, while the actor was at a casting, his apartment was robbed. They took the Xbox, the controllers, and the flatscreen. They took his coffee can filled with savings. They took his bike, his alarm clock, and his tablet. And they took his damn lamp.

6

*I*nside Loki's townhome, Eros was rifling through his index system and more of the unpacked boxes. He continued to organize while he searched for a Fountain of Youth, A Holy Grail, or a Philosopher's Stone that would help the Vampire King with his granddaughter's affliction. He hadn't been able to establish a timeframe or the necessary requirements since Loki had sped out of the situation so quickly.

Eros was sifting through his own notes and cross referencing them with Loki's scattered journaling. Loki had many artifacts that *might* have healed Josanna. The issue was that each item he found that seemed hopeful had specific wording attached about *reviving the dying,* or *anything living,* or *immortality to the mortal*; however, the girl in need was already a vampire, already dead, not living, and already, in a loose sense of the word- immortal. Given he wasn't sure how much time was at his disposal, Eros wasn't going to waste time on things that might not work.

Loki's hand appeared before him, spinning a small blue flower resembling a violet between his fingers. Violets were Venus's flower, and her temples were adorned with them. It was the official flower of Athens, and its smell represented sex.

"I prefer roses," Eros quipped and continued to flip through notes.

"I'll keep that in mind, but this isn't for you. This is for *Josanna*."

Eros looked up into Loki's proud face. "What is it?"

Loki straightened his shoulders, "So interesting you would ask! *This* is the Moon Violet of Mount Meru. Quite a task getting it. The locals were very helpful, though. It grows in a cave on the mountain side, and one can only escape the cave after having battled Mara, the demon who, by way of his seductive daughters, tempted Siddhartha."

"Oh," Eros smiled, restraining his snickering as best he could as Loki continued.

"Yes," Loki continued, "and this flower only blooms on a full moon, but if obtained, it lasts forever. *And* it is said to cure any ailment and to be an antidote to any poison. It's meant to mean poison to the soul, but still, sort of what deadman's blood means symbolically to vampires anyway. It's what we need. We steep it in tea, or maybe virginal blood, and have her drink it."

"Will it cure her Vampirism as well?"

"I don't know. I'm sure after what she's been through, though, that wouldn't necessarily be a bad thing for her."

"No, but I think Devereaux might be devastated. He really *cares* for this girl. I could feel it, but it was also tied directly into the loathing disappointment he has in his son. What was his name?"

"Alec VanGarrett," Loki rolled his eyes. "His heir, sad to say, unless something is done about him. The man's a nightmare."

"I've read about him in the papers, actually. He's opened up a rather... *popular* chain of clubs."

"Blood bars," Loki corrected, gently. "He is everything wrong with the vampire community."

"No," Eros corrected, less gently. "It's not *everything wrong with the vampire community*. It's just everything that is wrong with *people* everywhere. Greed, bloodlust, power-obsession. He just so happens to be a *vampire*."

"Fair point. I stand corrected. My apologies. But, the flower?"

"Right. I think it will work. Where was it hiding?" Eros asked.

"The windowsill in the kitchen. I figured she might like to see the moonlight, and given we have two moons, I thought it would help to keep her preserved."

"Well, *she* looks great, and if you're right, she'll do the trick."

"You think so?" Loki lingered, awkward and squinting.

Eros sighed and leaned against the desk, "Are you pandering for a compliment?"

"Yes. I believe I am." He grinned.

Eros tried to hide his humored expression by looking back at his notes. "Good job, Loki."

He feigned modesty, "No really, I can't take all the credit. I owe all of my success to the god of Luck and Cleverness."

Eros laughed silently and said, "Loki... that's you. You're the god of Luck and Cleverness."

"How you flatter and tease me! Stop it. I'm blushing! But, please, go on..."

Eros was actually laughing now.

Loki noticed Eros's gracefully parted lips and his closed eyes, covered by soft, thick black lashes. His etched jawline was raised, and his Adam's apple was defined. His laugh was milk and honey, and his sun-tanned skin beamed like morning rays.

Eros opened his amber eyes to Loki, "Your hubris knows no bounds."

Loki tried to blink the spell away, but the stupid dopey look on his face was still there, and he said, distracted, "No. I suppose it doesn't. Uh..." he again extended the flower to Eros, and said, "We should probably deliver this post haste."

Loki watched every effulgent beam radiating from

Eros extinguish, blown out quickly like a candle flame.

Eros went to take the flower. "Yes. Of course."

Loki should have walked away towards the door, to dial Devereaux, to grab their coats, to make their way to *Rose Noire*, but he never could let his curiosity down. He pulled the flower away. "Why do you do that?"

Eros blinked and pulled his brows together. "Do what?"

"Don't play coy."

Eros scoffed, "I don't know what you're talking about."

"Please! The moment you've realized you opened a door, you slam it back shut. Why?"

"Wha- I… Oh come on, you really want to have this conversation now?"

"Yes. I do."

"You and I don't need to have this conversation at all." Eros sidestepped past boxes so he could take his leave, as Loki should have done.

Loki let him get halfway to the door before he said, as deliberately as he could, "Well you have to have it with someone."

Eros stopped and let out the breath he was holding. He closed his eyes to consider the thought, and Loki waited.

"Now's not the time. Let's," he turned his head, and said over his shoulder, "get this to Devereaux, and- If you must know, we'll discuss it after."

Loki pressed his upturned lips together and gave a

small nod before hopping up to Eros. "Deal."

Loki held out his hand. Shaking a god's hand meant a magickally binding agreement had been struck, and there was no getting out of it. Eros squinted at the outstretched hand in uncertainty, but met it and shook. A zap of freezing cold shocked his system as the magickal contract was set.

"Your hand is ice," he complained as their hands fell apart.

Loki grinned, "I'm an ice giant. Sue me." He strode out ahead into the hall.

Eros rolled his eyes, "That's absurd. Sue you? For being wicked cold?"

They headed down the stairs.

"It's a joke," Loki said.

"Well, it's not a very good one, is it? Jokes have a point."

"My *point* was to be absurd."

Eros merely sighed.

They grabbed their coats off the coat rack that now stood inside the entry. Loki had found it in a closet and laughed at the redundancy when he had, because he could imagine what Eros would have said if he had seen the coat rack in the coat closet.

They stepped outside into the gray, and when they were halfway down the street, Eros snapped to attention and asked, "Where did the coat rack come from?"

Loki began to laugh hysterically.

Eros waited, but the laughter didn't stop. "Is this

another *joke* because. I know it wasn't there before. Loki?... Loki? Okay, nevermind, then." In spite of himself, Eros was laughing at Loki for laughing so hard about a damn coat rack.

Laughing felt good, even if it was over a ridiculous coat rack. As a matter of fact, being around Loki Laufey just *felt* good. There was no pressure to behave any particular way or no admonishing that the way he was behaving was incorrect. He could be snarky, and off-putting, and bitter, and he could be himself without Loki taking any offense or taking it personally.

Loki allowed free will to flourish in his presence. It was the way he challenged societal protocols by turning them all into a joke. It was the way he disrupted habitual patterns by questioning them directly, which is what had Eros in his current predicament.

He didn't really know *why* he kept himself locked away, held himself back, and now he was magickally obligated to speak about this after delivering the flower to Devereaux. Loki was likely to obliterate all the superficial excuses within the first five seconds of this conversation, leaving only the demotion, the divorce, and all the other real reasons. But the *real reasons* were a sticky, unstructured mess of emotions Eros didn't know how to articulate. And the fact he couldn't articulate them might have been another reason for keeping it all shut in.

But, trying to come up with a battle plan for this conversation was making his stomach churn, so he desperately searched for something to turn his mind over to.

"So... Um... What's Death's deal? In all of this? At my trial he and the Fates looked pretty cozy."

"Mmm..." Loki took a breath to soothe away the last of his giggling. "That is probably a conversation best saved for behind closed doors."

"Right."

"But, what I can tell you is... He's Captain. Our fearless leader. His greatest strength is his greatest weakness. He's a wonderful actor, and he plays the system like it's his own personal fiddle. I mean, well, fuck, he helped to invent the damn fiddle."

Eros shook his head. "Why then is he fighting the Fates?"

"He saw that this was going to happen. No matter what. And, so, if something is *going* to happen that you don't like you, put yourself on the ground floor of its implementation, so when the time comes you're in the best position possible to destroy it."

Eros thought about this. "In medieval art, the Wheel of Fortune is depicted as a wooden wheel people cling to as it goes 'round. Sometimes you're on the upside, but as the wheel turns you'll eventually be on the down-turn, but if you're in the center, the hub of the wheel, you're always in the same place. You're the one in control of fate."

Loki glanced down at him. "Exactly. Beautiful imagery. Very poetic. I'm a fan of proto-surrealism."

"Not surprising."

"You know," Loki made a series of hand gestures, "I take it back."

Eros stopped, and Loki then followed suit.

"Take what back?" Eros asked in earnest.

Loki put one hand in his pocket while the other continued to orchestrate his words, "Our deal."

Eros was silent, waiting for further explanation.

"I put you in a corner, because it was easy. I saw an opportunity. I bullied you. Forgive me. You owe me no explanation. I still want to know, but I should never have forced your hand… in a sense. You're no longer contractually obligated to tell me anything. I'll take the harder road- this time."

Eros blurted out a laugh and cleared his throat. "You think you *manipulated* me into this?"

Loki blinked, "I think I made you formally agree to divulge your very personal information. I-"

"You didn't *make* me shake your hand. I did that… on my own free will, *without* the influence of your *inescapable*," Eros was exaggeratedly breathy, "manipulation techniques."

Loki's expression was blank under the weighted scorn of Eros's contemptuous stare-down.

"You are such a pompous, arrogant arse! To think that you're that *clever* and that *guileful*, that the *weak* and *unsuspecting* little-me fell helplessly into your snare!"

Eros made a face of such disgust and revulsion that Loki became mortified with himself. His mouth went dry with the desire to take it all back, but it was too late. His ego, which hadn't known it had been inflated by his good-guy attempt, shrank and hid in his spine.

He couldn't apologize and say that wasn't what he meant, because on some level, that was exactly what he had meant. So, he stood there at a loss for words, which rarely ever happened.

Eros shook his head in disdain. With a snarl on his once beautiful and graceful lips, he pointed at Loki with a patronizing finger, which, each time Eros shook it, cut the giant down inch by inch like the sharpest axe. "You know- I agreed, magickally, contractually, so that I *couldn't* talk *myself* out of it. You think I had *no* understanding of what I was agreeing to? I- I wouldn't have agreed if I didn't *trust* you with that information- if I didn't bloody-well *want* to trust you with that information. So, screw you for taking all the credit. Screw you for thinking I'm that malleable! But fuck it- take away the obligation. Then, when I satisfy your vapid curiosity on my own free will, without the strings of your influence, maybe it will give your *ego* a reality check and remind you that you aren't the *Fates,* puppeteering people along. But you know- I appreciate your permission to do this on my own, because, well, I was *cluelessly under your spell.* But now, I'm weak in the knees. You've released me, and now you're taking the *hard road...* for me. What a hero you are! *Bravo.*"

Eros gave him one last nauseated glance and turned to walk away, leaving Loki standing there dumbstruck on the cobblestone.

Loki stood there, letting the lecture sink in. He began chewing on the corner of his lower lip and glanced up at Eros walking further down the sidewalk.

After a moment he followed Eros, but didn't make up much of the distance until reaching Black Rose Cemetery's bricked walls.

Loki cleared his throat, and Eros looked over at him, but then carried on like he hadn't heard him.

Loki said, "I- Uh, listen, that's not… exactly… the way I meant it-"

"What did you mean then?"

Loki struggled to find a way to reword it that would *sound* better than what came out the first time. Loki made several pondering-noises, gasps, snorts, groans, before his head dropped in shame. Letting his mouth run away from him wouldn't get him the result he wanted this time.

His hands moved around dramatically without saying anything, and as they turned past the gate into the Maison de Devereaux, Eros stopped.

"*This*," Eros waved his hand in a circular motion in front of Loki, "is exactly what you should have said to begin with. *Nothing*."

He began to walk again, and Loki glared after him. "I'm *trying* to apologize."

"Missed the mark. Try again." Eros snapped.

Loki snorted and caught up to him. "You know-" Loki was about ready to rapid-fire insults, but as he thought them over in his head - that Eros was impossible, cheeky, stand-offish, impertinent, pretentious, smug - he recalled those were all the things he liked about Eros. Because of those attributes they could banter. They challenged him.

"What?" Eros looked at him while pulling the bell chain before the mansion's door.

Loki pressed his lips together and released an aggravated breath. He snarled and sniffed and said, "Nothing." His eyes fell to the concrete.

"Good."

Loki's eyes darted back up, his countenance sporting a smile that was made of sharp, angry teeth.

The door opened, and both Eros and Loki smiled pleasantly at the doorman.

Loki cleared his throat, "Is the King in?"

"He's in his study. Follow me, sirs."

Loki let Eros enter first.

"May I take your coats?"

Eros pulled the flower from his pocket before shrugging off his coat. They were escorted up the grand staircase and through the ornately decorated halls.

Loki looked down at Eros and whispered, "I *really* didn't mean to upset you."

Eros bit down on the insides of his cheeks to keep from spouting off.

"And I think you know that," Loki continued.

Eros gave him a quick glare. "Can we discuss this *later*?"

"Here you are, gentlemen. If you could wait here a moment, I'll let him know of your arrival."

Eros and Loki gave him a nod, and he knocked on the giant wooden door before stepping into the study beyond.

"Of course," Loki began, "we can discuss it whenever *you* want… not that I'm giving you permission, of course."

Eros hissed through gritted teeth. "Shooting yourself in the foot, Loki."

"Well, that's just-"

"If you blame this on your *nature*, I swear to fucking-"

The doorman stepped back through, and Eros and Loki stood erect.

"He'll see you now."

Wordlessly, they stepped into the study where Devereaux stood awaiting their entry.

"Have you found an antidote already?" The King looked pleasantly surprised, but also seemed to be restraining his anxiousness.

Loki took a step forward, "Yes, *I* did. The Moon Violet of Mount Meru." The giant gave Eros a taunting eyebrow.

Eros held up the flower, while never breaking eye contact with Loki. "Yes," said Eros, "clever *Loki*, found it. Your knight in shining armor…"

The King's eyes darted back and forth between them, and he took a cautious step forward to take the flower from Eros.

Neither of them broke their piercing glances at the other, and Devereaux stood there holding the flower.

He shrugged. "What do I do with this?"

They finally both turned to him with fake smiles.

"You brew it," said Eros.

"In tea," said Loki.

"Or blood," Eros finished.

The King's gaze bounced back and forth, "I appreciate your sense of urgency on this matter."

"It was no trouble," Loki assured.

"But," Eros interjected, "may we see her? Josanna? I'd like to help if I may."

Devereaux pondered this for a moment before saying, "Very well. Let me send for a few people so we may begin."

Eros and Loki nodded before glancing at each other and looking away.

While the people were gathered and the violet blood-tea was brewed, Eros and Loki avoided each other expertly, maneuvering around the crowd separately.

It wasn't until they stood outside the door to an interior room, with several of Devereaux's sons and daughters, that they found each other standing side by side again.

Devereaux held a skeleton key in his hands. "Now, Loki and Eros have kindly provided their skills to help us with Josanna. We must get her to drink this concoction."

He held up a thin pitcher of the violet blood and cautioned the crowd. "She will think it is deadman's blood, and she will resist. She is much stronger than she looks. Do not underestimate her."

Loki bent down and whispered as Devereaux continued, "He's saying that because he *cares* about you. Not because he thinks you're weak."

Eros's neck tensed with rage. His face turned to stone, and suddenly Loki was filled with the overwhelming *desire* to bite down as hard as he could on his own tongue.

As Loki bit down, Eros heard the crunch, the wince, and could see Loki's hand jolt towards his mouth. All of the neighboring vampires noticed the smell of blood and turned to look, but their sense of decorum overpowered their bloodlust. Loki smiled and waved them away as the taste of copper filled his mouth. He dipped an inspecting finger in his mouth to feel the gash. His finger was red when he pulled it out.

He grimaced at the blood, "Ow." He shot a glare at Eros, who looked very pleased indeed.

Eros kept looking forward, listening and nodding to Devereaux's instructions, but there was a smirk on his face that looked good-humored, like maybe he was secretly enjoying their back and forth and might be on his way to forgiveness.

Loki pulled out his handkerchief from his slacks to wipe off his finger. He found himself sucking on the tongue-wound, feeling the strange way it stung.

"Ready?" Devereaux asked the crowd, and everyone nodded.

The Vampire King unlocked the door. Loki didn't

think about the blood in his mouth again until he was standing in the darkened room containing a rabid vampire-with the door locked behind them.

"Shit," he said aloud, as he barely made out the frail girl, cradled in a ball in the corner of the room. Her tangled black hair hung in her face. Her bony arms were raw from where she had been clawing herself with her untrimmed fingernails. Devereaux was cooing to her and showing her the pitcher of violet blood.

Eros perked up at the distinct change in Loki's tone. There was worry in his voice. "What is it?"

"I'm bleeding."

Eros's heart stopped.

He peered back at the girl, who looked up at him, her hair parting to reveal her skull-like countenance and disc-like eyes.

Vampires can move quicker than light, so the instant her gaze veered from him to Loki, he knew he had to be faster.

Eros teleported himself over the two feet it took to stand between her and Loki. In that moment, she was already on top of them, throwing all three of them into the wall with a bang. A picture frame dropped from its nail, and the other vampires in the room were already pulling her off, dragging her thrashing body to the four poster bed in the center of the room.

She growled, and cried, and laughed as they wrestled to hold her down.

Eros still guarded Loki while he tried to settle his rapid heart.

"*Can't get out!*" The girl cried as she writhed and scratched against the hands restraining her. "*It's so dark! The Darkness whispers!*"

Loki put his hand on Eros's shoulder. "Alright?"

"Yeah." Eros swallowed and stepped away. "Fine."

She chanted, "*Darkness come, and Darkness grow. Darkness come, and take my soul.*" Devereaux was shushing her like a mother does a babe and trying to pet the hair from her face.

Loki turned an ear to listen, to take note of her words.

"You must drink," Devereaux begged.

She jerked and convulsed as if possessed.

"*They made him so alone!*"

"I know. It's terrible, but you must drink."

Her fangs gleamed in the darkness as her jaw dropped down her neck, her mouth a yawning supernatural blackness, and she hissed.

And then her face was normal again, and she said, "*There is a desert rose in the devil's garden.*"

Five vampires struggled to hold her in place.

"*She never warned him!*" She laughed manically.

"Try to hold her still!" Devereaux commanded.

"We're trying!" One of the vampires yelled.

"*One for Death and four for a boy and seven for a secret.*" She tossed her head back and laughed into the madness.

Suddenly, she was overtaken with a thirst, a

bloodlust, a *desire* for the pitcher in Victor's hands. She blinked and calmed. Her episode ceased, and she lay perfectly still aside from her heaving breaths, making eye contact with Devereaux. The other surrounding vampires cautiously loosened their grip, but still held on. With her dark pitted eyes, she told Victor that she'd drink. She waited until he understood.

Victor Devereaux raised the mixture to her lips.

Josanna drank deeply, blood slipping down her chin.

"No no no!" Loki cried, looking at Eros. "Why did you do that?"

"I'd have done it sooner but-"

"But that was prophetic. Her words were prophetic!" Loki was anguished over the words he didn't get to hear. He covered his nose and mouth with his hands and kicked himself, not that there was anything he could have done.

Eros didn't bother to argue.

Josanna slurped and licked up all that was in the pitcher, collapsing into a magickal slumber the moment she swallowed the last drop. The King pulled out a handkerchief and began to dab the mist from her forehead.

The vampires were busily attending the sick girl on the bed, and the room suddenly felt more crowded than it had before.

Eros said to Loki, "Come on. Our work here is done."

One of Victor's progenies, Gabriel, showed them out of the room and all the way to the front door, promising to give them a report the moment they had one to give.

"How did that nursery rhyme go?" Loki asked himself the moment the door closed behind him. He had forgotten completely about their argument. "For counting crows and magpies? One for sorrow, two for joy? You know which one I'm talking about?"

Eros recalled, "Three for a girl, and four for a boy. Five for silver. Six for gold and seven for a secret never to be told."

"What the devil do you suppose she was referring to?"

7

Our hero hung in the Dark abyss, having an argument with it. It told him to abandon all hope, and he told it to quit quoting Dante. He preferred Milton. In Milton's poem even the fallen angels had hope, and he identified with them, having been kicked out of the Goddess's queendom and cast down into hell.

If he was going to be forced by the devil's right hand to kill, entertain, and grant souls all the *'riches that grow in hell'*, the abyss could damn sure bet on the fact that he was going to go down swinging.

And the abyss laughed and reminded him he already had. And the chains he was suspended from swayed ever so gently in a non-existent breeze.

A door opened and dim firelight illuminated the

shadows of the two demons and their rolling tray coming towards him.

His heart began to pound the adrenaline he'd need into his veins. Everything tensed. His breath grew rapid, and his body struggled instinctually for the freedom his mind knew was impossible.

And the Darkness laughed at this and said *I knew this would happen. I told you this would happen. You've already lost all hope.*

"Shut up," he told the Darkness, but his voice broke.

Shh. It's okay. You're okay. I'll be right here with you.

"How we feeling today, kid?" The gruff demon asked.

Our hero looked away. His pain, and shame, and misery reached unfathomable depths.

"Not so hot, huh?"

Our hero tried to swallow the overwhelming desolation bubbling up and festering in his being.

"You want us to stay or go?"

He choked on the word, the tormenting word. He'd rather be tortured than left alone. "S-Stay." And it broke him.

The demon grabbed his face and pulled it center.

"Look at me," the demon said without hostility. His voice was void of emotion. The demon said, "Not looking at me won't do you a lick. You look at me. You memorize my face. You see it?"

Our hero nodded, despite the feeling of drowning

in his own tears. They were sliding down his throat and burning at his lungs.

"You see past it, though, right? What's behind it?"

He swallowed and tried to steady the wracking in his chest. Our hero looked into his demon's all-black eyes. He looked through them and past them, and what he saw was the Darkness, the abyss. He saw, "Nothing."

"Right. Not a goddamn thing. Now, what's that tell you?"

The hunched demon with the cart giggled, "Nothing. Everything is nothing! *Hee-hee ho-ha ha!*"

The gruff demon grabbed bolt cutters off the tray, and again, the suspended body began to struggle and hyperventilate. Our hero closed his eyes, and gritted his teeth, and he desired stronger, harder than he ever had. He wanted it, wished it, longed for, so *fucking* much, to be somewhere else. Someone else. Dead. Never born. Gone. Empty.

The demon's monotone was almost comforting. "Hey. Look at me."

He did as he was commanded out of habit.

"It tells you you're not me." He paused for a long while, never breaking eye contact. "You will never be me."

Our hero didn't know what that meant, but his chest calmed, and his rationale began to prepare him for what was about to happen to his body.

"Okay." The demon brought the bolt cutters to his withering rib cage, about to start his work, but he stopped and added, "You might become *him*, though..."

Our hero looked at the crooked, cackling demon in the corner, and his face twitched.

"Food for thought," the demon said and began his work.

The demons left him with his chest cavity wide open. Blood still dripped off his toes and added to the lake of red beneath him. His body twitched as each gurgling shallow breath electrified every severed nerve. The chains creaked as he swayed back and forth in the still of the dark. His mind slipped in and out of consciousness and nightmares.

"That's rough, mate," said the blond man smoking a cigarette, standing before him.

The blond man bent his neck backwards to look up into our hero's face. "I mean... I thought *my* nightmares played rough. At least my nightmares are *fun*."

One eye was green, the other was blue.

His cigarette illuminated as he took in a drag, his fingers adorned with tarnished silver rings and his dirty nails covered in chipped, black nail polish.

He took a few heavy steps back. He wore bulky, buckled combat boots and a long black trench coat.

"Huh..." His mismatched eyes drifted all the way up the chain. "No wonder you're fucking miserable. This place is fucking boring! I mean there's no way to puzzle yourself out. It'd be more *fun* if there was a way out. You know, that's the hero's story, innit? Against all the fucking odds the hero makes it out alive. You can't die anyway. Not sure if you knew that, but you can't. Like… *ever*."

The blond man waited for a response from our hero, and receiving nothing, he shrugged and continued, wandering aimlessly around as he did.

"See! That's why they should add me to the payroll here. Spruce the joint up a bit." He snarled down his nose at the Darkness, "Sure it's a classic, *torture-torture*, but that's fucking boring! I mean… at least give them a chance to try to make their escape, and then, when they've almost made it- WHAM! Right back in their cell. I'm telling you," he mumbled with the cigarette between his lips, and he blew out a stream of smoke, "that will fuck a person up, that would. I'd take it up to the max- be better than this repetitive shit. Oi, what are you going to do? Cut up me innard-bits? And do the same tomorrow? And, let me guess, the same *fucking* thing the third day! Psht!"

He flicked his cigarette to the ground, and our hero wanted to laugh, but couldn't manage it.

"I'm telling you, mate. This place is third-rate." He sank his hands into the pockets of his leather trench coat. "You could do better. I could show you real torture, I could. Because I know your insides better than they do. The real insides. The fucking brain is where this shit's at. These people spend too much time making new fears, rather than playing on the ones you already have. They're missing out on making some serious fucking art out of your brain chemistry." He pointed at the hero and then dipped back into his pockets to produce another cigarette. With a click, a flame emerged from his index finger and he lit up. Then, he waved out the flame like a match.

"You're not listening to the Darkness are you? Because he, she, *it* is a fucking putz. Still owes me money." He stepped up to our hero and said, "Look, I'd love to help you out, mate, I would, but I'm sort of not allowed back down here after last time. So- Hello? Is there anybody in there? Just nod if you can hear me." Hypnos craned his neck to look into his face. His mismatched eyes were sympathetic, but he grimaced at the state of the hanged man, who could only manage to give him a glance and an uncomfortable wheeze.

Nervous, he wiggled his fingers and rattled his rings together. "Alright, so, here's what I can do. I'm going to help you sleep, and that's it! I mean it. I can't do anything else for you- Alright, fine. Jeez! Didn't have to break my arm over it. I'll see what I can do. No promises. If this shit goes sideways, I'm out! Get it? … Alright. I've got your back. That's what best mates are for, and you're my best mate. Not sure if you knew that, but you are. Just wait. You'll see."

And our hero drifted off to sleep without dreams or nightmares, just blissful nothing. When he opened his eyes he saw nothing, just Darkness. So dark, that if his hand had been in front of his face, as they say, he wouldn't have been able to see it. The only time he could see anything was when the door was open, which meant the conversation he'd had with the blond man was merely a dream. It hadn't been real.

His heart sank, and he discovered his ribcage

and flesh were back in their proper spots thanks to the regenerational magick put upon him.

He decided not to bring up the dream to the Darkness in case the dream had been real and was a secret. The man in the long black coat, whoever he was, wasn't allowed back down here after what had happened *the last time*. So, he would keep his mouth shut and not say a word about the punk rock phantasm who *had his back*. Because, that's what best mates were for.

***

Loki's mind puzzled over the prophetic words right up until he and Eros walked through his door and hung their coats on the rack, which snapped him out of his tangled train of thought. He glared at the coat rack for reminding him of their argument, and he whispered to it, "This is all *your* fault."

Eros plopped down on the second sofa in the sitting room. He lit up a cigarette, deeply inhaling. A look of relief spread across his face.

Loki clicked his tongue and with a breath went to sit down next to Eros on the couch. He rolled up his sleeves and propped his feet up on the coffee table, to which Eros rolled his head across the back of the sofa to give him a look.

"What? It's not your coffee table," Loki scoffed. Eros rolled his head back to look up at the ceiling and blew out a heart shaped smoke ring.

"I'm *sorry*," Loki said, folding his arms. His head was also resting on the back ridge of the sofa. "I mean it. You're right. My head was in the wrong place, and for that I am thoroughly apologetic."

"I accept your apology," Eros said simply. "Your head... well, I'm not even going to pretend I understand what sort of place that is."

Loki chuckled.

"But, your heart was in the right place. I know that. So, all's forgiven."

"Good." Loki chewed on the corner of his lip.

"I- um," Eros began, "even before Psyche, I never liked to show my *whole* self to anyone. I don't want anyone to... fall in love with *that* side of me, because anyone who sees it falls in love with it instantly. It is pure heart and passion and desire. So, I'm careful to keep that door closed. Not to let it out, because it feels wrong. Like cheating. Like taking away someone's free will, which sounds so incredibly vain, but in my case it happens to be true, so... there you have it."

He cleared his throat self-consciously and continued. "I've seen what actual, real, functioning relationships look like, and not saying I'm looking for that right now, but if I ever did, then that's what I'd want it to be. Honest, open. Not because of the god I am, but because of the man I am, and I don't even know who that man is anymore."

He groaned and rubbed his face with his hands. "Tell City was so stupid. I don't know what the fuck I was thinking. I just... I don't know..."

Loki tapped the top of Eros's hands that were still covering his face.

"I know you," Loki said, and Eros didn't glance up. "You are a bit weather-beaten and turned around, but you're intelligent, and witty, and you'll figure it out. Though the Cosmos may not see you this way, especially the Netherworlds, you're brave. And I'm not just saying this because you saved *me*, who is nearly *immortal*, from a vampire today."

Eros laughed and lowered his hands from his face.

"Which, I now owe you my immortal life," he smiled. "But, at least you're trying to pull yourself out of the same habits; the same rut you've been stuck in, no offense, for the greater part of your life. Which means you're admitting your shortcomings and trying to change. Changing is hard. It takes bravery. Gods must adapt, and so many don't. I think that you still believe in love, and in this desolate wasteland, well… that's certainly something."

"Oh. No. Please, don't stop. Go on." Eros turned on the sofa to prop his head up on his fist and face Loki.

Loki laughed aloud, "Are you pandering for a compliment?"

"Yes. Blatantly. Keep going." Eros leaned in.

"Well, I think that it's a damn shame you feel like you have to close yourself off like that, but I get it. I will respect that about you until your last dying breath."

Eros's amber eyes narrowed as they worked over Loki's expression and posture. Leaning casually on the sofa, the giant's fingers were laced, but his thumbs fiddled. He was turned towards Eros, and his crooked, scarred smirk was softly wrinkling his face. His sharp hazel eyes were inquisitive, yet smiling.

Then the giant said, "And then in the event of your death, I will pillage through all your personal possessions and ravage all of your hidden secrets like a filthy Viking."

Eros lit up, and he hid his laughing face into his hands. Loki let out a snort as he tried to keep his composure while Eros caught his breath. Loki, self-satisfied, stretched and put his arms over the back of the couch.

"You're awful!" Eros managed to say through the laughter, nudging Loki's shoulder.

"So I've been told."

"You turn everything into a fucking joke."

"One of my many charms," Loki winked.

Eros sat up and nodded, "One of many..." His eyes raked over the giant for a moment, taking note of his scarred hands, his stubbled jaw, and his built shoulders, and the giant gloated under his gaze.

"Come on." Eros stood from the sofa using Loki's knee as support.

Loki's brows pulled together. "Where are we going?"

Eros tilted his head and pressed his lips together in a coy smile. "We're going to move all those spears from off your bed..."

Loki's jaw fell open, and he blinked. "Are we?"

Eros leaned over Loki and gave him a stern look

before grabbing his tie. "We are."

He gave Loki's tie a small tug, and the trickster god raised his eyebrow, "Well, when in Rome…"

Loki gave him a nod and hopped off the couch. He followed Eros upstairs.

They shut the bedroom door behind them.

***

Loki lay in bed next to a dozing Eros, entangled in the satin sheets like a fucking Renaissance painting. The giant's body still hummed with the ecstasy of the pleasure he had endured for hours. He had heard tales of the orgies Eros had thrown back in ancient times before the god of Erotisicm was demoted, and Loki's imagination never did it justice.

He sat up in bed and drew the metal cigarette case from Eros's pile of clothing on the floor. He lit the end of a cigarette with magick and inhaled a deep breath of smoke.

This seemed to be more than ecstasy and pleasure, though. Or perhaps, it had just been that long since he had felt either of those things, and he was making it to be more than what it was. Or perhaps, all of this really was that he had just lain with the god of Desire, and this rush of feelings was a predictable result. The spell would fade, or worse, it might never fade, and he'd find himself fawning over the god for the rest of eternity like a damned fool.

He shouldn't have mixed business with pleasure, but

he was, after all, doing business with the god of Pleasure, so really it was a scenario just waiting to happen.

Loki tried to rub out the headache building up behind his eyes and stood. With his cigarette pinched between his teeth, he stepped into his pants and fastened his belt.

He told himself as he slipped from the bedroom that he wasn't going to glance back. He wasn't going to gaze upon the god sleeping in his bed, but he did. The bedside light illuminated and shadowed Eros's face, and neck, and chest, like an artist had fashioned him at just that angle. And Loki couldn't blame Psyche for what she had done, peering over the youthful god with an oil lamp to gaze upon his visage, because with the unquenchable burning rising up in his chest, Loki also wasn't certain whether or not he had just lain with a beauty or beast.

Loki shook his head as he closed the door behind him because he knew better. The most dangerous things in the Cosmos are also the most beautiful. The universe was a trickster that way, and he should have seen this punchline coming.

He walked outside onto the stoop to let the frigid night air clear and cool his senses. Loki had always liked chilled and icy air. He found it stimulating, and he realized, as he wiggled his toes against the cold concrete, stimulation was the last thing he needed.

He groaned and descended the steps. He wandered out into the empty street. It was filled with the crisp silence that came right before the dawn, when all the nocturnal things of the Netherworlds were making their way back to their mansions, and caves, and drug dens. With it being so close to dawn, he began counting on his fingers to add up how many hours he had actually spent in bed with the love god.

Over five hours. Over five hours of being completely enthralled and engulfed in a wonderland of sheets and sweat and sweet, sweet sex. And it was wrong of him to think this was all just Eros's spell because of what Eros had confessed to him earlier- and what? Was Loki going to fall for the propaganda the Fates had spread about Eros all those thousands of years ago? No.

But still, now he could see why it had been such a convincing lie and a fear that spread like wildfire even into Eros himself. To be unable to be loved without the other person thinking they had been lured in by his power… which is preposterous, because a person under his spell would be so undying in their love that they would never question it. Not that Loki was in love, of course. That would be dangerous. He was merely infatuated… though, Loki wasn't sure if that was any better.

Loki heard his front door creak open. Eros stepped out onto the stoop. He had dressed, but he had grabbed the wrong shirt. Loki's button down was swallowing him.

When Loki saw this, his smile stretched from ear to ear. He tossed his cigarette to the ground and made his way back to the steps. He leaned against the wrought iron hand railing and looked up at Eros, whose sleepy face was infuriated with the cold.

"What are you doing out here?" Eros asked.

Loki clicked his tongue and admitted, "Thinking."

"About?" Eros folded his arms against the chill.

A werewolf howled off in the distance.

"I don't know." Loki's eyes drifted to his feet, "About... how much I enjoyed tonight. I worry I enjoyed it a bit too much."

Loki looked back up at him.

"What do you mean?" Eros tried to disguise the hurt look sweeping across his face.

"I mean- Shit. I mean..." Loki, too, folded his arms, not against the cold, but because he was thinking. He chewed on the corner of his lip. "What... What is this?"

Eros didn't move an inch. He looked as if he were made of marble.

Loki's arms flew away from his chest, and he began moving them around wildly as he stepped up the stoop closer to Eros. "This? I mean... I can't stop smiling. My heart is hammering out of my chest, and I feel ill. My skin is shivering, but I feel like I'm on fire. But I feel so *incredible*, and those five hours were simply not enough. I need more, more of you, and, dear gods, I cannot stop looking at you. You are so... terrifying. I mean, what if this all goes incredibly wrong? Like, for instance, you laughing at me for believing there is a *this,* in the first place?"

Eros gave him a chuckle and a sympathetic smile.

Loki growled in frustration and stepped back down

off the stoop. "Am I losing it? Because my mind won't stop racing, which is actually rather typical of me, except I can't seem to make heads or tails of this. What- What is this?"

A cold and quiet moment passed between them with Loki standing in the street and Eros on the stoop to the townhome. Their breath turned to mist in the air.

Strangling all of his emotions, Eros said, "It's love. I can feel it."

Loki grimaced, "Are you sure it's not lust?"

Eros nodded.

Loki lowered his head. "Shit."

"You're in love with me." Eros's voice cracked. "Without arrows, without magick. You're in love."

"How long does it usually last?"

"Hard to say, really. It won't end well, though."

"No. The Netherworlds isn't going to tolerate it."

Eros shrugged, "And I'm not allowed to leave this world, so…"

"So, what do we do?"

"Enjoy it while it lasts… I suppose."

Loki dropped his head and walked up to Eros. "Which one of us do you think will get killed off first?"

"Probably you."

"Why's that?"

"It will hurt me most," said Eros.

"I wouldn't bet on it." Loki gave him a bashful smile. "Come on. Let's go in. You're freezing."

They walked inside with an ominous cloud hanging

over them.

Happily ever after doesn't last if you live long enough or die too soon, and the Netherworlds guarantees it won't last. It is a world of despair, heartache, and struggle.

And even without the help of the infernal world, the laws of Greek myth forbid it. Zeus cheats on Hera, who pines for her love's fidelity. Gaia had Cronus castrated. Hades and Persephone can only see each other for half the year. Every love Apollo chased was the one who got away, even the one who loved him back. Eros was the only one who had a happily ever after according to the myth, but in reality… divorce.

And Loki was just plain cursed. A horrible father to six children, and two ex wives, who maybe didn't hate him, but would just as soon never see him again. Cast out by the celestial kingdom and then damned by his adoptive family for… valid reasons.

It was plain and clear to both of them that their romance was fated to be doomed from the start.

8

Back inside the townhome, they should have talked about Loki's ex-wife Sigyn. They should have talked about why Eros formed a general distrust of love aeons before he even met Psyche, and how he didn't actually *believe* in love anymore... which would have led them both down a dark and dangerous rabbit hole. They should have talked about whether or not it was beneficial to indulge in the aura of their romance. They should have talked, but they didn't.

Immediately after shutting the door, Loki started to unbutton Eros's shirt- the one that was actually Loki's that Eros had thrown on, and Eros started to re-explore all of the trickster's many scars and tattoos as they kissed. The white dress shirt barely fell off of Eros's shoulders as their bodies pressed together, and they were both too absorbed in other things to remove it the rest of the way.

A crash and a bang came from upstairs, and a door creaked open.

They pushed away from each other, and Eros ripped the shirt back around him as Loki crept to the staircase to listen.

"Fucking hell!" came a voice. "Where the hell did the coat rack go?"

Loki buried his face in his hand as he recognized the voice, "Oh for fuck's sake."

Eros recognized it too and approached the staircase. "Hypnos, is that you?" he called.

"Yeah. Comin'." Hypnos appeared with his leather trench coat and his buckled boots at the top of the stairs. He looked down at the two men.

"Oi, Eros! What the hell are you doing here? I'm in the right place, right? Loki, this is your crib, innit?"

"Yes, it is," Loki said as Hypnos descended the stairs. "Shit, are you two shagging? Doesn't matter. Listen. I have, uh, a thing" He pressed his tongue against the side of his cheek as he began to reach into the pockets of his trench coat. The pocket swallowed his entire arm, and boxes and metal cans rattled around on the inside of it as he searched. "Hang on. It's in here somewhere. Ow!"

He ripped his hand out of his pocket and cried, "The fucker bit me! Little shit."

His entire arm disappeared into his pocket again,

and he made the face every man makes when he is grasping for something just beyond reach. "Got it!"

He pulled out a vintage, ruby red, Cape Cod cologne bottle slash candle holder. He held it out with a look which told Loki to take it, but as soon as Loki moved, Hypnos said, "Oh. Hang on! There's a prophecy that goes wiffit."

Hypnos began to giggle and buckle over, and he held up a finger, which begged Loki to wait until he caught his breath, and then he cleared his throat. "Okay. Okay," he said between giggles, "*Give this secret to the father of none, when you tell him he has a son.*"

"Alright… what is it?" Loki now gingerly took it from Hypnos's hand.

"What does it look like?" Hypnos gave him a condescending look.

Loki held it up and examined the way the light illuminated the cut ruby glass. "Tacky decor from the late 1800's."

"Well, that's what it is then. So, Eros..." Hypnos leaned against the stair railing, propping his heavy combat boot against it, "it's good to see that you're getting out and about. You know you could have been shacking up wif me instead of this stick in the mud? It's been a while, you and I?"

"Oh," said Loki pointedly, "You and him have…"

Eros flushed and shrank.

"Yeah," affirmed Hypnos. "Way back in the day. Can't you picture it? Dream and Desire. We made a pretty pairing."

Hypnos pushed himself off the railing and began wandering around, fiddling with Loki's belongings. "But then I got all self-destructive, and he got self-deprecating. We practically cut it off, but it was a mutual decision and all. I dig it. But *this joker*? Really, Eros? You should be putting him off for as long as you can, because as soon as you two hook up, that's the end... Oh, you already shagged, didn't you?"

Hypnos leaned towards Loki and took in a big sniff. "Yeah. You did. I can smell the shag all over."

Eros and Loki looked at each other, then back at Hypnos in unison.

"You did!" he accused. "Shouldn't have done that. Beginning to the end for all of us. Thanks a bunch."

Hypnos set down a whiskey glass that he had been peering through like a kaleidoscope. He made his way back towards the stairs.

"Oh, please!" Loki stepped forward. "I've had prophecies about Ragnarok hanging over my head for aeons, and they never came true. You can't convince me of this bullshit that him and I having *sex* is going to destroy the world." Loki set the bottle down on the coffee table.

"One," Hypnos said, "Ragnarok just hasn't come yet, so don't count your chickens. Two, it's not just sex, mate, and you know it. Three, why do you think endings have to be bad? Four, when I said *thanks,* I meant it. Never say that word wiffout meaning it, do I? That and the *s* word.

It's faery etiquette. Six, put the coat rack back in the closet. I put it there for a reason. Seven, don't forget the secret I just told you about. It's important. Me best mate depends on it."

Hypnos began to make his way up the stairs as Loki began to mumble the rhyme about counting crows to himself.

Eros ran to the stairs, "Wait! Hypnos!"

The Dream god looked down at him, his blond bangs hanging over his mismatched eyes. "Yeah?"

"What was five? You skipped over five."

"Did I skip five? Oh! Five was, uh… let's see. Five was… for silver. Oh! Maybe things would go smoother if you admit to yourself you love him back. You haven't said it yet. I've got to split."

Eros watched Hypnos disappear up the stairs, then he looked back to Loki for questions or answers. Loki was still counting on his fingers the counting-crows nursery rhyme, and without ever making eye contact with Eros, he walked away to find paper and a pen.

Eros grunted, rolled his eyes, and ascended the stairs, hoping to catch Hypnos before he vanished, unseen for another three-hundred years. At the end of the hall upstairs was a door, bursting from the seams with radiant golden light, and Eros saw the tail of Dream's coat and the heel of his combat boot disappear around the door. Eros jogged the rest of the way, knowing that it was too late, even if he place-shifted from there to the door, and it was.

He ripped open the door, and the closet light blinded

him and went out. Eros stepped into the closet and pulled on the chain to the lightbulb hanging above his head. There was nothing but a dusty closet with tweed blazers, wool overcoats, and dragonhide shoes.

The dingy closet smelled like Loki- expensive cologne, pipe tobacco, and brandy. Eros reached out and touched one of the blazers. Usually, he would snarl at tweed, but Loki pulled off the quirky professor vibe all too well.

Hypnos was right. Desire and Dream had made a pretty pairing, but dream and desire aren't solid things. And even though Loki was chaos and absurd order, both of those things were grounded in action rather than fantasy. Loki grounded him, and made him feel real. Tweed was a very grounding fabric, Eros thought. Not like silk or velvet.

And every pair of shoes Loki owned was dragonhide. Eros would have preferred something synthetic, dragons being too majestic and powerful to be hunted down for their pelts, but he supposed Loki wore them because of something symbolic, like having beaten his metaphorical dragons. Although in myth, when one dons a creature's hide, one becomes that creature. Eros wouldn't put it past Loki to become the beast everyone said that he was.

It was when he was flipping through and admiring Loki's vintage look that Eros remembered why he was led into the closet. A small glimmer of light refracted off a button and caught his attention. It came from inside the wall behind the jackets. He pushed a row left, pushed a row right. He moved some boxes and picked away at the peeling, tattered wallpaper, and a beam of the bright light shot through the seam.

***

Eros drifted down the stairs to see Loki mumbling to himself while sitting at the coffee table. He was furiously scribbling down what Hypnos had said on a scrap piece of receipt paper.

Loki didn't look up as Eros stopped at the foot of the stairs to ask, "Why do you keep your wings in the closet?"

Loki stopped writing. "Where else should they go?" he asked.

"Um... on your back for starters. Why are they in the wall, Edgar Allen? Why are they not attached?"

"I cut them off." He looked up from his scribbled notes.

"You *cut* them off?"

"Well, Odin helped..."

"Odin *helped* cut your fucking Angel wings off?"

"Well, not cut, more like *saw*. He helped me *saw* them off."

"That's...," Eros shrugged and made a disgusted face. "Why on God's green earth would you mutilate yourself that way?"

"God's green earth, indeed... I was making a stand, because I hadn't made one when I should have. I was mad at the universe. I didn't want a way *back*. I don't regret it."

"That's-" Eros began again, "Not even Lucifer himself cut- *sawed* off his wings."

"No, because he wants to go back one way or another, or so the stories say." Loki shrugged. "I have other opinions, but that would be one of many reasons why he never even thought of such a thing."

"Dare I ask what your other opinions might be?"

"Well I have a conspiracy theory. Lucifer was His favorite, and some would argue, out of all of us, Lucifer loved God the most. I think good and evil are dependent on one another. Evil needed to exist. God is omnibenevolent, so he couldn't do it and had to delegate, and if you had to delegate such a horrifically important task, wouldn't you want to put it into hands that you trust?"

Eros rubbed his face with his hands and restrained a yawn. He shook his head and said, "You keep your Angel wings in the wall, in the closet, because you and Odin sawed them off to give a giant middle finger to Yahweh?"

Loki nodded and leaned forward, elbows on his knees. "Yes. Yes it's true, and just think how much they're worth to the right buyer."

"You'd sell your own body parts?"

"Depends on how sentimental I'm feeling that day."

"Unbelievable. I'm going back to bed." Eros shook his head. Before he could turn, Loki grabbed the ruby red perfume bottle from off the coffee table.

"What do you suppose this is?"

Eros took it, looked it over, and uncorked the top. Loki flinched at the sound. If the item was magick, which undoubtedly it was, then Eros could have just let out a curse, a spell, a demonic spirit, hope, if the damn thing was Pandora's.

"What?" Eros shrugged, "It's fine."

"Well, it could have not been. Opening the thing could have depreciated the value."

Eros scoffed, "Yeah, the Jinni escaped. Damn thing's worthless now."

"Not how Jinn work, really, but wouldn't that be exciting!"

"I was joking, Loki…"

But Loki ignored him, "Jinn are incredibly rare and incredibly dangerous. But, if you swindle a person just right, depending on how stupid they are, you could persuade them to give up their house, entire art collection, their firstborn child, their soul, for a bottle that *might* have a Jinni in it. You could never be certain, however, if there really is a Jinni, because *you never open the damn thing*!" He finally made eye contact with Eros.

"Really? With how *rare* they are, why should I have assumed there was a Jinni in it? Because it has an *I Dream Of Genie* stereotypical vibe? Jinn containers can be in any shape and design. That's how they get you."

Loki cautioned, "I'm just saying you don't open *any* container until you know what it is."

"I'm just saying you can never know what's truly on

the inside unless you look," Eros rebutted.

"You're so Greek!"

"Well you're… so…" He struggled to find an insult, but his circling brain landed on something even worse. "You're Loki! Yes! B-Because that's what you do! *You* disguise yourself and trick someone *else* into opening up the bottle, so if there *is* a curse or a Jinni in there, it's on the other person, not you, but you still get to see what's inside. Rude!"

Loki shifted his weight uncomfortably. "Fine." He snatched the perfume bottle and its stopper from Eros's hand. "Just don't ever open anything *I* give you."

"I can't believe you just did that to me. You're terrible. I'm going to bed. And I hate you."

Eros slumped up the stairs.

"It's a reflex!" Loki cried up after him. He waited and listened until the bedroom door slammed shut. He smiled and laughed to himself. As far as first dates, or first hookups, went, this was good, even if it was the beginning to the end, which he knew was some sort of metaphorical riddle.

He sat down on the couch and continued his chaotic journaling. He wrote down the important phrases Hypnos had said, searched for their common themes or words, connected them to any dreams he had recently, none of which he could recall in full. He tried to connect the words to his own subconscious thoughts.

What does it look like?

Tacky decor from the late 1800's.
That's what it is then.

Was that Hypnos saying everything is relative, or was that him implying what Eros had just mentioned? Could this object change shape?

With the stopper off, he could smell the pungent perfume rising from the bottle. It wasn't bad, just very dated. The bottle had no markings aside from what it had been *made* to look like, but there was something underneath the surface. It wasn't *really* a pretty perfume bottle, but it *was* really good at looking and acting like one. He'd have to put the object under some major, but delicate, restorative ritual to figure out what it actually looked like.

Sleep began to overtake him, and he smiled as he laid his head down on the arm of the sofa and stretched out. He began to sing *Mr. Sandman* under his breath as he drifted off. One, because of Eros and the crazy twenty-four hours they had. Two, because he knew how much Hypnos hated that song.

***

Hypnos left through the closet as he had come.

He had put the coat rack in the corner of the closet as an oh-shit-handle, because when he crawls through the split in the wallpaper, he comes in at an odd antigravity-twisted angle and *falls* into the wall with the dragonhide shoes. So, the coat rack was something to grab onto in order to realign his center of gravity, and Loki moved it.

Nobody respects what he does for them, except maybe Eros.

Eros doesn't remember why, but Hypnos is okay with that.

He left a little trail behind for Eros to find.

He and Loki had a lot to talk about.

Dream didn't mind helping, as long as no one realized that was what he was doing.

He slipped through the corners of the Realm of Dream, taking a shortcut through the labyrinths, and avoiding the forest of spiders.

Dream didn't really like spiders. They gave him the heebies with their sprawling legs, like New Mexico highways and endless eyes, like black diamonds of wisdom.

He sank through the open grave he had dug for a nightmare.

He always buried the people he loved alive.

And the scariest part was…

The grave is empty.

It was *his* nightmare.

He stepped out of an oil painting of an open grave into an art studio.

His twin's art studio.

Death was sitting on a paint-splattered stool. He was in his white shirt, the sleeves rolled up. The studio's walls were covered with grayscale, anatomical oil paintings.

Death loves life.

But that was a secret, and so was this art studio.

Be very quiet, lest Death hears your breath, and takes it away...

His violin sat over by the window that looked out into *his* world, the world that Death hath made. He had an infinite amount of personal worlds, most of which had a mansion, but all of which had this art studio.

Infinite, infinite, endless, in fine night.

"What do you want, Hypnos?" came Death's whispering voice.

Dream snickered, "I have to have a reason to come visit my lesser half?"

"I'm not buying your drugs. I'm not bailing you out, and if you have a problem, I don't care."

The paintings on the wall begin to turn and come alive. The heart pulses, the lungs-

Death didn't turn to face Hypnos. He dipped his horse hair brush into the dark red pigment on his palette in a smooth rotating motion.

The lungs expand and collapse. The eyes blink and gaze around frantically. The still-lifes of flowers and fruit wither and decay.

"I don't need your money. I have my own... somewhere in me pocket. Listen, me best mate's in trouble-"

"I don't care," said Death, moving his paint brush, which had become a scalpel, to the painting of an open chest cavity, the muscles inside wriggling.

"See, I think you should, because the thing is he's y-"

"I still don't care." Death painted a line of dripping blood with his scalpel brush.

"Okay, fine. Be a putz. A prick, actually. A selfish, cocky shit."

Death moved his brush back down to his palette.

The paintings in the studio began to melt like wax. They puddle to the floor, and Dream hops around the scalding, bleeding, congealing paint up to his twin.

"Thanny-"

"Don't call me that."

"Thanatos. Brother of mine. Opposite side to me coin," Hypnos grimaced as he said it. "He's in Tartarus, and-"

Death stood, casting the blackest pall around the room. His nostrils flared as he said, "Hypnos, listen to me very carefully. You are not allowed back down there after what you did the last time. I am tired of cleaning up your messes-"

"My messes? You see this? Blood and paint and bleeding guts everywhere!"

Throbbing organs, hot stinking blood, pulsing paintings, slicing scalpel, twisting white canvas, dancing and singing gummy bears-

Thanatos pinched the bridge of his nose. "You're tripping. You're high. Of course you're high. Hypnos, you can't keep helping your *buddies* out of Tartarus. Things right now are *very* delicate with the Fates, and if I am ever going to outdo them, I cannot be constantly convincing them *not* to put you in there with your friends!"

"I think Tartarus would be fun, actually! I hear he's a great poker player!"

Death snarled and grabbed Dream by his coat. "Do you hear what I am saying to you? Do not go back down there! Do not *help* anyone escape. Look what your *help* did to Eros." Hypnos pushed Death away, and his boot slipped in paint that had coagulated into *organs* on the floor, while the canvases on the walls remained completely *white*.

"You fucking saying he'd be better off down in Tartarus?"

"I'm saying they almost threw him back down there after his *vacation* in the Mortalworld. The shit I had to do to keep him from ending up back down there would unsettle even you, and now *fucking* Loki is dragging him back into it. So, I'd appreciate it if all of you would do me a favor, and *not* help me!"

Thanatos sat back down in front of his masterpiece in-progress.

Living, moving, breathing masterpiece.

Hypnos nearly turned to leave, but instead snarled, "You can't do it all yourself."

"Yes. I can. It's better and more efficient that way. Why do you think I separated from you to begin with?"

"Psht. You didn't kick me out. I kicked you out! Fuck you! You and I being in the same body, the same head-space, was fucking maddening. *So* happy I'm not you anymore, because being you sucks!"

"Yes. It's a thankless job. Anything else?"

"Naw. I'm out, and you can go to hell, except you won't, because you're chicken shit."

Hypnos vanished the way he had come in, through the oil painting of an open grave. Thanatos leaned back to appreciate his work. It was the best one he had painted in a while. It was missing something, though. Scars. He mixed some dark fleshy tones together, and painted on the collar bone a magickal symbol for regeneration, a brand. You'd have to look for it in order to see it but Thanatos would know it was there, like a secret between an artist and his creation.

9

"What do you really look like?" The dark haired woman looked over at the boy sitting in her window sill. His eyes were older than his body. She noticed this as he rested his head against the window pane, watching the falling snow.

He instantly began wringing his hands, but he didn't answer her for a moment.

"There are more scars," he said, "than what you can see. Some people wish them invisible. They don't like to see them."

The woman nodded. "People hurt you?" She asked this as if she was speaking to a child, because to her he was. To her eyes he looked to be only eleven.

But, he laughed like a jaded adult. "Yeah. They hurt

me, but some are trying to help."

"Can *I* help?" She took a small step forward, her step echoing off the stone floors and walls.

"The ones who help are the ones who hurt me the most. You have to be cruel to be kind, in the right measure." He laughed at some joke the woman in the Victorian dress did not understand.

She walked up and sat down on the other end of the window seat. She could feel the cold seeping in through the welded seams of the glass. She folded her hands in her lap.

"Tell me your story, Jinni, so that I may know you better."

The whole story would take too long to tell, but he had been commanded, and he began to feel the unsettling pull in his stomach. If he didn't direct it somewhere, it would cause him to word-vomit out *everything* until he was commanded to stop. The woman had ordered a *story*, anyway, not a play-by-play, so as any good story-teller did, he catered to his audience. He left out the boring parts- a thousand years of nothing, or that time when he lived peaceably for nearly a decade masquerading as a fisherman's nephew in Prince Edward's Island. Instead, he told her tales of treasure-seeking and adventures- people who wished to travel to other worlds, or the moon, or the farthest star. But, he left out the spaceships needed to get there, because her world and time didn't even have home electricity yet. He didn't waste time trying to explain to her the concept of a *light-year*. He took out the parts that were too indecent for her sensibilities as well; the ones with rape, brutality, torture, and Stockholm syndrome. And he avoided the parts too hazy from time to remember.

His retellings made him shiver, made him cry, and he told her those were the tales, "...easiest to tell. There are worse, far worse memories that I can't-"

She put a delicate hand on his. Her touch didn't comfort him- it sent electric splinters all through him, but he couldn't flinch away. Her eyes latched onto his, "In time." She patted his hand, "All in good time. Do not think you need to protect me from your stories, *young man*. I too have tales which may terrify you, and I know from experience that stories can heal. You can tell me anything you wish and nothing more."

He would have rather told her nothing, but it was too late for that.

She stood and walked back towards the fire. "Do you even know what you truly look like?"

"No." He answered, "People wish me into convenient forms, so I can blend in, or suit their needs."

"How have you not gone completely mad?" She pondered to the fire rather than to him, and so he didn't answer. He resumed wringing his hands.

He had gone mad and back several times, because people had commanded him to *stop being crazy* or *act like a normal human being*, and other people with good intentions told him *just don't think about it, focus on the now, don't dwell on the past*, *just think happy thoughts*. Their *good* intentions helped our hero for a moment in time, but just because the bad thoughts, the haunting memories, the anxious habits weren't at the forefront of his mind, didn't mean that they were dormant. Beasts like that blossom in the deep.

"I do not wish for you to hide your true self from me. I will accept you as you are. Form is freedom."

He glanced up, terrified of what her good intentions were about to subject him to. Things had happened to him in his hellish dimension that hadn't affected his form outside of it. So many marks had been wished hidden away- brands of ownership, piercings of servitude, scars from punishments- not gone, just hidden.

He didn't get the chance to protest.

"I wish you to have the form of your true self."

As the wish was granted, he tried to fight it, tried to misdirect it to be symbolic of his true-self, *like how he felt on the inside*, but then he realized that wasn't much better or very different from what the magick was already doing. And this was a big wish. It took big magick, which was not something he could muster enough strength to fight.

He felt his actual bones cracking and moving. He grew taller, but more twisted. Teeth came loose and fell into his mouth. Muscles deteriorated. His wrists withered and disjointed. There wasn't a spot on his flesh that he could see which hadn't been marked by owners, or fire, or time.

He crumpled off the window seat and fell to the floor as his body convulsed under the magickal restoration of *him*. He choked and kicked as aeons of not eating, or drinking, or living took from him the toll he owed.

The woman sank down next to him and held his hand to comfort him during his transition. To be touched was the last thing he wanted. Centuries of hands had left him marred.

She cooed to him, and shushed him, and hummed lullabies to him until his rattling breath became less labored, and his twitching died into a light, all-over tremor.

"It's okay." The woman said, "I'm here, and I don't judge you."

Our hero's vision went black for a moment. These were the words of The Darkness. It was here.

"I think you are beautiful just the way you are..." she whispered, her voice cracking, "Scars and all."

Our hero decided she had read *Frankenstein* too many times as he looked at his knobbed and bent, quivering fingers.

She over-associated herself with the lonely monster of myth- The Doctor's Experiment, The Minotaur, Beowulf, the Jinni. All she wanted was to be seen and loved for all her scars. It was only human.

He was nothing but tattered skin, like a skeleton, like Death.

With one hand, she pet back the few strands of wiry hair that he had left, and picked up his broken teeth off the floor with the other.

He knew what happened next. She'd keep him *safe* in the sewers below like the Phantom of the Opera, or in a bell tower like the Hunchback of Notre Dame. She'd hide him in the basement of the manor, and he'd live there and sleep inside the walls. Or she'd sell him to whatever version of a circus existed in this time and place.

But instead, she helped him into the spare bedroom across the hall, his feet too deformed for walking.

Instead of sleeping in the walls, he'd be sleeping in a bed, reflected in the large oxidized looking-glass of the adjacent vanity. She stood him in front of it, and his stomach dropped. He might have dropped too if she hadn't been cradling his frail elbow.

His already rattling breath seized, and his heart trembled at the sight of the monster in the mirror.

The beautiful dark haired lady next to him smiled. "Do not be afraid of your true self. God has created you to be just as you are. You are special, magickal. This experience will give you power as you learn to embrace yourself. You have lived through all of this."

She waved a hand towards his reflection. He stared in horror at a face laden with piercings, eyes that were red with burst blood vessels, misshapen lips framing a nearly toothless snarl, patchy spots of discolored hair. His skin was raised and rough from tissue damage, and there were growths where there wasn't pitting.

"And in that way," she said, "you are free."

She left him alone in the room after a time, for him to settle into himself. He maneuvered from the bed, where she had placed him, to the floor, where he cradled himself in a corner until the coals of the fire were barely aglow.

Just before dawn, heavy footsteps approached him from inside the room. Before him, he saw two heavily buckled combat boots and Dream's leather trench coat bunched up on the floor as he knelt down.

"Hey, Mate. How's it going? Remember me?" He was beaming, and seemed unphased by our hero's new appearance.

"What's the matter?" He asked in earnest.

It had been an age since Dream had first made an appearance, and since then he would materialize in dreams to take him away from hell or his new possessor for a little while. Our hero, though, could only ever remember him when he was in Dream's realm, never before entry, and never after leaving. The memory of him only ever existed at the edge of his waking mind.

"You wanna get out of here?" Hypnos asked, and our hero nodded.

The Dream King held out his ringed hand, "Come on. Let's go."

Our hero reached out his hand, no longer withered and knotted, and he firmly grabbed a hold of Dream's wrist. Dream hoisted him up, and they were no longer in the manor, but on a ship with full black sails and a polished black deck. It was sailing in a sea of stars.

"Now, I'm Captain, and you're me first mate, savvy?"

"Savvy," he replied, but he was too preoccupied with the sight of his own hands. "It's gone." He said.

Hypnos looked back at him. "What is?"

"My…" He flexed his fingers. "Don't tell me you don't know what I'm talking about?"

"Listen," Dream almost laid a hand on his shoulder, but stopped and pulled it back, remembering his best mate didn't like to be touched, and realizing he had just given him a command. "Alright, I might know what you're talking about. Not gonna lie, but…"

He couldn't tell him it was his soul that mattered; that was just as scarred as his body. Magickal symbols are more than just skin deep, and mental scars are just as permanent. He couldn't promise it would go away or that time heals all wounds; that would have been a lie.

"In a way, the crazy lady's right. You are who you are because of what you've been through. It's the current which has brought you to this place, where mermaids sing, the horizon is the limit, and the rum is a-plenty enough to drink our filthy black guts out! Just don't trust the mermaids. They bite. You know how to sword fight?"

Our hero managed a fake smile. "Yeah. I know how to *fence*."

"Great! Work out that frustration!"

A cutlass appeared in the Jinni's hand.

"En garde!" Hypnos flashed around his own cutlass, which had also magickally appeared.

Our hero looked out at the sea of night sky and the billowing sails. He heard the call of a mermaid and shrugged. "What the hell…"

He raised his sword and dreamt he was a pirate.

After many hours of playing keep-away with the mermaids, they had a small run-in with the ghost crew who had previously sailed the dream ship. The Jinni and Dream won the battle, two against seventy-five, and headed to the captain's quarters for victory drinks.

Dream started off story-time by telling him of the gangs of vampires destroying his favorite city, Rippertown. It was a ramshackle city of burnt-out street lamps and toxic water. The vagabond residents lived for free wherever they pleased, under bridges and abandoned buildings, and they bounced from party to party, rave to rave. But, a Vampire Prince was destroying the anarchy with his gentrification and franchised blood bars.

Hypnos told him the story about how he lost his two favorite pistols in a card game with a methed-out cyclops on that very ship.

And then the Jinni explained why he was in the shape of an eleven-year-old boy. He had belonged to a six-year-old orphan in Carpathia, and the boy had needed an older brother to help fight off bullies. He found, in many realms, he wasn't treated any better as a child than when he was adult-sized. It was often worse, which broke his heart.

"Yeah… kids are great. I don't have any. My brother does, though. He's a good kid. *Hell* of an imagination," Hypnos said proudly.

"What's his name?"

"I don't know."

Our hero quirked an eyebrow, "You don't know? What do you mean you don't know?"

"As in I don't know. Don't be a git. Do you know your name?"

Our hero stopped, and wondered, and remembered not a name.

Hypnos narrowed his eyes, "Give you a hint, mate. It's not *Jinni*."

"I… I guess I don't remember my name, or if I ever had one."

"Well, that's okay then, because I've got a treasure map to help us find it!" Dream materialized a yellowed and tattered scroll.

Our hero took it and unrolled it. It was a map of worlds on top of worlds, sphere after sphere, with tree roots and caves and waterfalls connecting one world to another in faded black ink. There was The Firmament, Asgard, and Tartarus, over which there was a red dot and an arrow marked *you are here*. But there were other names that our hero found either unbelievable or unfamiliar like Avalon, Fairy-Tale World, Dream, Akasha, Faerie, Jontunhiem, Sheol, Umbraland, A'lam Al-Jinn, Cockainge, Diyu, and many, many more. The map took up every inch of the scroll he could see, and he was sure if he kept unrolling it, the map would never end, circle on top of circle, worlds colliding.

Our hero's eyes followed the red line going from *you are here* to *this is where you're going*, marked by a big red X drawn over a place called *The Netherworlds*.

The eleven-year-old shaped Jinni raised an eyebrow. "How?" was all he asked.

"Expand the image like you do on a touch screen," Hypnos told him, and he did as he was told. The map zoomed in to show the detailed passageways of Tartarus. He followed the weaving line through the canals into a dark pit called The Silence, where the line took a ninety-degree turn *down* into The Underworld. From there the line zigzagged to a plane called The Axis Mundi, where there was a pinpoint marked The Garden. A warped and knotted tree was drawn there, and at the base of the tree there was a hollow which would take him to *The Netherworlds*.

"That's how."

"It's hopeless," the Jinni said, despite the ember of hope burning him from the inside out.

"Why?" Hypnos asked.

"In... *Tartarus*- I can't get out. It's my-"

"Punishment?"

The Jinni snarled. "Fate."

"No. See," Hypnos leaned forward, his elbows on his knees and his fingers steepled, "this is a dream, a dream wiffin a dream, wiff Dream inside of itself."

"...okay?"

"I never get involved in politics, but when I do- No one plays fair if they think they can get away wiff it, and I can get away wiff it. Every adventure requires a first step, yeah?"

"Okay..."

"If you don't know where you are going, any road can take you there." He tapped a finger on the map, then to his temple. "How do you run from what's inside your head?"

The Jinni gave this some thought, "Fake it 'till you make it?"

"Exactly! Imagination, mate! Imagination is the only weapon in the war against reality, and reality is a dream, or a nightmare, however you want to look at it." Hypnos snickered to himself, then said, "Meself, personally, I like nightmares, but in this instance, you should take the shortcut."

Our hero squinted at the jumbled strands of logic. "You want me to *dream* myself out of my nightmare?"

"Yeah, pretty much. You dreamt up this map. This is *your* dream. I'm just the stuff it's made from. You have got to go *in* to get out, mate. Savvy?"

"I mean," his brows pulled together in a condescending scowl, "that sounds *nice*, but it *sounds* like hippy-dippy *bullshit*. You think I can just *wish* I may, *wish* I might, really, really hard and *dream* myself out? Are you fucking kidding me with this shit?" His voice was stern, but he never raised it.

"No, I'm not, but once you get the idea, throw it away, and if you can't get it, throw it away. I insist on your *freedom*…"

The Jinni's head tilted to the side, and his eyes wandered around the captain's quarters.

"...which is why you won't remember this when you wake up." Hypnos gave him a sympathetic smile, and our hero nodded.

The Dream King stood and gave his best mate a playful punch on the shoulder, "Come on. We still got a few seconds before dawn back in your world, and that's like hours here in Dream. Let's chase that horizon."

Our hero took a breath. "Okay, but this time I'm Captain. Set sail due East." He turned to look at Hypnos with a smirk.

"Aye, aye, Capitán." Dream smiled.

***

Death doesn't sleep. Death doesn't dream. He removed those needs when he separated Ego from Id shortly after the beginning of *time,* if you can call it that. Back then he didn't call the two parts Ego and Id, but Thanatos and Hypnos.

And with that separation, Thanatos did not dream. Despite this, he was dreaming of a flat gray reality, which was very cramped. The bleak horizon was uncomfortably close all the way around the gray, rocky plane, and before him were three women cloaked in dark rags.

The youngest sat at a spinning wheel, twisting fleece into yarn. The middle one measured the freshly spun yarn into lengths, some ever-so-long, others quite manageable and unremarkable, and a more-than-comfortable amount were shorter than your pinkie. The eldest one cut the lengths and laid the allotted threads down in a wicker basket as she went. She looked on at Death with empty sockets, holding her rusty shears open and ready to cut.

The youngest, Clotho, hummed a dreary tune to the rhythm of her foot pressing on the treadle of the spinning wheel, which creaked as the footman danced up and down. Though she was the maiden amongst her counterparts, her stained fingers, hollow eyes, and scabbed lips were hardly comely.

None of them were *beautiful* in the traditional ways goddesses appear: elegant, graceful, alluring, shapely. But, they were beautiful in their moroseness. The darkness contoured their countenance at drastic angles. Their lurching movements and draping fabrics were phantasmal, and with their black holes for eyes they were bewitching specters. Once you have seen your fate, no matter how gruesome it appears, you cannot unsee it. You cannot look away. You will see it in everything you do, and it will haunt you with its tenebrous beauty.

"Good afternoon, Ladies." Death addressed the Fates. "And how are we today?"

The Book of Fate levitated above its Romanesque pedestal a short distance off, and never did he think too loudly about how to steal it. If he thought it too loudly, if he let the thought form into words instead of a fleeting wisp, the three women might discover the thought and take corrective or preventive measures.

"What is so urgent-" *that it couldn't wait, that you couldn't send a memo, that you pulled me from my ever-important duties, that you found it necessary to disrupt my meeting,* "-that it needs my immediate attention?" The question still came off annoyed, but at least it wasn't directly insulting.

"*There are workings we cannot see...,*" began the eldest, Atropos.

"*...in the house of Laufey*" said the second, Lechesis.

"*Bring them out into the light...,*" said Clotho.

"*... and we will ensure your victory...,*" said Lechesis.

"*...in your next big fight,*" finished Atropos.

He knew they were referring to Loki and Eros. It would be easy enough to tell the Fates that it was business and nothing more, which was true, unless they already knew something he did not. And if he did what they wanted, then *victory in his next big fight* could mean damn near anything. He could rig the board for the *next big fight* to be whatever he wanted it to be, and the Fates knew he could and would do this. He and the Fates had made countless business transactions of this manner before. It was open-ended for his benefit, a perk of working with the Fates, but also a lure to get him to do things he'd otherwise never do. Then again, no one gets rich being honest, and when you're the Grim Reaper, ethics and morality are dismissed as a naive dream. They can't hold up to bitter, cold, dead reality.

Thanatos realized he had been silent for too long. The wheel had stopped spinning, and three sets of black sockets were burrowing into him.

He took in a breath and gave a slight cordial smile. "Of course." He bowed at the neck, and the Fates stood from their places. They glided up to him with an uncanny grace and twisted around him like funeral shrouds. Their discolored, bony fingers grazed his pure white suit. Their scaly cheeks pressed against his chest. A dry tongue somehow managed to lick the soft flesh behind his ear. He was towering, and they were small, but one by one he wetted their mouths of dust with the kiss of Death, and he was overwhelmed by their *absolute* power.

This was how deals were struck between the *Old Ones*. No one could remember why anymore. It had probably happened back when Eros had been a force to be admired, and desired, and feared, and worshiped. Only Desire would have invented a pact-sealing kiss.

As these formidable women spiraled around him in folds of dark linen, Death heard them moan, and laugh, and hum that dreary, dreary tune. He awoke, as it were, in his white office with a man in front of his desk, droning on and on about interest rates and real estate. Thanatos gave his head a light shake to clear it, and he nodded as if he had been listening to the man the entire time.

10

*E*ros awoke alone in Loki's bed. He sat up and stared at the gray light permeating through the curtains. His head was empty and numb, but heavy. The room was filled with the static of silence.

Eros remembered. Loki was in love with him.

With steady hands he unbuttoned the giant's shirt and left it on the bed with the tangled sheets. He picked his own shirt off the floor and made himself look as presentable as possible. He vanished the wrinkles in his clothes. He magicked his hair messy-on-purpose and his tie straight. He waved a hand so his body was perfumed with rose and frankincense, rather than reeking of ecstasy. If he had left Loki's home and stepped into the bustling afternoon street smelling like that, he'd instigate an orgy.

With shoulders broad and straight he trotted down the stairs, but slowed to the sound of sizzling, scraping, and humming coming from the kitchen.

Eros froze in terror as the fact he already knew sank deep into his gut.

This was going to be painful and awkward.

He might not ever see Loki again after this. Or if he did, Loki might hate him, and Eros knew what Loki's scorn looked like. He had seen it at Death's parties and other events. There was no one better in the Cosmos to make one look like an ignorant, simple fool in front of all of the gods than Loki. And Eros had suffered enough of that for a lifetime. Then again, his reputation couldn't get much worse than it already was. It would be adding insult to injury for him personally, but to the public eye it would only be a sprinkling of dirt on the trainwreck that was his life. They would hardly notice the offense being added to the toppling pile of Eros's existing indiscretions.

He closed his eyes, swallowed all the emotions, and walked into the kitchen, straightening his cuffs as he did. "Loki."

"Afternoon. Do you eat?" He didn't give Eros time to respond. "It's no bother if you do. I can make more."

Eros examined the plate piled high with flat cakes, fruit drizzled with honey, and nuts.

"Well, actually-," Eros began.

Loki cut him off, "I don't mind cooking. I know it's a bit mundane, but I quite like the art versus the procedure of it. You have a recipe, written out step by step, and you can follow that recipe to the tee, but it will always be missing something and won't be quite right, unless..." He plucked a blackberry off of the top of the towering plate and popped it into his mouth, "...you add a bit extra of this or that, or substitute something you're missing with something else. Otherwise, it will never taste the way mum used to make it, and that applies to everything in life." Loki leaned his elbows on the kitchen island, and folded his hands.

Eros found himself smiling and reset his jaw. "I'm afraid I can't stay. I have to go take care of... but it was nice of you to offer."

Loki's eyes bore into him, a wise smirk on his face. He just sat there smirking and staring without really even blinking. Eros almost made to turn and walk out a couple of times, but Loki's scrutinizing, unbreaking gaze had Eros fixed.

Loki watched Eros twitch under the breakdown of proper conversational structures with the prolonged silence. Eros panicked, not knowing what to do.

"Soooo... Err...?" Eros tried to break the silence. He tried to walk away, but Loki stared on, smiling.

Usually, other men whom Eros had put in Loki's position would start asking questions. Why are you leaving? What's so important? Or they would deflect to save their pride, or if Eros was lucky, they would politely walk him to the door. No one ever just stared that way for so long.

"Of course," Loki finally said. Eros visibly released

the breath he was holding, and immediately rolled his eyes at the realization that Loki was fucking with him. "I'll walk you out."

Eros wordlessly gestured around and eventually dropped his hand in defeat. "Okay…"

Loki stood abruptly tall, and took one long step to Eros's side. He smirked and escorted Eros to the front door-very slowly.

"I really enjoyed last night," Loki said, his hands behind his back. "The bit where Hypnos showed up. Oh! And, the falling asleep alone on the couch decoding Dreamriddles, classic!" Loki said in a cutesy tone.

"Oh?" Eros asked, confused and aggravated.

"I especially enjoyed the part where I tricked you into opening the bottle just in case there was a curse inside. What part did you enjoy most?" Loki had stopped at the stair rail when they finally reached it, and Eros hurried to grab his coat.

Eros glared at him, knowing Loki had a punchline coming. "Making you bite your tongue at Devereaux's house!"

"Yes! That was good. Oh, I know! What about that part where you told me I was in love with you? Huh, wow! Wasn't that crazy?" Loki's grin mocked him.

Eros lashed out at him. "Yes. Exactly! It was crazy. It shouldn't have happened. It was only a fleeting moment of lust. I was mistaken. It was just sex and nothing more. Can we please be adult about this and move on? I have to go."

Eros turned towards the door, but Loki jumped forward and grabbed the handle, acting like he was going to open the door for him, but he didn't.

"Yes, you have to go take care of your turtles."

"Right. My…" He shook his head and looked at Loki. "What?"

"Your turtles. You said you had to take care of your turtles. I completely understand. Turtles are high maintenance, and you've left them unattended for quite some time."

Eros fought a bout of laughter, "What are you talking about? My turtles. I don't have any turtles!"

"Well, I thought, if we were saying complete and utter bullshit to avoid dealing with an unpleasant reality, I'd go with pet turtles."

They looked into each other's eyes, Eros wondering if he should stay. Loki pondered, wondering if he should have just let Eros leave and leave this burning feeling nameless here forevermore. Was it sex and nothing more?

Eros's eyes had gone dark, dark with lust or anger Loki knew not which, and still they stood there, both transfixed. Deep in Desire's amber eyes peering, long they stood there wondering, fearing, doubting, dreaming dreams no immortal ever dared to dream before. But the silence was unbroken, and the stillness gave no token, and no words were there spoken-

-interrupted only by a rapping, rapping at the townhouse door.

The two gods' gazes remained unbroken, as their eyes implored unspoken, who the fuck is tapping, tapping at the townhouse door?

Loki slowly turned the handle, smiling to avoid a scandal, but their smiles flicker'd like candles, as he opened wide the door. Grins turned grim at the sight of the ungainly, ghastly, ominous, and ancient form entreating entry at the townhouse door. His eyes had all the seeming of a demon's that is dreaming, and the sunlight o'er him streaming, threw his shadow on the floor.

"Good afternoon, gentlemen." Death removed his hat. "Truly your forgiveness I implore, for dropping by unannounced-"

"Think of it nevermore, Thanatos," Loki waved away Death's apology sardonically. "To what do I owe this displeasure?"

"You mentioned the other day Eros was organizing your collection. I've come by to see it, unless you are currently indisposed?"

"Well, Eros was just leaving," said Loki .

"Yes, I have… turtles." Eros restrained a smirk.

Death ignored Eros's absurd comment. "You should stay." He made to step through the door, and Eros and Loki stepped aside to accommodate him. "You are the one who did most, if not all of the work, afterall."

Loki licked his teeth and looked away, aggravated and a little ashamed.

"Uh, yes," Eros said, looking into the eyes of Death,

who did not return his gaze. "Right this way."

Eros led Thanatos up the stairs and into the library. There were still scattered boxes and papers, given not much work had been completed the day before.

"We organized it," Loki smirked. "In categories, alphabetically, in chronological order," he added, hoping Thanatos's head would spin 'round.

"Obviously. That's the only efficient way to organize such a collection."

Loki's prideful smirk vanished, and when Death's back was turned, Loki made a face and stuck out his tongue.

Eros shot Loki a warning glance.

"What have you unearthed in this disheveled horde, Eros?"

Eros cleared his throat, "Um… lost Akashic records, Hand of Glory, Gabriel's Trumpet, Fenrir's Chain, mermaid tears, basilisk venom, a collection of bezoars, which is disgusting, the Pied Piper's pipe, Titiana's wand-"

"She's been looking for that," Thanatos mused as he scanned the shelves.

Loki grinned. "She can have it back when she hands over that first born child she owes me."

"You do know fairies do not produce children in that manner?"

"Oh, yes. I know. That was the point." Loki rocked back on his heels.

Thanatos gave him a slight humored smile, and replied, "Oh so clever, Loki."

"Might I ask," Eros interjected, "what sort of thing are you looking for, so that I can better assist?"

"Just window shopping. I was rather hoping Loki's infamous collection would have something outside the realm of the mundane, but as usual I find myself incredibly disappointed."

Loki maneuvered his position to stand directly in front of the box containing The Bowl of Fate. He leaned against the stack inconspicuously.

"Well," Loki reworked his frown into a self-conscious grimace, "of course there was no chance of my humble jumbled horde to even remotely compare to your refined collection, Thanatos."

"No, but it would be nice to see something in the universe that gave me even the slightest thrill of wonder or excitement… Something worth desiring in this world of chaos." He gave himself a rare and tiny smirk, which went unnoticed by the others.

"And you had hoped to find that here?" Loki scoffed. "You certainly came to the wrong place."

Eros shot a questioning glance at Loki, who answered the gaze by subtly tapping his fingers on the box he was guarding. Eros then understood Loki's intention. They needed to keep him believing there was nothing of interest to see here.

"Hope is the greatest evil," Eros added, looking back at the towering man with mismatched eyes.

"How unimpressively Greek of you, Eros." His eyes

continued to browse and never once made eye contact, "After all your people have put you through, haven't you thought of finding a new philosophy?"

That landed a damaging blow to Eros's pride as Thanatos had intended it to, but Eros coasted right along. "Like you, I'm so *bloody old*, nothing really excites me anymore."

From out of the corner of his eye, Eros saw Loki's jaw clench. But, he continued because Thanatos needed to be distracted from the valuable artifact. "There's hardly anything new to see."

Thanatos finally looked at Eros, but it was only for a second.

Loki stepped forward from off the boxes, "Well, I disagree with both of you jaded twits." Loki was as stern as a schoolmaster, his pride a little battered by Eros's comment. "Honestly, with both of you being *so old* you should know better. There are new things in the universe every fucking day, every bloody second. And all you have to do to see it is open your fucking eyes and look at what is directly in front of you, and then you'd notice! But you both are too fucking afraid to do so. Heaven forbid you do that. You might accidentally look into a mirror and see yourselves for what you've really become, and lo! What horror that might be! Excuse me." Loki took long strides to the door, leaving the box exposed to Thanatos's view.

"He's so sensitive," Thanatos hissed.

Eros moved to sit on the crate Loki had been guarding.

"That appeared to be misdirected anger of a sort," Thanatos observed. "Perhaps, I'll revisit at a later time."

Eros only nodded as Thanatos headed towards the door.

"It was good to see you in better circumstances, Eros. Farewell."

"Farewell." Eros looked down. He waited with bated breath for Death to step out into the hall, but he stopped short at the door.

"Ah! I almost forgot." He turned back. "I'm hosting another party next month for a far more... select crowd. Just collectors. Obviously, you and Loki are invited." He produced a designed invitation from his breast pocket that looked similar to the card on Eros's fruit basket.

"It's just the one invitation for the both of you. It would be rather silly to invite you separately, wouldn't it?" His tone was clear and pointed, and Eros knew what he was implying.

"Hypnos told you, did he?"

"No. Your eyes did. When Loki left the room."

"You know me too well." Eros's tone was flat as he took the invitation.

"You're still seeing my brother, I presume?" Death asked uncomfortably.

Eros's brows arched, "You mean *your other half*? Yes. Well, he only popped in, so no. Not in a while."

Thanatos nodded. "Do be careful using Loki as a toy. He tends to bite."

Eros's eyes fell to the ground. "He's not a toy," he said through gritted teeth.

"Aw, well... We shall see, won't we, Casanova?"

Thanatos exited the library. He made his way downstairs, where Loki sat tamping his pipe.

"I'm off," Thanatos announced.

Loki stood from the sofa and waved a hand over his pipe until it was perfectly lit.

"I'll be sure to call next time before I make an appearance."

"What a privilege! Most people don't get the chance to prepare before Death comes a'knocking."

"Very funny," Death deadpanned.

"I aim to please."

"Are you sure you know what you're doing?"

Loki's eyes darted around, "With… *pleasing*?"

"With Eros."

"Ah! Same difference. What do you mean, and how did you-" Loki's brows narrowed. If Thanatos already knew then who else did?

"Word travels fast."

"Evidently." Loki glared.

"You are aware of his *reputation*?" Death asked.

Loki blinked, partially offended and partially amused. "Are you aware of *mine*?"

"He's lost and disenfranchised. He habitually clings to men with money who can afford to support his lifestyle."

Loki scoffed, "That doesn't explain Hypnos."

"Actually, it does."

Loki blinked, "The very fact that you claim to have any interest in my well-being tells me this is a farce, because you have exactly *zero* interest in my well-being. I don't know what you're up to, but frankly, I'm already bored with it. Perhaps, you and I should just stick to business."

"Everything is business, Loki. Everything."

The ruby red bottle sitting on the coffee table caught Thanatos's curious gaze for a small glimmering moment. Then he put on his hat and ducked out the door.

"Well, that was unsettling," Eros's voice came from the top of the stairs.

Loki was chewing on his pipe stem. "Yes. It was a bit odd. He actually never shows up unannounced."

"And I doubt he often shows up here."

"*Never* would be a more accurate word, but he did want to see the collection."

"That's not what he wanted to see and you know it," Eros said condescendingly.

"How does he already know?" Loki sounded aggravated. "I mean, hell, it was just one night!"

Eros should have told Loki that it was a glance, just one glance that gave it away, but he didn't. He walked down the stairs.

Loki began, "I fear what we said last night might be more accurate than I would like. *The Netherworlds isn't going to tolerate it.* If this is of some interest to Death, then it's likely of interest to the Fates, and you're already on their list. You should probably go."

Loki dipped a hand into his pocket as he looked down at the beautiful god's burning amber eyes. He tilted his head.

Eros's eyes were on fire. "Why?" The Greek god snarled out.

"B-Because… they could leverage me against you in numerous, unimaginable ways to get you thrown into Tartarus."

"Then so be it." Eros held out Thanatos's invitation. "Take me to the ball?"

Loki raised an eyebrow and took the invitation. "The Collectors Gala?"

"He thought he'd save paper by making just the one invitation for both of us."

Loki grimaced. "Well…"

"Just think! They're already terrified because we spent just one night together."

"Yes, but…"

"Imagine how terrified they'd be if we decided to spend more nights... together? Apparently, we could destroy everything." Eros smiled deviously, recalling Hypnos's prophecy.

"That is ridiculous." Loki turned into the sitting room.

"Think about who that message came from though! *Beginning to the end* of what? The tyranny of Fate?"

Loki looked down at the notes he had left on the table from last night, happy Thanatos had not seen them.

"Let's not get ahead of ourselves," Loki cautioned.

"We'd be exercising our free will. Even if it's just to stand up against this horrid world, we'd still be *trying*."

Loki thought about chains, torment, and darkness for the rest of Eros's eternity because of one quick love affair, and the thought must have made its way to his face.

"Oh come off it." Eros protested, "It's not like you to play it safe."

Loki glanced over at Eros's exuberant face and the passion burning behind those amber eyes. They were dark and glowing again, the embers of dreams no immortals dared to dream.

Loki knew battles were more easily won when there was nothing left to lose, but they would never begin if there wasn't something to die for.

"Alright. You've convinced me. We're really going to do this then?"

Eros took in a deep breath. "Yes."

"Even if you have to tolerate my existence for the rest of your own?"

Eros blushed and looked away, only to look up at Loki through his eyelashes a second later. "Let's go on a proper date first?"

"Fair enough."

***

Our hero had learned a trick or two from Patrick

Swayze. He sang annoying, repetitive songs in Tartarus to keep the Darkness at bay.

"Fifty-eight bottles of beer on the wall. Fifty-eight bottles of beer..."

He didn't recall when he began calling his prison Tartarus, or even a prison for that matter. It had been his fate, a consequence of his actions, not even penance, because *penance* implies a sin had been committed. He never assumed he had committed a sin. He had done a *thing*, a thing which he could not remember, but that he did not regret, and this was what came of his decision.

Though at great despair, he had been resigned to this fate for most of his existence, but rebellion is borne from stagnation.

"Take one down. Pass it around. Fifty- What number was I at?"

Fifty-seven... The Darkness groaned.

"Oh. Fifty-seven bottles of beer on the wall!"

Please. Stop. You have been singing this fucking *song for weeks without end. I'm begging you. Just stop...*

"Okay, I'm Henry the Eighth, I am. Henry the Eighth, I am, I am-"

I will have the demons carve out your tongue!

"I've had worse." He would have shrugged if he were not suspended. "And then I would just hum it, and then they'd cut out my throat, and I'd just *think* the song really, really loudly. And then my body will eventually regenerate, and the process would start back over again.

You could just leave."

I am Erubus. I am the Darkness. Wherever light cannot prevail, I am present. I penetrate everything in this land; therefore, there is no escape from your insistent singing!

He was quiet for a moment, then, "This is the song that never ends. It goes on and on my friends. Someone started singing it not knowing where to end-"

May you never again feel the sun upon your flesh! May my quintessence fester in your soul for as long as it-

His vessel was opened, and he found himself kneeling in hot sand underneath a squelching sun.

The Jinni glanced up to see traveling people of the desert bow to him. The eldest of the men clenched the Jinni's vessel in his aged hands. It was currently in the shape of a ruby red perfume bottle.

"Great Spirit," said the man in an ancient tongue of a forgotten land. He did not look up from the ground, "we have summoned you for your wisdom and knowledge. We pray you show us mercy, and accept our humble offerings."

Younger apprentices in more modest robes shuffled to him, never taking their eyes off the sand. They set before him wineskins, and fruit, and honey.

"Will you accept our offerings and aid us in our journey?"

"What is your journey?" asked the Jinni in their language. His voice was a permanent rasp even when singing to the darkness.

The man almost glanced up, "Our journey is of self-knowledge and enlightenment so that we may better serve Him in this life and the next. Praise be."

"I am not a religious man."

"But, you are a Jinni?" The man said this in a different tone than our hero had ever heard before. Usually the phrase was of confusion, shock, or horror. But this man's tone was one of reverence. "I thought all Djinn are religious. You are one of His many designs. You are of Him." The man raised his head to look our hero's deformed countenance in the eye, without a trace of fear or disgust. "Have you lost your way, Great Spirit?"

"I guess you could say that." There is no direct translation of this phrase into the language they were speaking, so the closest thing to *I guess you could say that* more directly translated into a heavily sardonic and layered *Perhaps.*

The man gave him a generous smile that was wrinkled from sun and time.

"Then, perhaps, we shall journey together." And he bowed once more before standing. "We have prepared accommodations. We hope they are to your liking."

The frail Jinni tried to stand himself, but found the sinking sand to be unforgiving to his uneven gate.

The man offered him a walking staff, which he took gratefully. Though it helped him stand erect, moving towards the camp was still a grueling process. The old man walked beside him, never once complaining or losing patience.

They entered a large bedouin tent. The interior was spacious but bare. Brass lamps were hung from the center pole, and there was a small area on the floor for conversation. It was adorned with the few aged pillows and throws they possessed, and there was a tarnished silver tea set in the center of the seating area.

The wineskins and plates of fruits and honey, which had first been presented to him, were now carried in behind them by the apprentices.

"Seeking truth and spiritual peace, we have summoned many of the spirits from our holy texts, but none such as you. You are not one among the daemons we call. Your presence came to me in a vision of smoke." The old Sage sat on the cushions and gestured for him to do the same.

Our hero used the wooden staff to lower himself onto the pillows across from the Sage. His eyes followed the buzzing apprentices as they swarmed around him, setting down the trays of dried fruits and meats.

"A vision?" Our hero was skeptical of the Sage's story.

Previously, people had used magick summonings and locator spells to obtain his vessel, but he couldn't recall any time where a vision had been the source of that inspiration.

"It was merely a few nights ago, as the sun was dying, its red light bleeding out across the horizon. I sat before the fire. The flickering flames danced before me, casting shadows both of flesh and of fantasy before mine eyes. The twisting smoke took on both human and daemon form. The smoke figure was twisted and wrought, having witnessed all the tragedies of man. He turned to me, his face eyeless and atrophied. He spoke unto me through the crackling flame, 'When the fantasies of Arabian nights interweave with the mirages of desert days, all sense of time is lost to the sands. Memories are manipulated and forgotten. Dreams materialize against the haze of the setting sun, and all things tangible sift through your fingers, leaving in your grasp only a few grains of desert sand.'"

A quiet moment passed between them.

"What does it mean to you?" the Jinni asked.

The man's keen eyes narrowed as he looked into the face of the Jinni. "I have spent my life in pursuit of sacred, esoteric knowledge. I have lived in the fantastical world of spirits and visions and magick," The old man's face became youthful at that thought, but it quickly faded into wisdom as he said, "however, I did not notice how quickly the years had passed. I have, with my work, made peace with the darkest caverns of my soul, but I find myself grasping for meaning beyond my own salvation as my sun sets.

"Upon my vision in the smoke, I knew I must summon you, and that night while I slept, the ritual to do so was given to me as clearly as if I was truly performing the rite. Upon waking, before the vision slipped from my mind, I ordered the rite be completed as it was dreamt, and here you are- It worked! I will help you, Jinni, and thus you will help me," he said assuredly.

The Jinni shook his head gently in disbelief. "With?"

"*Meaning*. Purpose. I must leave this world holding more in my hands than just *sand*. And you, Great Spirit, must find your dreams."

Something deep and ancient stirred at the very center of our hero's chest as the command took hold. *You must find your dreams*, and he swallowed it before it rose up in manifested emotion. "As a rule," he began solemnly, "I do not wish. I do not want. I do not pray. I do not believe, and I definitely do not dream." This was all a lie.

Someone once commanded him to have *hope* and *belief* before. He didn't quite remember the circumstances, but the hope and belief remained. Despite wanting and wishing not to hope or believe, he did, and he hated himself for it.

The Sage's watchful eyes became soft. "Non-attachment is a profound spiritual practice. What you are describing is not the practice of non-attachment. What you are describing, you do for survival, not for growth, Great Spirit." The old Sage leaned in with passion and youth illuminating his ancient countenance, "There are dreams beyond this horizon, dreams you cannot comprehend, dreams so thick with blood and with honey, powerful enough even the Lord of Dream cannot control them. They are what keep you running and fighting, and they are what keep you dead." His sharp eyes narrowed. "You must make your way past this horizon. You *must* find these dreams."

Any other person who offered to help him, he shot down, but this time he couldn't. He had been commanded, and aside from that, he had *hope* that the Sage could set him free, if not from his prison, at least from his own mind. He did *believe* it, even if he didn't want to.

He wanted to hate the Sage, for on *this* horizon he could see only the ruin and despair that would follow this fantasy of false hope, but he couldn't. The foolish old man was so earnest and determined. What did it matter what was real or imagined if it made this man's life worth living?

Maybe the both of them could gain meaning and purpose by helping each other. Even if it was just more fantasy, smoke, and haze, the Sage didn't need to know, and the man could die a good death.

The Jinni bowed his head to the old man, "As you wish…"

11

The vessel had always been cursed to move on after a period of time. Our hero had never stayed in one dimension or time for very long, but as the weeks, months, and years passed without incident, he began to truly believe in this man's power of will.

With the magick symbols of their land, the Sage had placed the ruby red perfume bottle into a chest atop an altar. The chest was adorned with protection symbols, dressed with oils, and fed holy smoke. The altar was blessed with the protection of many different spirits.

The altar was watched over every hour of the day and night by apprentices appointed to keep the sacred flame on the altar from extinguishing.

The apprentices showed no want or greed for wishes.

Their passion for conquering their minds was a matter of pride. It was meant to be a long battle, the goal being to arise from the fight scarred and old, but humbled and wise. This result could not be granted. It must be lived.

All of the men and women of the camp knew him not as Jinni, but as *Great Spirit*, because that is all that the Sage called him. He was treated with honor and respect, both as an elder and a *god*.

He grew more comfortable telling his stories as more people asked him for his ear and his advice, as more healing men and women used his multidimensional scars and disfigurements to practice their healing art.

He grew less dependent on his walking aid. Towards the end, he could manage to walk from the flap of the Sage's tent to the cushions while leaving his staff outside, but he was slow and needed help to stand back up after hours of sitting.

Despite the man's old age of seventy-six, young compared to our hero's eternity, he had many stories to tell: his stories, the stories of others, and the stories of the land and its magick.

Our hero absorbed all the knowledge he could of their magick, and what he learned was this...

Everything had an energetic pulse. This electrical circuit, which existed in all things, could be rerouted to other circuits to affect change. A handful of sand could be electrified into a shard of glass. The passion of hate could be redirected into a passion of love. A symbol of life could be repurposed into a symbol of death.

The lines of symbols and written words, like the ones carved into our hero's flesh, were pathways for energetic currents. If the intent of the energy was changed, if the pathways were redirected, one could overload the circuit and break the connection.

The old Sage only ever made one wish. He did not wish for a copy of the *words* originally used to place the curse upon the Jinni's vessel, but he wished instead for a *map* of the curse's circuitry.

When it appeared, this map was filled with interlocking geometric symbols and allegorical imagery. The scroll looked more like a strange pirate map, rather than the modern electrical blueprint our hero had pictured when he had helped the Sage in wording the wish.

The Sage spent most of his days in his tent looking over the map, just trying to understand it, memorize it. He tried to get a feel for the topography, but he saved the *nights* for telling our hero stories and to listen to the stories our hero told.

They met in the Sage's tent each time the sun melted over the edge of the world, and they did this for years. The Sage tended to the Jinni's frail limbs, and the Jinni grew stronger. In return, the Jinni tended to the Sage as he grew older and weaker.

One night after a tale of senseless war, our hero said bitterly, "People just like to watch others suffer. Nothing you can do about it."

The Sage responded. "Well, despite this, one must still try to do the right thing..."

"True. But then, good deeds rarely go unpunished." They both laughed. "If people think they'll get repaid for doing *good*, they have been tragically misinformed. There's a far better payout for doing the wrong thing."

"But one should do right, not for the payout, as you call it, but because it is *right*." The Sage sipped his tea.

The Jinni reflected, "There have been plenty of times I've done all the wrong things for the right reasons, and all the right things for the wrong reasons. I don't think the *right* thing to do is always obvious, or cut and dry. I just think it doesn't matter what you do as long as you're willing to pay the consequences."

"But the ultimate consequence, the afterlife. Paradise. *That* is what matters and why we should always do what is *right*."

The Jinni looked into the face of his friend and asked heavily, "Hypothetically, what if you had to give up *your* Paradise? Go to hell instead to save somebody else from damnation? Would you do that?"

The Sage laughed. "Paradise is not a place. It is a soul's state of being. Being at peace within one's own soul..."

The Jinni thought and said, "But see, If Paradise is just a state of mind, then a person who is at peace with their actions, whether they be right or wrong, can achieve Paradise. So, does it even really matter what is *right*?"

The Sage rebutted, "Let us imagine, though, a person

who has committed atrocities with *no* apparent remorse. Now, they might *believe* they are settled in their soul, but when the end comes, they will see *truth*, and they will find no peace, because they have lied to themselves for all of their lives. This is why we seek truth in *this* plane of existence, for when we enter unto the next, we will know we have not been deceived. Honesty is quintessential, and I pity those who cannot be honest with themselves."

The Great Spirit replied, "But, this land is simple compared to other worlds I've had the pleasure of living in. It's easy to be honest with yourself here, where the temptations are few and far between. But, there are worlds where life is so complex, untangling the *truth* of right and wrong is an endless, meaningless agony. In some places, they can't even buy organic almond milk or a fair trade cotton t-shirt without contributing to global warming, or child labor, or some other evil. Everything they do is a part of a complex chain of events, and they *honestly* can't move without indirectly causing harm, so the only option they have is to just deal with the consequences."

"Well I pity them, and pray for their souls."

"I'm sorry, friend, but your pity and prayers won't do them any *good*."

The old Sage smiled and clasped the Jinni's hand. Our hero didn't flinch. He only smiled back, and the Sage helped him to his feet. Once standing, the old man put his hands on both of the Jinni's shoulders, which were beginning to gain shape and strength. He held the Jinni at arms length and studied his visage.

His sharp eyes narrowed and he nodded. "You have taught me so many things I did not know, Great Spirit, like the hymns of Aerosmith and Johnny Cash."

"Well-"

"They were wise prophets, and I am wiser because of them, and because of you. You have been both a teacher and a friend, and you should know you were the final key to my enlightenment." The old man removed a hand from the Jinni's shoulder and placed it over his own heart. "I am truly blessed by having met you."

The Jinni's head tilted to the side at the sudden outpour of affection. "Should I be concerned?"

"No. Not at all. You should be excited for a new dawn."

As he went to leave, the Jinni's peripheral vision caught sight of the scroll on the table at the side of the tent.

That night the Jinni lay awake trying *not* to think about freedom, a life without fear amongst his new fellows. They hadn't spoken a word about it, but he knew the Sage thought he had found a way to break the curse. A way to free him from the land of darkness and demons, a land he hadn't seen since the Sage had summoned him.

He tried very hard *not* to think about having the freedom to learn their magick. He understood it all in theory, but his magick was still not his own, and try as he may, his own energetic currents were still bound to that accursed bottle. Perhaps, after the sun had set the following day, they would belong only to him.

He tried not to think about belonging to himself, completely, wholly unto himself. To what, or whom, would he devote himself if he had the *choice*, the free will? Would he ever even want to be devoted to someone else again?

Perhaps in marriage, he thought, and he tried to push the thought out of his mind. He didn't want to think about how much he might like to be with a woman like some he'd met, the ones with hands graceful enough to paint or play an instrument. He thought about the women he'd met who would talk with him for hours about everything and nothing, and the women who were brave enough to stand alone, and the ones strong enough to command a room. He had met women like that, with long dark hair, and eyes that pierced like daggers, with diamond cut jawlines, and minds as quick as spring traps.

He felt a heat rising inside of him, and his heart skipped a beat. He had found his *dream*. That's what he wanted, and he shook his head and tried to squelch the desire. He didn't *want* to want to be in *love*, but there it was.

He was able to push all other thoughts away except *that* one, and it kept him awake until dawn.

***

The next night, all the elders and the best of the apprentices met in the Sage's tent. The Jinni joined the old man in the center of the congregation.

"For the last two solar cycles," the Sage addressed the men and women, "I have studied the curse of this bottle."

Two apprentices accompanied an elder who was carrying the intricate chest containing the ruby red bottle. She brought it to the center of the unfolding ritual while the Sage spoke.

"I now believe I have found the way to break this curse and unbind this Great Spirit from his container."

The room applauded as the trunk was opened. Nestled inside the trunk, the ruby red, glass bottle cast glimmers around the dimly lit tent. The Jinni shrank from all the eyes he felt staring at him.

The sage continued, "I will, however, require your assistance. I only ask that you hold the space, and lend me whatever energy you can." An apprentice reverently held the bottle out to him. He took it, moved forward, and set the insidious thing between himself and the Jinni.

He beckoned the Jinni to step forward, but the Jinni didn't move. The sight of that pretty red prison had him frozen. His brain hazed over, his gut wrenched, and his hands began to shake.

"Do not be afraid, friend."

He met the eyes of the Sage, who held nothing in his eyes but joy and comfort.

The Jinni stepped forward without fear, as commanded. The Sage took the Jinni's deformed face in his hands, the bottle between them on the floor.

Our hero felt the vessel's energy building a wall

between himself and his friend, but he felt no fear.

"As the great prophet, Johnny Cash, preached- *Now I've been out in the desert, just doing my time, searching through the dust, looking for a sign. If there's a light up ahead, well brother I don't know, but I got this fever burning in my soul, so let's take the good times as they go, and I'll meet you further on up the road.*"

The Jinni laughed, and the Sage lowered the Jinni's face and kissed his forehead.

"It will be alright," he reassured. He took the Great Spirit's hands. "Go find your dreams."

His weathered, but gentle, hands slipped from the Jinni's like sand.

He waved to the crowd like a conductor, and the choir began to chant and sing. "Everyone…," he gestured for them to join him. The Sage closed his eyes, and began to meditate.

The tent was still, despite the sheer number of people imbuing it with song. The reverence of the mass filled the tent like steam, and the hairs on our hero's arms prickled up as a bead of sweat trickled down his face.

Glowing gold symbols appeared on the cut red glass, and he took a step back to see them clearly. They were made of words, thousands of tiny words in rolling script moving down the bottle like binary code on a 1980's computer screen. The script began to glitch and crack. Full symbols and lines began to flicker and vanish as they twisted around the glass. Then, cracks of light began to splinter and refract from the bottle.

The Jinni looked up at the crowd, wondering if they too were witnessing this phenomenon, but their eyes were closed. The entire room was working towards his freedom, and he realized he had never been in a place like this before, where he felt like he belonged and was loved.

The curse was breaking, and he watched the glowing script move up his own skin, words and phrases and symbols flickering and breaking out into shards of light, like he was breaking out of himself, shattering his connection to that damned bottle.

The wind whipped up, and the tent panels began to bellow and kick. The ropes strained, and seams began to tear.

Sand began to swirl around the room, and the Jinni could feel the energy of the people becoming unsure and distracted. Despite his own uncertainty, the words continued to break on both his flesh and the bottle. Then, the sand stung at his eyes.

He had felt this ripping, dragging feeling before. He had been in this sand storm before, once upon a time, inside a mirage...

"Wait," he called out. "Wait!"

Magick was warping around him in what sounded like thunder, and his hands were disappearing from sight. The Jinni could barely make out the Sage as he crumpled to his knees in the sand.

Our hero was suspended in darkness.

"No," he said through the thudding in his heaving chest. "No…"

Yes. Said the Darkness. *It's okay. I'm here for you. I'm here…*

***

The Sage was dead in the sand. His eyes were glazed over. The people of the desert stood back in awe and confusion, the loss to their community yet to sink in. The wind and sand had settled.

"Where did the Great Spirit go?" asked one of the elders.

"Gone," said a strange voice from the back of the room. "Back to Tartarus."

A pale man with mismatched eyes who stood in the corner of the room lowered the hood to his long black cloak.

"Lord of Dream!" some exclaimed upon the recognition of one of their deities. The crowd bowed down in the sand.

Dream grimaced and began to tiptoe around them in his awkwardly heavy boots, not made for tiptoeing or sand. He nearly fell over as he entered the center of the tent where the ruby red bottle still sat, looking defiantly unscathed. He righted himself and raised his arms. "It's good! I'm good! Nearly face-planted there, alright, so…" His gaze landed on the Sage, smiling in death upon the floor, and the congregation stared.

"He died to save his friend. The bugger knew it would happen. Planned it that-a-way. And it worked! I know it doesn't look like it, but it totally paid off. He uh, the Great Spirit," Hypnos waved his ringed hand around, "who is actually me best mate, was unbound from the, uh, *thing*." He had forgotten the words *vessel, bottle,* and *container.* "But, see, his *real* body was someplace else, Tartarus. The body you know, well it was still real, but it wasn't. Do you get it? It was like... *Astral!* That's the word. It was like his spirit body. His spirit body was the thing bound to the, uh- the bottle! Yeah. So you did save him, in that his soul is now detached from this bottley-thing," he gestured at the red cut glass, still glimmering audaciously in the sand. "So, give yourselves a pat on the back!"

No one moved, but a young child began to cry.

Hypnos grimaced and shrank, "Okay, so I'm not explainin' it right, but this is a good thing! I'm just gonna..." He picked up the bottle and stuffed it in the pocket of his cloak, then began to make his way out of the wind blown tent.

"Lord of Dream," an elder called out, and Hypnos froze as if he were caught doing something bad.

"We may not comprehend what it is you are explaining to us, but pray... tell us... what has become of our eldest member's soul?"

Dream looked at the body on the floor.

"Has he too been released, unbound from this mortal plane?"

"You see, my brother, the Lord of Death, has taken him… from this plane… to the next, ya know? Land of the Dead! And... lots a' things can happen after that. But, I gotta go deliver this... *thing,* so catch ya on the flip side."

Hypnos saluted and stepped from the disheveled tent. Hurrying to the next tent over, where the altar was kept, he stepped into the eternal flame and vanished, entering the Netherworlds from a public bathroom mirror on the other side.

He exited what turned out to be a women's restroom and crept down a hall echoing with Frank Sinatra's crooning voice. He dashed behind a ficus to survey the restaurant's seating area before him. As a waiter walked past, Hypnos conspicuously slipped after him, shuffling and crouching in a fruitless attempt to stay hidden in the shadows. As this absurd conga approached the corner table, Hypnos yelped when he saw Loki and Eros, who were giggling over plates of fine cuisine and red wine. He leapt into a conspiratorial crouch next to their table.

They both jumped at the presence of Dream. "What the hell, Hypnos!" Eros snapped in a whisper.

"I've got something for you." Hypnos began to rummage through his pockets.

Eros and Loki glanced at each other.

"Damn it! Where is it?" he said as he tore through his pockets.

Other patrons were looking over, concerned at Hypnos's rough appearance and raucous display.

"Hypnos," Loki said in a patronizing tone, "we're actually on a date."

Hypnos ignored him, "It's red, and glass, and it's really important!"

Loki's brow scrunched.

Eros leaned forward and gently laid his hand on the table, "Are you referring to a ruby red perfume bottle?"

"Yeah, that's the one! Here it is!" He pulled from his pocket a needle and thread and frowned.

Loki growled, "Dream, *that* is a bobbin! Listen, you already gave me the bottle."

"I did?"

"You did," Loki said.

"Whoops…"

"Yes. Whoops. Do you mind maybe talking to us about this later? We're trying to…" He gestured towards the table.

"Right, you're trying to get into Eros's pants. I forgot. I wouldn't do that if I were you. As soon as you two shack up-"

"We've already had sex!" Loki shouted, and the restaurant fell silent.

Eros took a breath, "Well done, Loki…"

Loki waved apologetically to the crowd, who less than politely turned away and began to whisper.

Loki covered his forehead with one large hand and began rubbing his temples.

"Right," Hypnos stood at his full towering height and

shoved the needle and thread back into his pocket. "Time's a bitch to keep track of. So, if you're here, and he's there- Oh shit! I'm late!" He picked up Eros's glass and slammed back the wine. He made a face. "Too dry. Gotta split. Call me?"

Eros gave him a thin smile and a nod while taking back his empty wine glass. Hypnos ran from the restaurant, nearly knocking over a waitress, with his coat flapping behind him.

Loki closed his eyes and took a breath, "Well, this has been a disaster." He slammed back his own wine. "The waiter is a snooty prick. The food is bland. Hypnos has amnesia, and apparently the wine is too dry."

"Yes." Eros nodded along in agreement with every beat. "Want to try something else instead?"

"Like what?"

Eros shrugged, "What about the theater?"

"You *would* be a thespian."

"I like musicals."

"I like opera," Loki said.

"I think a compromise can be found. And after we could grab a drink?"

Loki leaned forward. "Want to dine and dash?"

Eros leaned in. "That would be wrong."

"Live a little." Loki smirked, and before Eros could compose an argument, Loki stood and made for the door.

Eros jumped up to follow him, but turned around and fumbled some demonics from his wallet. He hid them under a napkin before hastening up to Loki, who was

205

outside hailing a cab on the corner.

"You slipped a note on the table, didn't you?"

Eros avoided eye contact. "I have no idea what you're talking about."

Loki's crooked smile overtook his face, and a cab rolled up next to them. The giant opened the door for his date, who deliberately sat in the middle seat, which Loki took as a very good indicator as to how the night was actually going.

He lowered himself into the cab as Eros leaned forward to tell the driver to head to the performing arts center.

Eros pulled out his phone to see what was on the playbill for the night, and Loki grimaced at the illuminated screen. "Why do you have one of those?" Loki stretched his arm over the back of the seat and settled into the corner.

"It's convenient." Eros did not look up from his phone, but crossed his legs and slightly leaned into Loki's side. "You should get one."

Loki snorted. "No."

"You have a home phone. What's your number? I'll add it to my contacts."

Loki shrugged and made to look out the window. "You don't need it."

Eros's eyes finally rose from his phone. Loki could feel Eros's body tense and pull away as he snapped him a glare. "What do you mean?"

Loki continued nonchalantly to peer out the fogging

window. "Well, if you ever need to talk to me, you can just come over. Day or night."

Eros relaxed a little. "Very smooth." He didn't think it was that smooth. "Just give me your damn number in the event that I need *you* to come to me, and you should get a cell phone for business purposes."

"Fine." Loki cleared his throat. "Six. Six. Six."

Again, Eros looked up from his phone. "Is that a joke?"

"Yes. It is. I was drunk, and Lucifer had said something to piss me off the night before."

"So to get back at him you made your phone number the mark of the Beast?"

"...You had to be there."

"Oh. Okay. Six. Six. Six." He entered it into his phone, and immediately realized that he really didn't need to save the number. He was never going to forget it.

Loki added in a childish tone, "Death's number is just *four*."

Eros put his phone back in his pocket. "Is there a story behind that as well?"

"Well, in the Chinese language, the number for *four*, *sì*, sounds much like their word for *death,* so it's bad luck."

"And you lot think *my* family is strange."

"What's Hypnos's number?" Loki asked with faux jealousy. "He did tell you to call him..."

"That's not still a thing-" Eros began to justify.

"Please," Loki looked at him steadily, "I wouldn't

care if it was."

Eros readjusted in the seat to face Loki, *"Really?"*

"Really, really. Jealousy has never been a color of mine. Well, actually, I do like the color green, but I'm not the jealous type. Never have been."

"Oh."

"But, please, tell me his number is just as ridiculous."

Eros blinked rapidly. "I don't actually have his number."

Loki raised an eyebrow.

Eros readjusted his cufflinks, "We just, um... drop by whenever we want to see each other. Oh, look. Here we are!"

The cab stopped, and Eros slipped to the other side of the cab and out the door.

Loki laughed and stepped from the car. He paid the driver through the window, calling out to Eros over his shoulder, "But I have to *call* if I want to see you."

"That's not what- I'd just like to be able to get a hold of you!"

Loki jogged up to his side.

Eros continued, "Hypnos is my oldest friend, and we've always been this way-"

"Then why would you try to convince me it's not a thing?"

Eros stopped and looked up at Loki in the lights of the performing arts center. He only offered Loki a shrug.

"I am not-," began Loki. He stopped and sighed,

hearing the words Thanatos said the other day about the types of men Eros apparently clung to. He stuck his hands in his pockets and readjusted his footing, "This is about to become a very serious conversation. Is that alright?"

Eros blinked, "Uh, sure."

"I really do think that you and I- Well, we work well together, and we are attracted to one another, yes?"

"Yes..." Eros's face was stricken with confusion and worry.

"Good, then." Loki rubbed his face, "I'm not your father, as a matter of fact I'm a terrible father, and as a result, I'm not going to tell you what you can and cannot do. I'm not going to be one of your boyfriends who parade you around like divine arm candy. I've seen you play those boys like a fiddle, and I'm sure you've seen that I don't let people play me like a fool. I have a habit, or a flaw if you will, where I accept people for what they are- good, bad, or indifferent. If Hypnos is a part of your life, or anyone, or anything else for that matter, then- If I want to be in your life, I have to accept those things, don't I?"

"Okay…" Eros nodded as he rolled this over in his head. This was why he was attracted to Loki- his directness, his self-awareness, and the beautifully strange way his mind worked. Eros might have just been hanging around all of the wrong people, Hypnos aside, for much of his existence. "While we're at it, then, and if I can be honest?" Eros said.

"Fire away," Loki invited.

"I have self-destructive tendencies. I push people

away before they can leave me, so I don't bother letting myself get too attached to them. But, I think you're so clever it makes you stupid sometimes. I think you make yourself intense to scare and to test people, because if they can make it past one layer, you'll let them on to the next, and the next. I wish I could do that, and I think it's incredibly sexy how you bite your lip when you're thinking, and you smell *so* amazing, and you man-spread more than anyone I've ever met! And, you really don't mind?"

"Mind what? *Hypnos*? Lord no! Of course not. I mean, he's Dream. He is literally everyone's dream-guy. I've probably had a few sex dreams with him myself if we look at it that way. And you being who you are, Erotic Desire, I would think asking you not to be *that* would be a tall order to fill. I want to let you out of your cage, not put you in a new one."

"You keep saying all these pretty things, and I don't believe any of them." Eros shrugged helplessly.

Loki appeared disappointed, but said, "Well that's alright. I'll enjoy proving your disbelief wrong time and time again. Sound like a bargain?"

Eros looked him up and down. "Fine. But we're not shaking on it after what you did to me the last time."

"Deal." Loki bowed his head and wrapped his arm around Eros's shoulder as they stepped into the theater.

Eros muttered, "And I'm not in a cage…"

Loki grinned. "Of course you're not."

12

Our hero's mind was focused. He concentrated only on the rising heat of anger in his chest. They had been *so close*, damnit! So fucking close. He hated how much he had let himself hope and dream of pointless freedom. And now his friend, possibly the only one he'd ever had, was dead, and that was his fault. And he was back in *fucking Tartarus*. He scowled at his bound hands above him, eyes burning ire into the chains, almost as if trying to will himself free. He could feel the Darkness watching him. It didn't say a word, almost as if weary of his quiet rage.

He worked his fingers and his toes, trying to relieve the tingling numbness. The numbness and the Darkness were threatening to envelope him and pull him back into helpless misery, but he wouldn't let it. Not this time.

Fuck the Darkness.

And the numbness.

Fuck. This. Entire. Place.

Then a bright light blinded the corners of his eyes, slicing through the Darkness, and he welcomed it. The demons left the door open, as always, to illuminate their way to the hanging corpse.

"You're back," said the demon with the voice of smoke and whiskey. "It's been a while. You were away the last few times we dropped by. It's good to see you."

The demon looked up to see that our hero's eyes were latched onto him. Our hero's breath was steady and calm.

The demon made a pensive face, taken aback by this audacity, "You want us to stay or- "

"Stay." Our hero didn't hesitate. He was sure. He wanted the pain.

The demon stood in front of him and looked him over, studying the determined wrath simmering deep in the blackness of the prisoner's eyes.

Our hero looked back. His defiant gaze never wavered.

"Hm," the demon broke eye contact first, sucking on the insides of his cheeks. He licked his teeth and looked back, "That's good that you can look at me like that... That's real good... Hey, dipstick..."

The bent and crooked one peered up with a savage smile.

"Hand me the lid speculum, would you?"

"*Hee-hee ho-ha!* Didn't see this coming…"

"Quiet." The demon's gruff voice was stern, but not angry.

The little metal speculum looked like a strange, wiry eyelash curler. He held it up for our hero to see. "Now, you make it through this without making a sound… I'll let you off the hook." His eyes glanced up the chains, and centered back onto our hero. The demon's chin was raised, his eyes were narrow, but calm, seeking understanding. "Got it?"

"Do it."

"Good. Let's get started then." He flexed the speculum in front of our hero's face before placing his other hand over the hero's brow, his thumb on his lower eyelid. He shifted his thumb down until our hero's bloodshot eye was exposed and bulging. The demon put the speculum carefully on our hero's eyelids, and our hero's heart went from hammering to explosive as he felt the spring tension pulling apart his lids, keeping them from blinking. His eye was watering and drying out from the exposure.

"Hand me the Wescott scissors, the tiny scissors."

The laughing demon handed him the scissors. He sang, "There was an old man in Thessaly, and he was wonderous wise. He jumped into a thornbush, and scratched out both his eyes. *Hee-hee-heh! Ha!*"

The gruff demon brought the scissors up to his eye.

The laughing demon continued his song, "And when he saw his eyes were out, he danced with might and main..."

Our hero felt the pressure of the sharp, cold metal in a place only the random stray eyelash had ventured before.

"Then he jumped into another bush..."

Our hero felt and heard the first snip and strangled the scream that nearly belted from his chest. Warm liquid streamed down his face, and his body began to tremble.

"...And scratched them in again," the bent demon sang.

The gruff demon said, "Good. Four more cuts to make... on this eye."

Our hero's vision faded in and out until the last snip. Then there was only static.

Through his good eye, he saw a small metal scoop come towards the minced socket. The demon forced the scoop in, making squishing watery sounds as he went, and the pressure built up until there was a final *pop*.

With one hand holding the instrument and the other holding the back of our hero's neck, the demon didn't bother to catch it as the lumpy, slimy ball of tissue plopped onto the floor.

"There's one." The demon scooted it out of his workspace with the toe of his boot, lest he step on it. "One more."

"He-he-he-he ha! He-he-he! Ho!"

"How you holdin' up, kid? I'm going to remove the speculum. Don't scream." His voice was almost kind. He removed the speculum and the lids had nothing to close around.

Our hero threw his head around, trying to shake off the pain and the emptiness.

"Hey. Hey." The demon grabbed his face and pulled it center. Our hero's jaw chattered in agony within the demon's hand. "One more. Just one more." He patted our hero's cheek, grabbed the back of his neck, and brought the speculum to his right eye.

Our hero began to struggle, and the demon held him tighter.

I can't watch this anymore... said the Darkness.

"Then leave," the gruff demon said. "Turn a blind eye..."

The bent and crooked demon laughed and laughed at the joke, and the gruff demon gave three sharp, but silent, chuckles of his own.

"Just one more," the demon said, "and then it's all over. You understand?" He shook our hero to get his attention. "You understand?"

Our hero nodded feverishly.

"Okay. Don't make a sound. I want to get you off the hook, you understand? I want to help you. Not a peep."

He pried apart our hero's lids with the speculum.

***

Dream was late. He was late, and he felt sick. He should have been there. Not that it would have changed anything, but he should have been there for his best mate.

Our hero was curled up on the floor, body trembling.

Hypnos crouched down next to him.

"Hey, Mate, so, listen. I wanted to tell you sooner, but I'm really bad at telling time. That's me other-half's job. The old man did it right, though. You're no longer bound to the bottle. You're free! You just have to carry yourself the rest of the way. Too bad I can't do much to help. Can't afford to lose me head... but..." Dream pulled the spindle of thread and the needle from his pocket. He set them down on the floor next to the eyeless hero's hand.

He didn't move. His sockets weren't black like that of the Fates. They were white tissue and pink with blood.

Hypnos nearly gagged, but swallowed it. He fell back to sit on the floor, his ankles crossed and his arms around his knees.

"The way of things is a fucking mystery to me." He pulled a pack of cigarettes from his pocket and lit up. "Your magick belongs to you now, you know? From here, it will be easier for you to get out. Only a few find the way, some don't recognize it when they do, some don't ever want to. Just let your need guide your behavior. You'll be out of here in no time. You're about to wake up. I should go." He stood and ashed his cigarette. "I'll come find you when you get out, Mate. Promise."

Hypnos vanished, and our hero began to stir. Upon waking, he had no idea where he was. His arms were free, but he still saw nothing but static. He sat up, and his hands flew to his face, knocking something over in the darkness. He heard the thing roll a short distance before stopping. His fingers began to explore the crust on his face as the memories started coming back, explaining his headache, and the soreness, and the sharp stinging in his… not eyes, but eye sockets. He tried to shake his head, to pull away from the feeling, but it was in his sinuses, and it wasn't going anywhere.

Losing balance, he fell back on his side. Again, he hit something, which started to roll. Relying on his hearing, he reached out a blind hand, feeling for the object. When he found it, he inspected it with his fingers.

It was cylindrical and smooth on the top and bottom, with something soft wrapped around the middle. He felt a wooden bobbin, and its tail of thread had a needle secured at the end.

Our hero pricked himself upon its inspection. He thought about the threads of current within all things, between all things. He thought of the Sage and the sandstorm. He remembered a time when a charming man tried to destroy his lamp. Hell was not a metaphor. The mind is its own place, and you had to go in to get out, mate.

The vessel must have been destroyed. He must be stuck in the hell dimension on the other side, where his body had always remained, even when his astral self was off granting wishes in other worlds.

He had so much hope that when the damn bottle turned to dust, he'd be able to use his own magick, the magick the Sage and his people had taught him.

With thread in hand, he began crawling on the floor, his hands becoming powdery with ancient dust. His fingers outstretched, his palms out flat, he felt around for two things, smooth and sticky.

He didn't care if it was unlikely. He had no room for *unlikely*.

He found rocks and dust, then blood and grime. He kept searching and probing until his unsteady hands found the first of the ravaged eyes. He rolled it around in his fingers to find which end had been the front and the back, the back having nerves, and veins, and muscles tendrilling off.

The outer layer made a *pop* as he jabbed the needle through the back of the eyeball. Like weaving a needle between the holes of a button, he twisted and pushed the needle back out, so that the deflated organ hung off the thread like a pearl. Then, he brought the needle to the empty socket, his chest racketing and his breath doing nothing to calm his heart. His too-big and clumsy fingers ran the needle through the slimy exposed muscle of the exposed socket.

His heels kicked in the dust as he popped the needle in and out of the back wall, pulling tighter and tighter, until the eye was just outside the socket. One hand held the ball steady, and the other hand pulled the thread and tightened the loop, until the eye was fitted and seated right back into its hole. Then, he let his heart and his breathing free to do whatever they needed to do to prepare for the next one.

That was just one eye. One more to go. It was almost over. Just one more.

He cut the needle free with the sharp edge of a broken tooth, and he repeated the whole harrowing process on his right eye, using the thread to secure the delicate organ back in its home.

With both eyes in place, he lay on the ground and focused on his breath. He remembered how the Sage's tribe had preached that meditation was the foundation for art, clarity, and magick. He centered himself and covered his eyes with his hands. He focused on the electrical waves the eyes sent to the brain and how the brain translated those signals to see light, and color, and beauty, and emotions. He needed his eyes to do *that* again. He didn't even have to change the pathways, he just had to reconnect them.

If he could make alternate realities and dynasties for others with only two simple words, *I wish*, he could do this for himself. He was free…

He focused on the heat rising in his chest. He had never had this feeling before the Sage's ritual. The heat. There was fire inside of him. It was his soul.

The heat scorched his eyes from the inside, and he let out a scream as he rolled on the floor until the searing went away.

Gingerly, he moved his hands down away from his face, and blinking, discovered he could move his eyes around without pain.

He started to laugh with joy, and release, and power. *Power.* And then, he began to cry and sob between the fits of laughter as he rolled on the floor. He could feel his own soul, his own being, coursing through him. He was him, and he belonged to himself, and his entire body was embracing his soul like a lost twin brother.

Well somebody's lost his mind. Can I join the party? the Darkness purred.

Our hero glared into the Darkness. It had seen him... naked, his emotions, his soul spread open and vulnerable. He was filled with shame. He wiped the tears from his face, and slowly stood.

He felt the rumble of the fire stirring in his chest. It was scorching him from the inside out. He clenched his jaw.

"Fuck you," he said.

Getting feisty, huh? I like it when you fight back... the Darkness teased.

He moved the fire in his chest to the palm of his hand. It ignited like the tip of a match.

Where did you get that trick? the Darkness laughed nervously.

He smiled. All the power he had as a Jinni was now his. He took a sharp inhale and slowly released the rest of the fire building up inside, and the room was set ablaze.

The Darkness screamed as the room ignited, and flames licked its every shadow. In the brightness of the fire he could see the abyss hadn't been that big. It was actually quite small. His eyes darted up the chains to where they were suspended from nothing.

He blinked. And the chains twisted as they fell and coiled on the dusty ground of what looked like a warehouse. The walls and floors were concrete, and pipes lined the ceiling.

He walked to the door on the far side of the room. He blew it open with a blink of his eyes, and the flames spilled out into the hallway of rolling carts. The sprinkler system clicked on as sirens and red lights overwhelmed his senses.

A voice rang over an intercom system. *LOCK DOWN IN BLOCK C. PRISONER ESCAPED. LOCKDOWN IN BLOCK C. PRISONER-*

Through the rain, smoke, and fire he saw his demons exiting a room down the hall from his door. His cell was at the corner of two adjacent halls. To his left, he saw the demons. When he peeked his head around the corner to his right, he saw that the hall was empty. That hall seemed to be the only means of escape, but he didn't know if he could get far with his weakened bones.

Before he could make a move, the gruff demon began to walk towards him, waving to his counterpart to stay put. He was casual as usual, hands tucked into his pockets despite the circumstances. "Hm…" He looked up at the full height and newfound power coursing through this strange, yet familiar creature. He clucked his tongue as our hero's ragged breath snorted down on him. The demon peered into the monster's burning eyes. He slipped a metal instrument into our hero's hand, and patted it gently. Our hero glanced down at the scalpel.

Three demons in suits, carrying metal sticks like cattle prongs, were assembling down at the other end of the hall.

The gruff demon smiled, "Here we go..."

Our hero nodded and took a deep breath. Gratitude and a million years of hatred for this personal demon of his, warred inside him in the space of that breath, and when he released it, his fist was clenched around the scalpel. He jammed it into the demon's eye socket.

Magick was pulsing up his arm, sucking back the years that our hero had lost in that torture chamber. Despite the heat of the flaming hallway, the demon's skin grew cold as his corpse turned to dust, like a million years had passed in the span of just a few seconds. Our hero felt the newly gained years giving him strength.

Half shocked, half relieved, coursing with newfound life and adrenaline, our hero dropped the scalpel and ran down the hall to his right before the hordes of hell could catch up to him.

Our hero slipped in the water pooling on the floor from the sprinklers. The rejuvenation from the demon's life force had gotten him surprisingly far, but he was losing steam. He dipped into a doorway to catch his breath, wracking his brain for a spell, or some kind of magick he could use to get the hell out of here.

He could hear dogs baying down the hall over the sound of the sirens. He popped his head around the doorway, and saw something sniffing its way through the water. It looked like a giant charred jackal with flaming eyes, rather than a dog. It had no jowls to cover the sight of its gruesome black teeth. Another of these creatures appeared around the corner, and our hero pulled his head back into hiding.

The fire in his chest had dimmed, and he couldn't seem to summon anything to magick himself out. He had to run. He had to find a way out, but he had no idea where to go or what he was looking for, let alone if he would recognize it when he saw it. Surely there wouldn't be an *Exit* sign... but, then again, he hadn't expected this concrete maze of a prison either.

The hellhounds were getting closer. He needed a way out, and he had to face the beasts. He knew he couldn't outrun them. He needed the fire back, and he only knew one way to summon it.

He stepped out from his hiding spot.

The hellhounds perked up and latched onto him with their hellfire eyes.

Their muscles flexed, and they bolted at him. Black, talon-like claws scratched against the tile floor, their serpentine tongues salivating.

Fear rose up in his chest. The fear quickened into rage, and the fire inside of him returned. The first hellhound lunged, and he sent it flying back at a glance. The second hellhound grabbed hold of his bony leg. He tried kicking it to shake it off, but was unsuccessful, while the first hound had regained its footing and resumed its attack.

Together, the two hellhounds were ripping and prying at more than just his scarred and tattooed flesh. They were eating his soul.

He summoned enough magick to throw them off one at a time, but they just kept coming back. The trio was stuck in a relentless cycle, but the hellhounds were prepared for this dance, and the Jinni, though now free to use his own magick, was still learning how it even worked. His magick was sputtering like a drowning candle flame in a puddle of wax. It kept coming and going with his concentration and emotions.

The dogs of hell were quickly wearing him down. They were on top of him, tearing him apart bit by bit, prying away flesh, and bone, and something invisible. He could feel his soul detaching and pulling away from him inside out.

And when they ripped greater parts of it from his body, they shook their heads, like shaking a rag doll caught in a monstrous tug of war between two vile toddlers.

A whistle sounded, sharp and piercing, and both hounds retreated to the three demons with cattle prods at the head of the hall. The hounds obediently stationed themselves at the demons' sides as they approached our hero's bloody mess.

"Unholy shit! Get up!" one exclaimed. The demon approached with his prod extended, making contact with our hero's side. "I said get up."

Our hero put up his hands in surrender and made to get up. The demon took a small step back, foolishly letting down his guard *just enough*.

Our hero snatched the demon's wrist and twisted, wrenching the prod from his hand. In the same swift movement, he connected the prod with the demon's ribs, electrocuting him with a magickal current. The demon fell, and the hellhounds resumed their attack.

The heat and anger welled back up in the Jinni. With a glance, he threw one hellhound into a wall hard enough this time to knock it unconscious. The second demon tried to stick him, but found her arm bent backwards, and her own prod connected with her neck. The second hellhound went after our hero's bloody leg, and ended up with a mouthful of magickally boosted electro-shock.

The third demon, who had been frozen with uncertainty, now stood very still to embrace what he knew was coming. Our hero casually touched the end of the prod to his chest.

The demon vibrated for a short moment before collapsing.

Our hero stood there breathing, waiting for the ringing in his ears to clear, and for the sound of sirens to return.

He looked at his new weapon and smiled. The emblem on the stick read *Grim Enterprises*, and he chuckled. On the other side it read *32" Soul Shock*. He liked the weight and balance of it in his hands. It felt like a saber.

The baying of hellhounds rose over the sound of the sirens. It was a blood curdling and unholy sound. With the Soul Shock still in hand, he began to hobble down the maze of white hallways lined with doors. The whole place was made even more labyrinthian between the flashing red warning lights and the wispy threads of intuition guiding him.

He left a trail of blood behind him as he walked, having tried and failed to heal the hellhound bites with his magick.

His right shoulder was gnarled and chewed along with several other spots around his ribs and arms, but his left calf was shredded. He was already skin and bone, but now there was hardly any skin remaining on his lower leg.

Either their bites had a magick of their own that went beyond his capabilities, or he was doing something wrong. No matter what he tried, the wounds wouldn't heal, wouldn't reconnect. With little time to waste, he ignored the searing pain and kept moving through the paths of Tartarus.

He had to find a way out.

There had to be a way out.

You have to go in to get out.

But like any labyrinth, he had no idea if he was getting closer to the center or further away.

The white halls transitioned abruptly to stone, and he stopped at its edge.

He knew where he was standing was hell. He knew it wasn't safe, but the primordial road before him was unknown. The straight-edge conformity changed to the jagged rocky terrain, and he gathered himself. This was the way out, which had seemed impossible to find. Now he could see it clearly. There had always been only one way out, and this was it.

No way in hell was he going back.

He rested the Soul Shock against the white wall, and stepped over the threshold, moving onto sharp, black rock with bare feet. Eventually, the flashing red lights faded, and he was in Darkness. He felt safer in the Darkness. He felt concealed, but not for long.

There you are! We've been looking for you. Just come back to what you know. I know you missed me, Erubus, the darkness, purred.

He ignored it.

And you know you won't make it out of here, don't you? What are you even trying to escape to? There's nothing and no one out there for you, even if you do make it, which you won't...

He wiped away the tear that fell as his anger began to rise.

Oh, baby, your feet won't carry you. You're weak. It's okay. You just don't have the strength to pull this off. You're going to break. Spare yourself the pain. Listen... I'm only trying to help here.

"Go away," he growled as he climbed over boulders and stone.

Nope. Can't. I exist everywhere the light cannot touch... which means I am inside of you. In your heart. In your mind.

Can't you see? There is no escape.

He felt the fire rising up inside of him.

"Maybe not, but I'm damn sure going to try."

It will only end in heartache.

"Pain is temporary."

Erebus laughed. *So is happiness, and unlike happiness, I will never leave you, old friend.*

The rocky tunnel opened to an all encompassing expanse that reached in all directions. The black void washed over him and left him as hollow as the endless cavern around him..

The tunnel had been dark, but this pit was darker. It was filled with the permeating stillness of Silence.

It is the Silence which follows absolute trauma. It is the Silence which follows the pivotal moment when your life changes forever. It is the Silence that becomes you right after your soul dies.

Unlike the illusion that was his prison, this was boundless, eternal, and filled with empty nothingness.

His toes found the edge of the world, and pebbles fell over the ledge and never landed.

Our hero could feel his oldest friend roll its eyes. The Darkness groaned.

And the chasm yawned.

Our hero asked the Darkness, "What is this?"

It scoffed. *The Silence, and despite his name, he's a real chatter box.*

"The Silence?"

You know that space between life and death?

"Not personally."

Well, now you can say… you've met him personally. Come on. Nothing to see here. I told you there was no way, and now you see, I was right. The cake was a lie. This was all a fool's errand. A dead end.

Our hero nodded in complete understanding. "Good."

He felt the Darkness squint.

"Then I'm out of options. There's only one left."

Our hero felt the ledge underneath his toes, and he swan-dived into the chasm.

***

Our hero was floating in nothing. He felt snakes slithering and constricting all over him. His brain sent signals telling his body to move, but there was no response.

He was floating in nothing.

Well, hey there. There he is. How you doing? A smooth male voice permeated his mind. The disembodied voice was everywhere. It was inside his head, echoing.

Our hero told his mouth, his throat, and tongue to respond- but nothing.

What's your name?

Our hero pondered how to respond, while trying to move and beginning to panic. The constricting snakes rolled across him as he levitated. He couldn't see. There was nothing to see.

I see, said the Silence. *You don't have a name. That's fine. I have no use for names. Everyone's just passing through. But you. You jumped. Why is that?*

I had to, our hero thought.

He tried again, in vain, to move, but his body wouldn't listen. The feeling was similar to when a wish forced him to move and act in ways he would never, but that had been his body betraying him. This was like not having a body at all. That was why he couldn't see or move. His consciousness was lost in the Silence.

You had to, the Silence pondered. *But where were you trying to go?*

I didn't plan that far ahead.

The Silence laughed. *Well, if you don't know where you're going, any road can take you there.*

Any road is good with me if it gets me out of here, our hero quipped, the smooth scales rolling across him.

Okay. Fine, hot shot, the Silence was amused, *I can point you in that direction, but you'll be going the wrong way.*

The wrong way?

The wrong way, the Silence teased.

There is no other way. Our hero thought.

When you come home- do you want to come home the wrong way, or do you want to come home right?

I have no home.

The Silence said, *Home is going to be wherever you land, and that's what I'm saying. You don't want home to be at the end of some road some stranger sent you down. You want it to be down the road you chose. So choose. Where are you going?*

I… Our hero struggled over this thought. He had trouble enough admitting to himself what he wanted, and he knew better than to speak his heart's desire aloud. But, then he realized, he didn't have to speak it aloud for the Silence to hear. They hadn't been speaking with words, but thoughts. Even without having said it, he knew the Silence knew it. His silence had been louder than any words he could have uttered.

The Silence clicked his tongue, despite not having one, and the sound slithered around our hero. *That's a long, hard road you just picked, but there you have it. Enjoy the thorns.*

He felt every snake tail slip away one by one, and as if he were suspended by fraying ropes, he began to drop. First an elbow, then an ankle. Then, completely untethered, he tumbled through the Silence, and woke just before he crashed into a pile of bones.

***

The world was as gray and as flat as Kansas, but instead of yellow corn or green cities, or red poppies, bones grew up from the ground. The corn cobs were made of teeth instead of kernels. The trees and bushes were literally skeletal. The ground was littered with broken shards of mirror.

He saw a dirt road. He grumbled and cursed under

his breath as he carried his raw, shredded, useless feet, stuck and sliced by the mirror fragments, for miles and miles.

He wanted to lay down to sleep, and if he died before he woke... The thought was nice at first, but then the fear of waking up back in Tartarus kept him going. He couldn't collapse. He couldn't sleep. He had to keep going, so the past couldn't catch up to him.

He walked onward until the bones and glass disappeared, until the bleak sky faded to purple, and there was nothing but cracked red dirt spreading across the flat landscape.

Our hero could see, small in the distance, what appeared to be a tree. It was the only landmark throughout the entire plane, and he made it his goal to reach it. If it was the only thing visible in this god forsaken desert, it had been put there for a reason.

The tree grew bigger and bigger against the horizon as he trudged forward. He fell many times, and each time he thought he wouldn't manage to stand again. But again and again, on shaking limbs, he brought himself back up to his feet. There wasn't another option.

He was still nowhere near its trunk yet, but the tree was larger than life. It *was* life. Its branches reached to heaven, and its roots ran down to hell.

The tree was just as warped, knotted, and scarred as our hero's twisted body. It was like looking at his reflection for the first time, but with his new eyes.

Tears began to stream down his face when he was

finally close enough to reach out his stained fingers to touch her deeply-grooved bark. He put his palm flat against the trunk, and he closed his eyes.

The Tree sang. She sang and she cried, and loved, and breathed. She was free in her own form. The Tree of Life, The World Tree, had a million worlds existing inside every ring. She looked so still, but she was vibrating with the singing-bowl harmony of infinite multiverses dying and being born.

He pulled his hand away too soon, but not soon enough. Beauty and bliss was not something he could see in himself.

He looked down in shame, but saw a large hollow at the base of her trunk. It was black, and oozing, and smelled of something foul. A wet bubbling came from the hollow as the wood writhed with larvae. Our hero laughed a cynical laugh and shook his head.

After seeing the blackness eating away at the very foundation of life, he felt better. Nothing in this universe is sacred. Existence at its foundation is flawed.

He crouched down and peered into the black hole. It was more than big enough for him to crawl through, and he knew there would be plenty of room for him inside the rot. He slipped into the hollow and sat for a moment in the tree's womb, and he felt her hum vibrating through him. He vaguely came to understand- the rot wasn't poison.

All that is born must die, even existence itself. The rot was death and time. It was inevitable. It was ineffably part of the Great Tree's tenebrous beauty.

Now he was ready. It was time to forget.

He crawled on hands and knees through the tunnel of black, moldering decay until there was nowhere else to go. He dug his way through the soggy wound until his hand breached into humid damp air. He pulled and squirmed his body out of the earth until he was free. He emerged from the hollow at the base of a different tree. A mangrove tree in a shadowy swamp.

He collapsed in the moss. Bugs and gnats were already swarming around his eyes and ears. He didn't bother to fight them off. He was exhausted, sore, and free. He sighed a breath of relief.

13

*E*ros and Loki were sitting at the bar of an uptown lounge in the theater district. The lounge was Loki's choice. It was bright and classy with rich cherry wood and it smelled like a humidor.

"Okay, Desire," Loki set down his glass, "what are your secret *desires*?"

"Well, they aren't really secret, are they? I already told you."

Loki waved him on with his hand.

Eros rolled his eyes and brushed back his bangs, "Okay, um… same as anyone really, to be loved and respected for who I am in a healthy way. To feel safe, secure, not like the relationship could go to hell at any moment. I want something," he looked into Loki's eyes, "*real*."

"Hm." Loki pondered with a cocky smirk and picked his drink back up.

Eros's eyes zeroed in on that grin, wondering what exactly it meant. No doubt, Loki was restraining from debating the definition of the word *real*.

So, Eros put on a coy smile and tilted his head just right in the light to ask, "And what are your inner desires, Chaos?"

Loki snorted mid sip and had to cough the burning bourbon out of places it shouldn't have been. "My desires?" He coughed, wiping the liquor off his chin.

"Yes. Your desires," Eros prodded.

"You mean beyond kinky foreplay?"

Eros flushed and bit his lip, "Yes, beyond that."

"Well, you're Desire. You tell me."

Eros leaned in. "Not how this game works." He didn't break eye contact as he sipped from his glass.

"Inner desires…," Loki pondered. "I don't think I live in the realm of desires. I live in the world of what I have right in front of me." He gazed at Eros, who smiled and looked away.

Loki continued, "I also think in terms of cause and effect, and I don't necessarily do so to reach a desired outcome, but just to see what the outcome will be."

"And what do you think the outcome of tonight will be?"

Loki chuckled, "Kinky foreplay. But I don't think that is the question."

Eros cocked his head.

Loki continued. "The question is *why*?"

"*Why?*"

Loki repeated, "Yes, *why*. Why are you truly here with me? To piss off the enemy or because you're actually fond of me? Because we both know the answer, and you're avoiding it, or making excuses for it. I'm not rushing you to proclaim your undying love for me, but if you have feelings for me you should at least own it."

"Fine. I'll own it. Yes, I have feelings for you, and pissing off the enemy is a wonderful side-bonus," Eros confirmed, finishing off his drink.

Loki looked away deliberately to relieve the pressure he assumed Eros was feeling.

Eros slipped his fingertips over the giant's knee to his inner thigh.

Loki's attention snapped back to Eros, "But *why* is that?"

Eros's hand stopped. He glanced at his hand then back at Loki.

Loki said, "I mean, what is with all the fuss? First, Hypnos shows up with that damn bottle and prophecies, then Thanatos shows up to make a scene." He was chewing on his lip again.

Eros's shoulders slumped.

"And he told us to piss off with one hand and invited us to the gala with another. Hypnos might have given us direct prophecies, but the message Thanatos gave us was more clear. Someone put him up to this."

Eros blinked, and said flatly, "The gala is a trap, is it?"

Loki drummed his fingers on the table. "Most definitely."

Eros sighed, and nodded to himself, surrendering to the fact that this was what it was like to date Chaos. He patted Loki's knee and removed his hand. "Well then, we should probably get back to work. Finish cataloging the collection-"

"And then *make* a catalog," Loki added.

"And make a catalog," Eros agreed. "Find out everything we can on that bottle, make a battle strategy, buy new suits, and really, truly get to know one another."

Loki thought on all of this for a moment, finished his drink, and stood. "Perfect. We should start at your place."

Eros, still sitting on the bar stool looked up at him, "My place?"

"I haven't seen it yet."

"Okay, well, I do still have a very expensive bottle of champagne, courtesy of Grim Enterprises, which has been begging to be opened..." Eros stood.

"Begging to be opened?" Loki raised his eyebrows. "You and the champagne share something in common, then."

Eros side-eyed him as they exited the bar, Loki laughing under his breath all the way to the door. Once outside in the cold, Eros bumped intentionally into Loki, and Loki wrapped his arm around him until they flagged down a cab.

***

Loki was intrigued, rather than surprised, at the sight of Eros's minimalist black and white apartment.

"Well…," was all he said upon entry, "we'll never be moving in together."

"No, probably not." Eros shrugged off his coat. "Champagne?"

"Please." Loki took off his coat and set it down on the back of the couch, while Eros headed to the bar.

Loki put his hands in his pockets as he took in the wall-to-wall window, overlooking the city lights scattered under a firmament of falling stars.

"Where were you before you were sentenced here?"

"Bouncing around in the Mortalworld." Eros popped off the cork, and a bit of bubbly overflowed from the bottle. "This is the first place I've lived in aeons that is actually *mine* rather than someone else's, so I suppose the sentence could be worse."

"They were talking Tartarus, yes?"

The memories of his trial made him uncomfortable. "Yes. They were. But, enough of the jury decided my level of involvement wasn't enough to warrant that sort of verdict. I was charged with border infractions, mortal coercion, second-degree abuse-of-power, and aiding and abetting

Clermiel's conspirators."

Loki's eyes narrowed as he took the glass of champagne Eros was offering him. "Hm. What was the difference in charges from those who were sentenced to Tartarus?"

"They were charged with more of the same, just to a higher degree, and of course the charge of actually *conspiring to dismantle the natural laws.*"

"Did you get off easy because of who you are, or rather, *what* you are?"

"It's possible, but I'm sure it had more to do with the fact that I'm irrelevant." Eros self-deprecated.

"No. You're not any more *irrelevant* than Strife or Charon. In fact, you're far more relevant."

Eros let out one bitter laugh.

"It was either out of respect for the fact you are Primordial, or because they have you right where they want you. You wouldn't do them any good if you were in Tartarus."

"I don't do them any good now."

"Or so you assume."

Eros and Loki looked at each other pointedly.

"Or so I assume," Eros agreed.

Loki scoured Eros with his eyes, studying his energy. Only now did Loki truly understand how *old* Eros was. He was probably older than Death, and Dream, and the Fates. It wasn't long after Eros's inception that he had been degraded and removed, forced to hide everything he was, or risk eternal imprisonment- never mind that a life like that was a prison all its own. Eros was so much bigger than he appeared, bigger than he could possibly recall or admit to. It was no wonder his desire was to be loved and accepted. It was no wonder the Fates would want him where they could see him, where they could use him if they ever needed- somewhere accessible and easily manipulated.

However, Loki knew that there was a fine line between cornering a mouse and cornering a wolf. Too much pressure in the wrong places turns cowering submission into gnashing ferocity.

The Fates couldn't see that manipulating Eros would be the equivalent of manipulating a dangerous artifact. One wrong move could set it off, and setting it next to a similar object could cause a world-melting reaction.

They *were* afraid of what he and Eros could do together.

Eros smiled, "Why are you looking at me like that?"

Loki reached up a hand and brushed back Eros's bangs, "Daydreaming," he replied. "Just daydreaming."

Eros pulled Loki's tie from out of his vest. "Anything I can help with?" He looked up at Loki through his lashes.

Loki raised Eros's chin, again oblivious to Eros's flirtatious lure.

"Listen to me." Loki's gaze was unwavering, "No matter what happens between you and I, I will stand between you and them every time, no matter what your protests might be."

Eros dropped the tie. "Loki, has it escaped your notice that I've tried multiple times tonight to *seduce you?*"

"No. It hasn't. But do you understand me?"

Eros walked away with a frustrated laugh. "No! Not in the slightest."

Loki took a breath and walked up to him. "I think you do."

Eros glared at him. "I understand what you're saying. What I don't understand is *why* you're saying it, and why we have to be having this conversation *right* now."

Loki's voice tensed. "Because it came to mind, and it flew out of my mouth, and I'm glad it did! You need to know where I stand, so that you know I'm not using you the same as all the rest."

Eros sat on the arm of his sectional and brushed back his hair. "I know that."

Loki calmed himself and stuck his hands in his pockets. "Well, it's still nice to hear sometimes, even if you already *know* it."

Eros shrugged. "I'm not used to hearing it. At all. And, frankly, it's a bit much..."

"Fair enough."

"And I don't believe it."

Loki nodded and took a breath. "I'll enjoy proving you wrong."

Eros folded his arms, and Loki stood still for a moment with his hands in his pockets.

Loki rocked on his heels and he looked at Eros,

whose eyes were on the floor.

Loki cleared his throat.

He rocked on his heels again.

"So," he removed a hand from his pocket to rub the back of his neck, "where do you want to go on date number two?"

Eros dragged his eyes up to scowl at Loki.

***

A beautiful young woman was crumpled on the damp banks of the swamp. She cried ceaselessly as she watched the bugs crawl and buzz by her. The grief in her heart immobilized her, but her body trembled with the echoes of her heartache.

The young woman knew it was unwise to wish her heart's desire aloud, but her sorrow drowned out this wisdom, and she wished with all her might, "Please, I wish this curse was taken from me."

A shadow slipped across the swamp, and turned into a man before her. He crouched in front of her. Despite his human shape, he was hardly human. The dark creature before her was twisted in unnatural ways, and was covered with magick symbols and swamp muck. His head was nearly bald and tilted to one side, perked and curious like an animal, peering down at her with blotchy red eyes.

"I grant wishes," he said strangely through gnarled lips.

The beautiful woman managed to pull her palms under her and push herself up from the ground to take in the strange creature before her.

Our hero leaned closer and insisted with a gravelly voice, "Wish it again."

The woman wiped away her tears with the back of her hand. She knew the danger of wishing wish her heart's desire aloud, because you never know who is listening. But, this was her chance to remedy the past. The rules she lived by before had failed her. It was time for a new set of rules. With a raised chin she gathered her conviction. "I wish I was no longer beautiful."

Our hero raised his hand of his own free will and clicked his fingers.

She watched as the knuckles on her hands knotted. She felt her back roll into a hump. Her mouth began to bleed as her teeth fell from her gums. Her eyelids began to twitch as one eye went lazy and bulged from her skull. She ran her boney fingers through her hair, and many coarse black strands came out in her hands.

She stood up, looking down at her new talon-like toenails and her calloused bunions, then looked up at the creature before her. With a joyful and toothless grin, she asked, "Am I still beautiful?"

Our hero lowered his bloodshot eyes to hers, and he fell deeply into the hidden depths of her soul. Tumbling, as if he had fallen blindly off a cliff. With a shake of his head he reemerged, overwhelmed, with tears in his eyes.

The bugs crescendoed around them.

"Yes," his already unsteady voice cracked. "You are... I'm sorry."

"Come," she invited, and she began to shuffle through the swamp.

His own tattered, deformed body lurched after hers, taking her words instinctively as a command.

She led him through the reeds of the swamp where the worlds meet.

Glowing eyes followed them the entire way. The eyes peeped out of the Spanish moss and the mud puddles, but the moment our hero turned to look at them, they blinked and disappeared.

The short walk ended when they reached a stilted house on the edge of the water.

"This is the place my family banished me to when I became pregnant out of wedlock. The man, he... He had been one of my sister's suitors," she said as she climbed the stairs up to the door, "but when my spiteful sisters cursed me with beauty, he set his eyes on me instead- and took advantage of me. He was wealthy and powerful, and he told my father I had bewitched him. So, they sent me here to give birth to my girl... but they took her from me today... to be raised by my mother."

"I'm sorry," he said.

"You are new to these parts aren't you?" She opened the door to her one-room house.

He answered, "Today I crawled from the roots of a

mangrove tree, and I can't remember where I came from before that. I remember walking a really long way, but that is all." He didn't walk far into the house. There was a bed in the right corner, but everything off to the left was for food storage, cooking, and mending clothes.

"Well, in this place, it's rude to say the words *sorry* and *thank you*. It will get you in a world of trouble."

"Where is *this place*?"

The woman looked at the set of drawers by the bed. One of the drawers was open. Clean, pastel-pink sheets were bundled around the edges, so that a baby could lie swaddled right in the center.

"This swamp is a portal between many worlds, but the forest beyond the swamp is called The Netherworlds. It is a world ruled by Death... and it shows."

She slid the drawer closed.

The painful memory she was reliving in her mind was written all over her face, and tears began to fall as she wrapped her arms around herself. She turned her face away and sat down on the bed as the tears and sobs came without hesitation.

He wanted to help her. He knew, but could not remember how he knew, that with the snap of his fingers, he could fix all of her problems- even reshape her reality. Then again, he also inexplicably *knew* that snapping reality into a new shape didn't truly solve your problems. It just gave them a new form. Either way, she hadn't asked for help.

Finding a chair by the fire, he pulled it up close, but not too close as to invade her space. And he sat there with her in silence, safe inside her house, while the swamp around them crawled.

14

*E*ros didn't remember falling asleep. He and Loki were tangled in each other, fully dressed on the couch. Half empty glasses of champagne sparkled lacklusterly in the gray morning light. The bubbles were stagnant, and the light illuminated the sticky fingerprints speckled across the glasses.

Eros turned around to face Loki. He watched Loki's face carefully to make sure not to wake up the giant as he tried to slip away. Upon gazing at the giant's peaceful face, Eros felt as if he had been struck by one of his own arrows. He smiled and stroked Loki's blondish stubble.

He liked that they had stayed up all night simply talking, and drinking, and occasionally kissing. He knew Loki better now, after hearing the trickster's myths from his point of view. It had been quite a comedy sketch. Eros had nearly rolled off the couch with laughter.

In turn, Eros had told Loki about his life of romance and sexual intrigue. Loki had been gripped by the tales of scandal and betrayal, but he had enough trouble trying to keep track of the various characters and their backstories, and the bubbly hadn't helped. At one point he had threatened to take notes to keep it all straight.

"Do you miss that life?" Loki had asked.

"Of course I do, but," Eros had looked up at Loki through his lashes, "I'm really enjoying being here... with you."

Loki hadn't kissed him. He had just locked eyes with him and brushed back his hair. That's when they had fallen asleep, Eros recalled.

Loki's eyes blinked open as Eros was petting his cheek.

"Good morning." Eros smiled and moved his fingers from Loki's stubbly cheek to his ear.

"Good morning."

Eros looked away, suddenly bashful.

Loki tried to shift back into Eros's line of sight with an adoring grin. "What do you want to do today?"

Eros readjusted to lay his cheek flat on Loki's chest. He played with the buttons on Loki's gray vest. "I want to shower and wash the bubbly away. We need to finish organizing the collection, which will require coffee, and I want to stop by Devereaux's tonight."

Loki groaned. "Fine."

Eros hopped up with more bounce than Loki anticipated and knocked some of the wind out of his chest. Loki laid there making a face.

Eros started to leave, but turned back when he realized the giant wasn't behind him.

"Loki, are we not going to do all that together? As partners? ...*Together*?"

Loki was confused. "Yes..."

"Then why aren't you getting up?"

Loki sat up sleepily, "I thought you were getting in the shower?"

Eros stared him down until he understood.

"Oh… right! We'd be saving on your water bill if- Two birds, one bar of soap…"

"Loki?"

"Yep. Coming." Loki stood and followed him into the master bath.

***

Later at Loki's townhome, Loki tried to help Eros organize, but Eros was very meticulous and Loki was easily distracted. When he found an interesting artifact he had forgotten he had procured, his direction shifted entirely to playing and experimenting with said artifact. Once his mind was set on a new play thing, the legions of hell wouldn't have been enough to steer him away, let alone Eros.

"Loki." Eros set down his pen. Eros was buried in boxes and wood wool, logging the items he was uncovering in a ledger, while Loki lay on the floor holding a book over his head.

"Hang on." Loki held up a finger, "I think I've almost found it..."

"Loki, why not instead of looking for..." Eros trailed off, motioning for Loki to finish the sentence.

"The lost Arthurian curse of the Ring of Dispell," Loki dead-panned.

"Yes. That." Eros rolled his eyes, "Which is undoubtedly very important, but, maybe, you could work on something *more* important."

"Such as?"

Eros pondered over what might get Loki out of his way for a bit. "The bottle. The one Hypnos brought us. You haven't looked at that since the night he dropped it off."

Loki lowered the book to his chest. "No. I suppose I haven't. I'm not sure exactly where to start with it really."

"What about taking it to an expert?"

Loki turned his head. "You're trying to get rid of me, aren't you?"

"Yes. When you *clean* something you take three aeons."

"Fair. Well, the only expert is Thanatos, and I don't trust his motives right now... I suppose there is Christopher or Shmeaglebobenzoar."

"*Who*?" Eros asked.

"Shmeaglebob. Second to Thanatos in the artifacts business."

"By the time we're done here, he will be the third in the business..."

Loki stood, "More than likely. We haven't even thought about the warehouses yet."

Eros sank. "Warehouses? Loki, did you just say you have *warehouses* of this junk?"

"I best leave you to your work before I make you too distraught." He grabbed and kissed the top of Eros's head just before he disappeared downstairs to grab the bottle.

Eros screamed at the ceiling "Loki!"

***

Bottle in hand, Loki appeared outside a polished stone building, whose narrow face looked out onto the street corner. It looked like an old bank with its column-framed, arched doorway. The front doors were open, and when he stepped inside, he was immediately tussled between busy men and women running around the hectic office floor. He made his way to the brass metal gate of the elevator, and took it to the top, executive floor.

The secretary let him in without a fuss when he revealed he had a magickal artifact the boss would find interesting. Once inside Shmeaglebobenzoar's office, the old demon with a monocle poured him a brandy as Loki set the bottle on the bar.

"I heard you were preparing for business. Will you be at the Collectors Gala this weekend?" asked the demon, as he examined the mysterious red bottle through his monocle.

"Yes. I'll be attending with my new partner-in-crime."

Loki sat comfortably in a leather Queen Anne armchair with his freshly poured brandy.

"And who's that?" Shmeaglebob asked distractedly, "Is this safe to open?"

"As far as I can tell. And Eros is my new," Loki questioned the word coming out of his mouth, "partner."

Shmeaglebob eyed him from across the office.

"Well," he looked back at the bottle, "that pairing seems only fitting."

Loki grinned and sipped his brandy.

The demon opened the bottle and waved a hand over the top to send the aroma to his large beak-like nose.

"Hmm. Ozone... I believe this object is broken."

Loki listened intently for the explanation.

"It appears this container could shapeshift, but the hydrix has degraded. It also has a diatomic element that would suggest it was once a portal to another realm."

Loki sat up in his chair. "What does that mean?"

"Well, the shapeshifting element could imply many things- Jinn, faery, witchcraft, but the portal element is interesting. One might assume that someone created this as a secret portal to carry around with them. However, someone with that sort of power would also have the means of teleportation, and so wouldn't *need* such a device as this.

So, it looks like what you might have is a portal someone made for a person of weaker power, who might need to escape in a jiffy. In any case, it is highly specified and made for a particular use for a particular person, but since all of its functions are offline, it is hard to determine specifics. Right now, it is merely a perfume bottle that once was not."

Loki said, "Not that I question your abilities, Shmeaglebobenzoar, but this particular perfume bottle was given to me under very interesting circumstances, and I wonder if there is anything else you might be able to discover if you thought it might be more than just a *vexing perfume bottle*."

"Hmm." He looked at it again. "It will take a while. Could you leave it with me for a bit?"

Loki grimaced.

Shmeaglebob removed his monocle. "Or I suppose you could… stick around."

Loki smiled and shrugged.

***

When Loki returned home many hours later, he could hear music blaring from upstairs. He walked into the library and saw Eros had expanded his workspace to the floor. His sleeves were rolled up, his tie loosened. A cigarette hung off his lower lip as he scribbled in his ledger. His fingers were stained with ink. His hair was standing on end from where he kept brushing it out of his eyes, as he bobbed his head along to some punk-rock pandemonium blaring from the phonograph.

The shelves were almost filled up, but there was still a plethora of boxes to be gone through. Loki decided to fix that problem later.

With the wave of his hand, he turned down Eros's music to twenty percent.

Eros popped his head up for a moment, "What did you find out?"

Loki walked further into the room.

"It took a bit of fuss and quandary, but... it's currently broken. It once had the ability to shapeshift. It was a portal to an unidentified location. It was made for a specific person in mind- very specialized and protected. Despite the fact its basic defense functions are all fried, spells to look back into its history don't work, which means- and this is the fun bit- The item exists outside of time."

"Very cool, but still broken, yes?"

"Yes."

Eros gestured to the boxes, "Add it to the rubble."

Loki frowned. He sat down at the desk and put the bottle in the center.

The chair creaked as the giant leaned back and pondered over the artifact. At this point it was just like all the other artifacts he had hoarded - useless.

Eros saw the look on Loki's face.

The trickster clearly didn't want to give up on the bottle just yet, and he kept rolling it over in his mind, with his desire to *know* what the bottle was.

The youthful god stood and unrolled his sleeves. "Come on. Let's go check on the Devereaux girl."

"The VanGarrett girl, you mean." Loki didn't take his eyes off the bottle. "Alec is her sire. Alec *VanGarrett* is the one who turned her. Not Devereaux."

"Yes. But, either way she is under Devereaux's care. So…"

Loki sighed and stood while Eros grabbed his blazer and put it on.

"I feel like it's talking to me," Loki said.

Eros scrunched his face. "You mean the bottle?"

"Yes. It's…" He made a mess of hand gestures, and felt Eros scrutinizing him. "Okay. Fine. Let's go."

Loki stormed past him while aggravatedly chewing on his lower lip.

Eros watched him pass, but turned his eyes toward the bottle.

Eros felt it pulling at him, as if he was a damaged ship being pulled to the bottom of the ocean, but he ignored it. He shut it out like a bad memory and closed the library door behind him.

***

At the Devereaux mansion they were led through the ornate hallways to the room that had previously held a rabid vampire.

The door to the room was wide open, but the bedchamber was still dark. No lamp was lit, and every curtain was drawn tight.

Together, they cautiously entered the room to see Victor Devereaux sitting in a chair next to the girl's bed.

Loki and Eros approached the opposite side of the bed from where the Vampire King sat. Devereaux looked up, his youthful but exhausted face filled with gratitude. The girl, however, looked at them with cautious curiosity. She appeared to be mostly stable, from what they could tell. Her dark hair was plastered to her face, and she was pale, but that complexion was typical in vampires. Her eyes were still dark saucers, teetering on the brink of madness, but she was calm.

"Loki. Eros. I give you my truest gratitude." Victor Dexereaux beamed at the girl, who in truth was too old to be considered a *girl*. "These are the two gentlemen who procured your treatment."

She was past the gateway into womanhood, but to gods, and to a centuries-old vampire, she was but a child.

"How are you feeling, Josanna?" Eros asked with tender care.

She tilted her head and inspected him with her wide, dark eyes. *"As sharp as thorns and as red as petals of blood. The sweet steam of passion and the pang of disprized love."*

Confusion etched itself across Eros's face, and he turned back to the others, "Uhh...was that to *me*?"

Devereaux stood. "If you'll forgive her, she's still

out-of-sorts."

One of Loki's eyes narrowed, "Are you sure she doesn't *always* talk like the Oracle of Delphi?"

Devereaux smiled, "No. She doesn't."

Eros ignored Loki's implication and spoke to Josanna again, "We're glad to see you're feeling better." He leaned in closer, and she lunged for his wrist.

She began sniffing it.

Devereaux reached out a hand to pull her off, but Eros made a gesture to stay him.

She pulled Eros down suddenly, his face level with hers, his breath moving the oily hair that hung over her eyes.

"*Desire, you're hungry,*" she breathed into his face.

Her breath was rank from having drank fresh blood. He wasn't afraid of her, but he was very concerned for her, and he didn't pull back.

Loki moved towards the bed, not out of fear or protection, but out of curiosity. The glow in his eye, and the smirk on his face, implied he just wanted a close-up to whatever would happen next.

Josanna's eyes landed on Eros's forehead, and she began to trace the creases in his brow with her delicate fingers. "*You're all locked up in there. You never really escaped, did you?*"

Eros and the girl had locked eyes with each other, her wild blown-out gaze boring into his puzzled one. She was making less and less sense.

"What do you mean?" Loki asked, eagerly pushing for more clues.

Devereaux walked around the bed to the gods. "I'm afraid she doesn't know what she's saying-"

"*Hell.*" She answered before she moved to Eros's ear and nibbled it, whispering, "*The Red Room.*"

Then she began to laugh in his face.

She shrieked. "*You don't remember!*" and cackling, she threw his arm out of her grasp.

She collapsed back onto the bed, and wriggled in the sheets. Her tangled dark hair an ominous black halo around her, as she warmly looked up into Devereaux's face. "*He doesn't remember, daddy!*"

Devereaux shrugged, "A-again, she's still not well. She needs a great deal more blood to regain sense, but the deadman's blood is out of her system at least, thanks to your flower." He moved between them to pet Josanna's forehead.

Loki nodded, muttering loudly to himself, "I'm not so sure about that."

Hearing this, and circumventing the conversation around it, Eros said sincerely, "We're glad she's better. Is there anything else we can do to expedite the process?"

"She just needs more time." The Vampire King gestured towards the door with a smile.

"I do have time saved in a bottle somewhere if you're interested." Loki grinned.

"*Bottle, bottle toil in trouble. Fire burn and cauldron*

bubble!" The girl on the bed was looking pointedly at the giant with a wicked grin of her own.

Loki glared back at the girl. She was clearly teasing him about his vexing perfume bottle, and the sodding Fates, or witches, or whatever they were! He knew it, and she knew it, but the other twits in the room were ignoring her words outright.

She looked him in the eye and sat up on her elbows. *"Baby boy finally found his way home."*

At this, Loki gestured wildly in the clever girl's direction, sputtering out incoherent bits of sentences, all along the lines of "-See!?"

Searching valiantly for a compromise between Loki's excited theory and Devereaux's decorum, Eros offered, "We'd love to come back and visit you some other time, Josanna. If that's alright?"

She nodded and smiled sickly-sweet, with two sharp fangs and childlike eyes.

Devereaux looked up at the gods. "You're welcome whenever you like, of course."

"We appreciate it, your *highness*." Loki's forced smile was almost a snarl, but the expression was subtle enough that Devereaux might have missed it.

Loki bowed at the neck facetiously, and Eros followed suit. They quickly walked towards the exit.

Just before reaching the door, Eros paused and turned back. "What is her name?"

"...Josanna?" Devereaux tilted his head in feigned

innocence and then looked at the girl on the bed.

Eros clarified, "Devereaux or VanGarrett?"

The Vampire King's eyes were dangerous when they snapped to Eros's face. "*Devereaux*. After what that boy did, he cannot claim her as his own."

Eros nodded simply and again bowed politely to the King, and left the room.

Loki was waiting for him in the hall with wide eyes speaking a thousand words. Eros only nodded in agreement to what Loki's eyes were saying, wordlessly cautioning him to stay silent until they were out of earshot. They left the mansion and were around the corner before Loki blurted out, "*Well?*"

Eros's jaw was set. "He loves her like she's his own."

"Is she? She did call him *daddy*."

"I never painted Devereaux as a dishonest man."

"Exactly. No one pictures him that way, which means his kingdom would fall if ever something disgraceful were to mar his name..."

Eros continued the train of thought, "So, he lied and said the girl was Alec's to protect his reputation? It's plausible, but certainly not the whole truth."

"Well, of course not. As I've said before, that girl is psychic... By the way, what's the Red Room?" Loki asked.

Eros stopped and gave an earnest shrug. "I honestly don't know, which is why I'm not entirely sold on your psychic theory either."

"But, you know she was picking up on our gift from

Hypnos and his prophecy."

Eros looked confused.

Loki aggravatedly waved his arms. "Blah, blah, *father of none when you tell him he has a son.*"

"Oh!" Eros recalled, "And she said *Baby boy... came home?*"

"*Finally found his way home.*" Loki corrected.

Eros nodded in agreement. "That's right. But, if she is spouting prophecy- Does she have magickal genes? Victor said he was good friends with her mother, didn't he?"

"He did, but didn't say where the girl came from. It would likely be one of the neighboring worlds, since she was evidently human before."

"Or a witch. She could have come from Hawthorne Grove."

"Possible, given she has some obvious magick."

Eros made a disagreeing face.

Loki justified, "Well, I think it's obvious."

"Fine."

"I wonder if Alec will be at the Collectors Gala..." Loki pondered.

"Uh... Does he collect artifacts?"

"I have heard he's getting into the business."

Eros's eyes narrowed, "Why?"

Loki shrugged. "It's profitable, and essentially, if you want to be a part of the *in crowd* you have to collect magickal artifacts."

"It's such a waste, all of you collecting so much

expensive, useless junk."

Loki chuckled. "The rich aren't rich if they are not amassing a dragon-den's worth of useless junk."

Eros rolled his eyes.

"It's history, though." Loki justified, "It's art."

Eros sighed, "I know. I'm just bitter. It's just that when we first began organizing your collection, I was looking for a weapon, a clue to escaping Fate, and well, even though I'm happy to have found other things," he pushed himself into Loki as they walked, "it's a bit frustrating."

"It's an uphill battle."

"Meaning we're Sisyphus, and it won't amount to anything."

Loki tutted, "You see, I always imagined Sisyphus as being *happy.*"

"*Happy*? He's in Hades, rolling a bleeding rock up a hill *for eternity*. Why would he be happy?"

"It's the symbolism to life-"

Eros protested, "Which is fucking miserable if you never achieve anything, never finish anything."

Loki wagged a finger, "But. But… You could view it as a challenge, and a test of the spirit. If you're constantly working to achieve the impossible, you know that you will fail, and you will fail and fail again, and maybe never get it right, but it is the intellectual pursuit, the physical challenge, the test of stamina that keeps you going. You keep trying, and you carve new paths and innovate new means, and that is what makes the human spirit happy. It's the puzzle, the fight, the near-misses, the almost-successes."

"Sure. Well, enjoy your symbolism. I've met Sysiphus. I've seen him down there, and trust me… he's not very happy."

"Well, then, he's doing it wrong," was Loki's curt reply.

15

The swamp where the worlds meet is a very dangerous place. Under the muddy water's surface, lurk monsters that if dreamed of, could wake a demon from his deepest slumber. Betwixt the shadows of drooping Spanish moss and twisting vines, live the nastiest of all malicious and vicious pixies.

But she was safe inside her little house on stilts. She had hung herbs over doorways and anointed the thresholds with oils for protection, but that wasn't the only reason she was safe. There was something about her new friend that made the swamp things skittish.

Before, the pixies might have come up to her window and made faces at her and her nurses. But the nurses were gone, her baby too, and now the pixies and sprites peeped in for only a second before slithering away.

The pixies now weren't even touching the sweetcakes she left out on her front steps as an offering to them. They were shunning her because of her new visitor. There was something about him they didn't like.

Her new friend couldn't stay with her long if she was going to make the swamp her home. The spirits might have been leaving the offerings alone out of fear, but if it went on for too long, they would leave her offerings untouched as a sign of rejection. Her new friend's ominous pall would have them both shunned, and being shunned from the place she had been shunned to was more than she could bear to think about.

But her new friend was kind and helpful. He helped around the house and gave her plenty of space. She did the same for him. It was as if they both were ghosts, habitually moving around the house, sliding unnoticed past each other, lost inside their own memories.

Every now and again, she would stop to cry, and he would become quiet with whatever work he was doing. He would never say a word. He would just check on her with his eyes, and if hers ever met his, he'd give her a sympathetic smile. But, she never spoke about her tears, and she was happy he didn't ask.

Then, at night, he would try not to sleep. He'd fumble and fidget throughout the night, trying to stay awake. At times, she would think about saying something. When he did fall asleep, sitting in the chair by the fire, it didn't take but a few short minutes for nightmares to set upon him. Sometimes he'd thrash and wake himself up. It always took him a few moments to regain a sense of where he was.

She'd give him a sympathetic smile, and he would gesture for her to go back to sleep.

One morning, when he was collecting wood for the fire, she made herself busy with her herbs and her oils, and when he returned, she presented a small dark jar to him.

"For your nightmares," she said, while he was stacking the small logs and sticks by the fireplace.

He eyed the jar and stood, holding out his hand. She placed it in his palm.

He asked in an inhuman voice, "Do I drink it?"

She shook her head, raised her hands to her temples, and demonstrated where to anoint himself with it. He mirrored her circular movements as she moved her fingers to the soft flesh behind her ears, then her wrists, then her forehead.

"Thank- I mean, I appreciate it." The customs of this world did not abide by the words *thank you* and *sorry,* because people often do not mean those words when they say them.

He nodded and set the tincture on the fireplace mantle.

He also wanted to apologize for disturbing her sleep with his night terrors, but he went back to work, restacking the kindling before going out for more.

When he stepped out the door, he stopped on the

porch. On a small china plate, which was the finest thing she owned, there still sat the two sweetcakes. She made them fresh every night as an offering to the swamp.

He knew he couldn't stay long. The memories coming back to him told him this was his way, and he needed to be getting on.

That night, he anointed himself with the oils as he sat in his chair before the embers in the fireplace.

"Dream well," The Swamp Witch said.

He nodded, "You too."

She rolled away to face the wall, and he took a steadying breath before closing his eyes.

***

Our hero was suspended from a rope, secured to something beyond the open skylight.

"Hurry up, Mate! Don't just hang there!"

Our hero pulled himself up and released the clip holding his safety harness to the rope. They were in a marble ballroom. All around the room were pedestals holding empty glass cases, and each case was lit. Aside from the lit cases and the red lasers crisscrossing the room, it was dark.

"What is this?" Our hero asked the man in the leather coat.

The man was shadowed in the dark hallway on the other side of the red laser beams. "It's the opposite of a heist." The Dream King lit up a cigarette, "Come on."

In his dream, our hero was *normal*. He had no scars and no piercings of servitude. He was young, but not a child. He was healthy and fit.

He examined the red lasers, and mapped out a path under this one, over that one.

Matrix, limbo, back flip, arabesque, half-moon pose, pin drop, cart-wheel, and he stuck the landing.

The Dream King looked at him with wide eyes through the haze of his lit cigarette.

"You know those weren't activated right?"

All the red lines across the showroom faded.

Our hero blinked, "And you're just telling me this now?"

"Because, that was fucking awesome, Mate! You were like this, and then you did that-" Hypnos excitedly mimicked his moves as they made their way down the darkened hall. "And then what the fuck was this thing? Are you a ballerina or something?"

He nodded, "I lived with one." Our hero stopped. "Hang on, I just remembered that..." His eyes drifted out a window towards the purple sky, dripping with falling stars.

"Yeah. You're dreaming, so this is where all the things you left alone in your subconscious come to run amuck. It's to be expected your memories are all out of sync. My buddy, well, kind of my boyfriend, but not really, he can't remember any of the time we spent together in Tartarus." He resumed walking, and our hero followed.

"You've been in Tartarus? You got out?"

"Not exactly. Just… You're not the only one I sprang from the joint… but, if anyone asks, I had nothing to do wiffit!"

Our hero blinked, "I don't even know what you're talking about."

Hypnos pointed his cigarette at him, "Good. Because you won't remember anything when you wake up anyway. Hey, sorry I wasn't there when you got out. I meant to be, but I was at this rave, you see, and things got a little-" He wiggled his fingers around his temples.

"We're not supposed to use that word here. *Sorry.*"

"Not unless you mean it, and I do mean it. Here we go." Dream approached a door and held his hand over the handle until the pins and tumbler clicked, and the door swung open.

They walked into an office with dark, rich wood shelves lining the walls. It smelled of scotch and decaying paper. There was a large wooden desk on the opposite side of the room.

Hypnos unlocked the desk drawer the same way he unlocked the door. He dug through his pockets until he withdrew a black velvet bag.

He saw our hero's curious expression and poured out the contents, which were tiny black gemstones in tear dropped shapes, into his hand.

"What are they?"

"The tears of my brother." Hypnos said.

"He cries rocks?"

"No. His tears turn into rocks."

"Ah... got it."

"And these," Hypnos looked dejectedly at them as he moved them around in his palm, "are all the tears he's ever cried."

Hypnos funneled them back into the bag.

Our hero cleared his throat. "Ever?"

There were only twenty-some odd stones in the pouch.

"Ever."

"Wow."

"Yeah... he um..." Hypnos tossed the pouch into the drawer and kicked the drawer closed. "He has a problem with his emotions. He's been looking for those. So, I thought I'd give them back... He's going to need them. *We often call a man cold when he is really just sad.*"

Our hero thought for a minute about the quote, "Longfellow?"

"Who? What? I'm talking about my brother, Thanatos. Pay attention."

"Right. My apologies."

Hypnos nodded back towards the entrance, "Now that that's all said and done, and you're a free man... We should get a drink!"

Hypnos opened the office door, but instead of the marble hall, they entered the graffitied back hall of a bar. The walls were littered with torn black and white posters and it smelled like sour-boozy vomit.

Hypnos yelled over the pulses of an electronic beat, "I bet you're a whiskey man. Me too. Thanny drinks scotch, though."

"Um… question. I mean, I have several, but…"

Hypnos turned to him, and our hero pointed at his own face. "Do I still look eleven years old?"

Hypnos looked him up and down. He yelled, "You look fine," and he walked into the bar.

Our hero pressed his lips together and said to himself, "Not what I asked." He followed the Dream King anyway.

They slid into a booth, which already had a bottle of Jack Daniels waiting for them. "You know you can be whatever age you want, right? You're free now. You get to start anew, do whatever you like, *whenever* you like."

"I don't know if that's really what freedom means."

"How would you know?"

"Good point."

"Listen, I'm free, and let me tell you what- I can smoke, I can dance, I am a free agent. I make me own rules, and there's one rule here in Dream: There are no rules!"

The ex-Jinni smiled and leaned back, "But, that's still a rule."

"So?" Hypnos took a swig of whiskey straight from the bottle.

"You're essentially asking me what it is *I* want."

Hypnos handed him the bottle, "Yeah. What do you want?"

Our hero sighed and looked around the bar for his

answer. He noticed the patrons of the bar were all people he vaguely recognized. There were two demons smoking and drinking at the bar. There was a scruffy waiter practicing different accents on the people he served, and a woman in a Victorian dress talking about humanities with an interior designer from Cali, and a fisherman from Canada. There was a fairy prince arm wrestling with the undefeated champion at a corner table.

Everywhere he looked, he saw different people from different points in his life, spinning around the room in a whirlwind of memory and colors. He took a swig from the bottle and pinched the bridge of his nose. "I don't want to remember."

The orphans of Carpathia walked into the bar with wide eyes and ragged clothes.

"I want to forget," he said.

An old Sage held out his glass as a ballerina poured wine into it from a red perfume bottle.

"In order to be free I must be free from my past. I can't- I don't *want* to remember *this*." His fingers were pulling through the hair he knew he didn't have. He ripped them out of his hair and shook from the mental strain of differentiating reality from dreams and memories forgotten.

Hypnos pulled the bottle of Jack back to his end of the table, "I know you've only had a sip, but I think you've had too much to drink."

Our hero laughed, "What about being able to do whatever I want, huh?" He stole the bottle back and drank deep.

"You know...," Hypnos cautioned, "in the future, you tell me you can't run away from your past, and that a strong man can face his weaknesses."

"Yeah, but I'm tired of always being responsible for my own sanity! I'm tired of being strong! For holding it together when there is nothing to hold onto! I know nothing but pain and loss, and I have told myself lie after lie to keep myself sane... to survive! I can't. If I get to start over... then I'm going to start over. You are certainly right when you say I won't remember any of this when I wake up."

He took one more drink, and the fire inside him brought him to his feet.

"Wait, don't leave yet!" Hypnos reached for him.

But, he was gone.

"Shit." Dream brought the booze back to his side of the table as he sat in an empty and silent bar.

***

Our hero awoke to the sound of the Swamp Witch coming through the door with firewood. He rubbed his face then his bald head as he groaned, trying to recall the mess of faces he saw in his dream. He turned to her and she smiled.

"I thought I'd let you sleep," she said. "Did you have bad dreams?"

He thought and said, "I don't remember, but I did have an epiphany."

"Oh?" She crouched down to set the wood next to the fireplace.

He leaned forward in his chair as she stopped to listen.

"If-if you could forget *everything*, would you?"

She took in a deep breath, and her eyes drifted across her tiny house. "Parts. I'd want to forget parts, but not everything."

"Why?"

She swallowed and stood.

"I want to remember… so that maybe I can keep it from ever happening again."

He thought about this and nodded.

"And my life wasn't bad. There were good parts, and I cherish those memories." Tears began to well up in her eyes as she wrapped her arms around her chest. "I still love my daughter. I still love my sisters, and I don't want-," she swallowed, and her lip trembled. Then anger strained in her throat, "But, I don't want that man to take more from me than what he stole. I won't allow him to take everything from me." Her head fell, but she took in a breath.

She laughed despite herself, "Why do you ask?"

He bit his tongue and shook his head. "Forgive me. I shouldn't have…"

She moved to the work table behind him. "Are *you* going to forget everything?" She looked back at him.

He thought for a moment and turned in the chair to face her. "Yes."

She nodded and sniffed, "Well, I hope that works out for you."

He wasn't sure if she meant it. He wouldn't blame her if she didn't.

Her face softened, and she asked, "Do you need help?"

He did have magick of his own, though it was sporadic. Sometimes it would fizzle away like a weak firework. Other times it worked seamlessly and would come as naturally to him as breathing.

He smiled, "I'd like that very much."

She turned to her table and took inventory of her jars of oils and herbs. "We'll need a few things."

"I'll get the fire and breakfast started," he offered.

The Swamp Witch looked over her shoulder at him. She had a million thoughts in her mind, and she decided to leave them there. She opened the door and descended the stairs into the swamp.

She returned an hour later with a basket of ripe, fresh fruit and a jar of swirling glitter. Our hero raised an eyebrow at the jar.

"Pixie dust." She answered his questioning gaze.

He arched his eyebrow further, "And how did you manage that?"

"A witch doesn't reveal her secrets." She wagged a finger.

"And how is it going to help? I just think happy thoughts and fly to the second star to the right?"

She stiffened. "Where I'm from, we use pixie dust for a number of glamours. Pixie dust tricks and distracts. It will help you blend into the world by hiding your scars."

He nodded.

She continued, "...And the fairy food," she looked at her basket of fruit, which made his breakfast of swamp fish stew look even more sickly, "It will help you forget, just like the Lost Boys of Neverland."

"Then I will do what I can to change my-," he looked down at his hands, "shape, and to lock away the memories that keep surfacing, and this will do the rest?"

She nodded and stepped forward, "Are you certain this is what you want?"

He took a breath. "Yes."

She raised her chin and set down her basket of fruit on the table. "I appreciate your friendship and what you've done for me. I wish you luck."

He cringed, but couldn't put his finger on why.

She said, "But, I warn you, we will meet again."

He smiled, "I don't doubt that."

16

The day before the Collectors Gala, Thanatos was patrolling the showroom floor. Collectors had been dropping off their artifacts all week to be put on display. The glass cases had to be locked and sealed with magick after the usual technological security protocols were put in place.

Over the epochs, so many artifacts had been stolen from places, despite all of their magickal protections, with some mundane modes of thievery. When one relies solely on the complexities of magick, one tends to make trivial and detrimental oversights, which thieves who think themselves Indiana Jones take full advantage of.

Death would never allow himself, or his company, to be disgraced by such mindless mistakes. Thus, every precaution was taken on nights like this: ample security guards, cameras, motion lights, weight sensors, heat detection, and other anti-theft systems. These measures are taken long before they apply the aura detectors, magick blocks, force fields, protection symbols, devil's traps, and hex charms.

Thanatos is not a nervous or paranoid man. He is observant and prepared.

With his deadly reputation, no one had ever tried to infiltrate one of *his* Collectors Galas. In the event someone ever did, his reputation as a fierce and powerful businessman would be soiled, so Thanatos made sure many would die before that became possible. If anyone stepped onto the property with even so much as a thought of stealing from one of his clients or himself, they would incinerate so suddenly, no one would ever know that they had been there. Not even a speck of ash would remain to be swept up by the janitorial staff.

A grating and familiar voice broke his concentration. "Thanatos."

Death turned around to see a short man. Everyone was short compared to Death.

The man with shoulder-length blond hair approached him. He was dressed in expensive turn-of-the-century French attire, and he sported an ornate cane for fashion purposes only. It was tucked under his arm.

"Alec. What can I help you with?"

With his top hat in hand, Alec gestured towards the

offices, "I was hoping I might have a private word with you."

"If this is regarding your night clubs, I've told you before I'm not interested." Death made to brush the Vampire Prince off.

But, Alec quickly added, "Though, I hope to change your mind on that particular subject, I hope to speak to you about a more *private* matter."

Thanatos then knew that Alec wanted to speak with him about his sire, Victor Devereaux, and Death's curiosity got the better of him. He publicly supported the Devereaux House and was well aware of the drama Alec was concocting. Perhaps this was his chance to belittle some sense into Alec. The prince was young and rebellious, and would soon learn the error of his ways.

Thanatos nodded and led the way to his office. Alec followed with the pretentious sound of his cane echoing off the stone hall.

They entered through a large wooden door, which Thanatos magickally unlocked with the slightest flick of his wrist, without so much as missing a step. The walls were lined with shelves of books, and Death moved behind the desk, gesturing Alec to sit before him.

Alec rested his cane on the arm of the chair and placed his top hat in his lap.

Thanatos's decorum forced him to have to wait for Alec to situate himself before he could finally sit. He leaned back and steepled his fingers.

Death said, "Say what you've come here to say."

Alec readjusted in his seat, reading his mental notes with haste, "Thanatos, I've come here, as you are a man my father and I both greatly respect. I trust you are aware of the rift growing between my father and myself?"

Thanatos didn't bother to restrain his boredom, "Yes. I am."

"I am beginning to worry that this chasm is going to mar my reputation as a businessman."

"You don't say?" Thanatos said as patronizingly as he could manage.

Alec clenched his jaw to regain his composure. "Yes. His personal feelings about my business operations are starting to sway my investors to withdraw. He is slandering my name. I was hoping, as a friend and a business partner to my father, you might be able to mitigate our private disagreements so as to have our differences not affect my future in the business world."

Death chuckled, "Alec-"

"*Mr. VanGarrett*, if you would..." the Prince interjected.

"*Alec,*" Death sneered. "Everything. Everything is business. I am not a *friend* of your father. I am not *your* friend, and I am certainly not a family counselor. If you are concerned about your *private* affairs affecting your businesses, perhaps you should clean up your private affairs.

"Because, in business, nothing is private. Your

investors and your clients are going to care about what you do behind closed doors, because how you handle your house is how you handle your business enterprises. Your *father* knows this and has been trying to teach you this lesson by disowning you from his family, because he doesn't want *your* private affairs to sway *his* investors and clients to withdraw from his businesses."

Alec's face was beginning to twist with rising rage.

"I do not apologize if this reality I am explaining to you is harsh." Thanatos continued, "Reality *is* harsh. The sooner you learn that, the better. Your best bet, as a businessman, is to repent and seek your father's forgiveness. That is your only way to secure the success of your future. Your sire is the Vampire King. To go against him is to go against the *entirety* of your client base."

Alec stood, his hat falling to the floor, "The new wave of the vampire community is exhausted of the old regime! My father and his merry men are tired and antiquated. We want a free market. We want industry and freedom from our oppressors!"

"Calm yourself. Just because you can't do whatever you want doesn't mean you're oppressed, *Prince Alec*. Your sire-"

"My *sire* is painting me a monster because I challenge him and his failed ways. He is trying to destroy me because my ideas frighten him."

"I know about the girl, Alec. Everyone does."

Alec's nostrils flared, "That story is much more

nuanced than he tells it. Victor is *lying!*"

Death smiled and corrected, "His royal highness, Vampire King, Victor Devereaux, if you will..."

Alec took a breath and nodded in frustration. "Very well, I'll prove it to all of you."

Thanatos stood as Alec picked his hat up off the floor.

"Very well. We'll see who the *free market* supports. Will you still be at the gala tomorrow night?"

"Yes. I appreciate the opportunity to meet other collectors and expand my collection." He nodded as he took up his cane and made his way to the door.

"You'll be happy to know your father will not be in attendance," Thanatos added, as a minute gesture of peace.

"That does brighten my spirits, although I assumed that he wouldn't be present, given that all he's collected for decades... is *dust.*"

Alec exited the room, and Thanatos fell back into his chair. Alec was a punk and a trouble maker, who no one took seriously, but Thanatos wondered for a brief moment if thinking that way was a mistake.

He opened up the bottom drawer of his desk where he hid a small decanter of Macallan scotch, but next to the crystal container was a small velvet bag he vaguely remembered. It had been so long since he used this office, he was uncertain of its contents.

He opened the bag and sprinkled the loose items into his palm. Jet. Black. Teardrops. He looked around the empty office to make sure that it was indeed empty, and no one else but him had seen the prized little gemstones.

He had been casually looking for these little tears whenever he strolled through one of his vaults or reliquaries. He had hoped he had just misplaced them, never wanting to accept the idea they had been stolen or lost, even though that could have been the reality.

Thanatos released a sigh of relief, then an inward snarl at himself for this idiotic misstep. Why would he leave them here in this old office of all places? How careless and irresponsible. Death of all people should know better.

He entertained, for a small moment, that he would have never done such a thing, that someone else had placed them there for him to find. But, he quickly dismissed the paranoid thought. It denied fault and responsibility, and if Death was anything, he was *responsible*. He was responsible for *everything*.

There was a knock at his door, and he quickly replaced the tears into the velvet bag and shoved it into his pants pocket.

"Come in," He barked.

His secretary opened the door and blinked at him through her cat eye glasses, "Sir, the head of security would like you to sign off on his work for the day."

"I appreciate it, Patrice."

Death grunted, closed the desk drawer with his foot, and exited the office.

***

Death walked through the streets of New Bedlam from the venue to his office building, which he could see towering over all the other edifices and rooftops. His office building was the tallest skyscraper in the city, and it was all white, just like his suit and just like his Lincoln.

It was a monolith. It was a symbol, a reminder, that Death is pure and that Death is looming, and that Death ruled all, and no other god could obtain his domain, nor could they escape it.

Except maybe the Fates.

He did not enjoy the power they wielded over him and his world, controlling the ins and outs of his job, taking lives whenever it fit their power-hungry agenda.

To him, their manipulative works were a threat to the *balance of things*, over which he kept an ever-vigilant eye. Keeping the *balance of things* was his true nature.

And the Fates were threatened by any of the ancient gods whose power surpassed their own, like Eros, or himself, or his brother Hypnos. Those three sisters saw anything that existed before them as a danger to their reign, and they would see to the submittance or non-existence of anything potentially detrimental to their plans.

Fate was everywhere, and it could control you without you ever even knowing.

Death would not be controlled. He would not allow himself to be strung up like a marionette. He would only play their game long enough to win it. But, he made sure not to think on this for long and to resign himself to boiling that frustration down into a constant discomfort in the back of his mind.

Amongst the hustle and bustle of the congested sidewalk, a homeless child bumped into him.

It startled him and shook him from his thoughts. The child with a slight limping gait apologized with fear in his eyes, and he quickly ran off with a pack of other dirty children.

Thanatos grunted. The homeless children were beginning to pour out of the rundown communities like Rippertown. Most of them were demons, but an increasing number were humans.

The real currency of the Netherworlds was not demonics, but power, which humans had little of, and as a result they were literally on the bottom of the food chain. Wealthy demons and vampires kept them as pets and cattle. They were expensive to buy and to keep, and if they escaped, they ran away into the sewers or the woods. Both hiding places were dangerous and would also end with them becoming something's lunch, but they did it anyway for the dim chance of freedom. Somehow, more and more had managed to survive, and they were beginning to run amuck.

He'd have to find a solution to *fix* the problem before it got any worse. Perhaps adoption. The upper class demons would enjoy the ego stroke they'd receive for *adopting* a human, and yes, the human would quickly perish, but death comes to all creatures. It is the balance of things, but that way of handling the issue appeared more humane than literally leaving them to die in a gutter.

Thanatos pushed open the glass doors to his skyscraper and admired the clean lines and open floor plan of his offices. He went straight to the coffee shop on the first floor. Death prided himself in the care he gave his employees. He provided them with a living, along with living arrangements, life insurance, a great deal of accidental death and hazard insurance, along with many other perks to their job, which included the coffee shop. It was identical to the one across the street. To be honest, it was good for his employees *and* for him. They took shorter breaks, given that they didn't have to leave the building, and he, of course, profited off the coffee shop as well.

"My usual," Thanatos ordered the cashier, who nodded nervously and told the barista they needed the boss's order *on the fly*.

Death stood there with his hands in his pockets as he waited for the baristas to steam the milk and ready the espresso.

It took much longer than it should have for him to notice his pockets were empty.

He double checked his breast pocket, his back pockets, his front pockets again, but the little velvet bag was missing.

The barista handed him his warm paper coffee cup. With a large smile, he took the coffee. Calmly, without raising alarm, he strolled back through the grand entry. The moment he pushed through the double glass doors and his shoes hit the sidewalk outside, he dumped his coffee in a trash can and sprinted down the pavement. He wove in and out of the crowd as he heard them ask in shock as he ran, "Is that Thanatos?"

When he reached the spot of his mugging, he brushed back his hair and composed himself as he tried to recall which way the group of children had gone.

Thanatos tugged at his suit jacket and his sleeves as he looked over the street and the crowd. He turned down the alleyway he suspected the children had disappeared into, and he saw that the solid steel cover to the sewer was slightly askew.

He stepped up to it, noticing the Grim Enterprises logo stamped into the steel. With the flick of his wrist, the drain cover slid away to reveal a rusted ladder descending into the dark pit. He snarled and took off his suit jacket, laying it on a nearby Grim Enterprises dumpster.

Thanatos descended into the New Bedlam underground.

His white shoes sank into the muck when he finally hit bottom. It was rank with the blood of Alec's nightclubs and the general waste of the Netherworlds. Rats with glowing eyes scampered past him on pipes and rails, and bioluminescent scum grew on the damp stone and lingered on the opaque surface of the water.

He waded ankle deep through the canals. However,

whenever he found a drier walkway, it was disrupted by the giant blocks of ancient temples felled in the bygone days of the Netherworlds, forcing him to to continue traversing through the mire. Eventually, he heard the laughter and cries of children echoing off the walls, and Death crept like a shadow closer to the congregation.

He could sense how many were demons and how many were human, and his senses landed on his thief, whose gait was slightly gimp, whose aura at first glance was purely human, but something tasted off. Thanatos could taste the death of all things, and this *human* boy had no expiration date.

The boy was only pretending to be human, and this *thing* had no death date. Everything had a death date. Every ocean. Every star. Every god. The only *thing* without a termination date was Death himself.

At that realization, he quit lurking in the shadows and stepped out into the mass of children, like a dragon descending onto a town of villagers. They scattered, human and demon alike, except his thief, who unlike the other children, had no internal instinct to run from his own mortality.

Death came upon him like a Titan and took him by his throat. He could feel the boy's heart racing underneath his grasping palm, and he knew the pulse was a lie. He wasted no time removing his velvet bag from the boy's pocket, and instead of pocketing it again, he teleported it to a secured vault where it belonged. Never again would he make such a mindless mistake.

"What are you?" he asked the gasping child, whom he promptly dropped onto the damp sewer floor.

"What the hell are you talking about?" The child responded with strength and aggravation. "Look, I stole your stones, because I was aiming for your wallet. I had no idea. I was just going to sell them to buy us all some food."

"You were just going to *sell* them," he mocked. "Do you have any idea what those stones *are*? Do you even- It doesn't matter what they are. What matters is what *you* are. Tell me."

The child was looking for a way out, but Death had him cornered, so our hero stood his ground. "I don't know what you're talking about."

Death lowered himself to the child's face. "You're not human."

The boy laughed in his face. "Yes. I am."

Death smiled and looked away. "Maybe you think you are," he looked back up, "but you, my boy, shouldn't exist, and we are going to find out why you do. You are coming with me."

He grabbed the kid's arm, and took him away.

***

Our hero was strapped to a stainless steel slab in a dank basement. When he tilted his head back he could see the old wooden stairs leading to the floor above them.

"What is your name?" asked the towering man in the white suit.

Our hero had to think for a moment before he answered, strangely, as if only just remembering it himself. "Damien." The creepy old lady he had met in the swamp had told him his name was, "Damien Warrick Parker." The way he said his name- it was as if he was saying it for the first time.

"And where did you come from?"

"I come from the water," he sang, then quickly corrected, "the swamp."

"The swamp." The man in the white suit echoed in disbelief.

"Yes!" Damien protested Death's questioning and patronizing tone.

"And *why* were you in the swamp?"

The swamp witch had told him that when she had found him, he had just survived a terrible accident. His brows pulled together, "I don't know. I woke up there."

The creepy witch had healed him and had told him it was time for him to leave the swamp.

"Where were you before the swamp?"

He had no recollection of where he had been before. "I don't remember."

"I find that hard to believe, thief. Do you know where you are now?"

He had spent days wandering from town to town, sleeping in abandoned houses and shacks until he found other children like him- lost, and hungry, and wandering. They had made homes in the sewers and begged for money when they weren't picking pockets and digging in dumpsters. The demons in that world ate strange food.

Damien rolled his eyes. "Enlighten me."

At this blatant disrespect, Thanatos laughed. It was further proof the boy was not a boy. "The Netherworlds. *My* world."

"Oh," Damien quipped, "you're the douche bag on the front page of the papers?"

"Yes," Death snarled, "That *douche bag* is me. I am Death, and I am the ending of all things, and you, *Mr. Parker*, have no ending. I don't believe it is a coincidence that you happened to be the one to *steal* something very important from me. Do you think it is a coincidence?"

"The universe is never so lazy." Damien sighed as if he had said that line a million times.

"My sentiments exactly… The Fates sent you."

Damien wrinkled his nose, "Huh? You mean like the goddesses, the Moirai?"

"Yes. Exactly. You apparently know *nothing* else, but you somehow know who the Fates are?" Death scoffed.

Damien offered unconvincingly, "Amnesia can be selective?"

Death gave him a condescending *hmph*, and began to move up the table, trailing his long white fingers along the stainless steel.

The metal slab on which he was laying became cold as

Death faded from view. He began to shiver uncontrollably, and a familiar but unnamable fear sank into his bones.

Damien began to tug at the restraints as an inner voice shushed and cooed him, and another one said *Hey, look at me.*

His heart slamming against his rib cage, he tilted his head back to see the blond man with mismatched eyes looking down at him. The blue and green eyes were lifeless and cold. Damien looked through them, and past them, and saw nothing. He saw the dark nothingness of lifelessness after death.

Thanatos put his hands flat on the table on either side of our hero's head.

Here we go...

Damien steadied the tempest in his chest.

"Let's take a quick peek and see what's going on inside that head of yours."

Death put all ten fingers on the sides of Damien's head. He wiggled through the hair until his fingernails scraped the boy's scalp. His touch turned our hero's blood to ice.

That cold second passed like a decade in a grave.

Don't scream, said the distant voice.

Then ten spikes penetrated into his brain.

And he screamed.

17

*E*ros had decided a week ago that he was comfortable enough to walk straight into Loki's townhome without knocking, and Loki never corrected this action. So, on the night of the gala, Eros glided straight through the door without pause, until he mindlessly went to hang his coat on the rack, and his coat fell straight to the floor in a heap. The rack was gone. The youthful god grumbled and picked his coat up off the ground.

"Loki!" Eros called.

Loki's voice called back, "Upstairs."

Eros ascended the stairs, "Hypnos moved the coat rack again!"

"I know. I thought about buying a second one."

Eros rounded the corner to see Loki in the process of

buttoning his shirt, his tie draped over his shoulders.

"But, then I thought… fucking with him is so much more entertaining." He flashed Eros a wicked smile.

Eros pulled his brows together when he saw Loki was having trouble with his buttons. Eros offered, "Let me get that."

Loki's arms dropped in exaggerated defeat.

Eros reached up to Loki's collar, and Loki snorted, "Are you sure you don't need a step ladder?"

Eros glared and nodded, "Maybe you won't be such a *giant* dick if I choose to bite it off next time, yeah?" He smiled, patted Loki on the chest, and commenced fastening the buttons.

Loki readjusted his shoulders, cleared his throat, and hazarded, "You'd need a step ladder for that too."

Eros nodded, and when he tied Loki's tie, he choked him with it. Loki let out a small gurgle before Eros asked, "Too tight?"

"Not at all," Loki gasped, bringing his hand to his throat. He loosened the knot. "Ugh. You tied a Windsor. I prefer a Pratt."

Eros had moved to sit on the trunk at the foot of the bed. "You look better with a Windsor, and Pratt knots are for prats." Eros blinked.

Loki shrugged and began looking madly around the room. "Now, where the devil is my jacket?" He stormed off towards the closet. "I just had it!"

Eros suspiciously eyed the suit jacket laying on the

trunk right next to him. "Loki?"

From inside the closet, Loki returned with an aggravated, "Yes?"

Eros handed him the jacket, cautiously. "It was next to me on the trunk."

The giant sighed and snatched the thing from Eros's hand.

Eros frowned and felt Loki's aggravation, and grumbling, and sharpness within himself. As the giant slipped his arms into his suit jacket and shrugged it on, Eros *felt* everything Loki was feeling: *The process took too long. The damn thing fit too tight. The arm was slightly twisted. He needed a stiff drink and to smoke before they left to go to this god awful party, filled with awful gods who would make the experience perfectly awful.*

Eros turned from Loki and slipped out the door.

Loki threw back his head and kicked himself for ripping away the jacket the way he did. Eros hadn't done anything wrong and didn't deserve the brunt end of his... his... whatever the hell was wrong with him.

He sat on the trunk and ran his hand over his face. Then, he groaned at his stubble. He had forgotten to shave.

Eros popped back in the room, having grabbed one of the pipes and a glass of scotch from the library. He offered them to Loki without a word.

The giant marveled at the Greek god for just a moment before Eros thrust the items into his hands.

Eros sat down next to him.

First, Loki threw back the burning scotch, despite the fact it was for sipping not gulping. Then, he waved a hand over his pipe, simultaneously filling it with tobacco and lighting it. Lastly, he waved a hand over his stubble to clear it.

He preferred tamping his pipe and shaving the *hard* way, but Loki didn't find it hard, he found it ritualistic and meditative.

He pulled in a big cloud of smoke and held it in his mouth until he could feel its effects, and he let it go. Finally, he was relaxing.

Eros had made himself small next to Loki, and finally felt safe enough to say, "I'm scared too."

Loki spat out the rest of his smoke. "Scared? I'm not scared. I'm Viking. We don't get scared."

Eros pressed his lips together.

Loki blurted out a laugh. "Scared of *what*?"

"I don't know... of what Odin and Thor will say?" Eros's eyes went wide, "Or my *mother*."

Loki blurted out another laugh. "Please. I'm used to the gods demonizing everything I do. I'm the universe's scapegoat."

"Just because you're used to it doesn't mean that you enjoy it."

Loki put his forehead in his hand. "I hope our ex-wives aren't there."

Eros grimaced, "Same. I mean, this is different for me. I'm a stereotypical playboy and the god of homoeroticism, so I'm only worried that they aren't going to take this seriously. Like... *typical Eros.* "

Loki just threw up his hands dramatically and shrugged.

Eros continued, "You, well, I mean at least the Greeks *sometimes* approved of homosexual activities, but *your* family... "

"Maybe they won't be there." Loki began, "I mean, this is a Collectors Gala after all. All the cool trinkets my family has came from *me*. Because, *I* tricked some dwarves into making them. They won't even be there, and if they are- No matter what I do, they will always think of me as *cowardly* Loki."

"You're not a coward."

"Well, Thor would disagree-"

"Not bothered. Let him." Eros shrugged. "Mjolnir can't stand up to my sharp wit. I'll shoot him in his Achilles with my arrow and make him fall in love with an ass."

Loki grinned. "Promise? Can I help? I'm very good at getting people to shoot *other* people with arrows, you know."

Eros looked up at him through his lashes. "Sure. You can help."

They both laughed, carrying on this way for as long as they could.

Eros stood and faced Loki to loosen and straighten the giant's tie. "I actually liked the stubble."

Loki reached out and kissed him hard on the mouth,

but he pulled away slowly and tenderly.

Eros pressed his lips together, savoring the taste of tobacco and scotch Loki left behind. "You know... the gala starts in fifteen minutes and... we should be fashionably late..."

Loki blinked, "Thanatos would kill me. I'm his rock at these functions. Believe it or not, I keep him sane. He has a very short fuse. The last time I wasn't there to hold his hand The Black Plague happened."

Eros pouted, "Why do you think I want to be fashionably late?"

Loki squinted, "For appearance's sake?"

"Try again." He looked Loki up and down through his lashes, while biting his lower lip.

"Oh! Oh..." Loki's eyes went wide.

"Right, I really don't get how you miss what I'm putting down like *all the time.*"

"I don't get it either." Loki shook his head and added, "But, but... I'm afraid I can't do that to Thanatos. And, if we wait until *after* the party we'll have a reason to leave early."

"Or we can arrive late *and* leave early," Eros offered suggestively.

Loki grinned. "At that point we might as well not show up at all."

They both gave this significant consideration.

Simultaneously, they both sighed and rolled their eyes.

"No. No, we have to go," Eros pouted.

Loki groaned like an old tree when he rose from the trunk. "Do we have to?"

"Yes. We have to. Come on." Eros begrudgingly took Loki's hand and dragged him from the townhome.

They pulled up to the event venue in Loki's classic Bentley. There was a line of cars in front of them, and one by one people in suits and cocktail dresses stepped from the vehicles, which were swiftly taken away by valets.

At their turn, Eros and Loki stepped from the Bentley and approached the endless stairs leading to the lit-up, columned building. There was a small crowd of bored reporters standing behind a red rope, flashing cameras, and taking notes, and yammering incoherently.

"Well, are you ready?" asked Loki.

"Yes," Gulped Eros. "It's not a big deal. We were overreacting. Are you okay?"

"Fine, yes. Fine."

The sound of a revving engine and squealing tires caused them to turn. Loki's Bentley was hardly out of the way when a red Viper slammed to a halt in its spot.

Hypnos jumped out of the hot rod and tossed his keys to the valet. "Not one scratch on Sasha, you hear me? If I find one scratch, I'll give you nightmares for six months!"

The valet nodded and hurried to the car.

"Oh, dear Lord." Loki rolled his eyes.

"Oi! Wait up! Eros, you're looking... well, that *is* a look. New cologne? No. That's just Loki's musk all over you. It suits you." He peered heavily into Eros's eyes.

"I appreciate it," Eros coyly smiled back.

Loki interjected, "Hypnos, why are you here? Do you really call yourself a collector?"

Hypnos scoffed, "You call what you do collecting? Because the rest of us call what you do *hoarding*. And I collect dreams, baby. Subconscious secrets. People pay a lot of dough for that kind of intel. But, don't get me wrong, Thanny would never invite me to this sort of shindig. I'm crashing." He popped the collar to his leather trench coat and posed provocatively for the cameras. Those pictures would be posted in the papers the next day with both Loki and Eros in the background, looking on in perplexed amusement.

Hypnos flashed them a grin over his shoulder, "All the cool kids *crash* parties. See you poofs inside."

Hypnos continued posing for the journalists, who suddenly turned into the paparazzi from Hollywood dreams.

Eros and Loki stepped into the grand hall of the venue. The building was illuminated by crystal chandeliers cascading from the muraled ceilings. Servers dashed around in red tailcoats carrying trays of champagne and hors d'oeuvres.

Neither of them were struck by the grandeur of the event. An event such as this was a normal occurrence in the realm of the gods, and the pair wasted no time being distracted by the vapid glamor and glitz. They headed straight towards the cocktail reception, held in a barroom off the main showfloor. It was more darkly lit, and it was cluttered with round tables surrounded by collectors of all races and sects.

They both paused just beyond the archway to scan the room and assess the catastrophe they were in for. They saw Shmeaglebobenzoar and The Lizard King, Xepherus Xypherus. Morgan le Fay and Queen Mab were attached at the hip while making their rounds. The two ladies were speaking with King Vollmar, the current Dwarf King.

Loki grimaced and averted his eyes. He had a long history with the dwarves, and they still had several warrants out for his head.

There were dragons, demons, faeries, and angels, but surprisingly few gods.

Eros and Loki gave each other a small nod before entering further into the bar.

"Just because they aren't here now doesn't mean they won't be later," Eros pointed out.

"Yes, but by that point I hope to be drunker than a sailor and have no recollection of conversing with them when I come 'round."

A deep voice hissed, "Loki!" And Loki jumped like a frightened cat.

Eros rolled his eyes at the man in the white suit towering over Loki. Eros hated how Loki would *literally* jump when Death called.

Death was looking at his pocket watch. "You are fifteen minutes late. You are always here on time and *this* time when I actually *need* you, you're late! Why?"

Eros stepped up to Loki, who was making a face and waving his hands around trying to explain, but he wasn't actually saying anything.

"Thanatos," Eros smiled, oozing condescending charm, "it's a pleasure to see you. Loki was late because of silly ol' me. You recall that we were arriving together? And I have to apologize for keeping him from you for an extra *fifteen* minutes. I had him quite... tied up... in the bedroom, you see."

Thanatos glared down at Eros. "Of course you did. Loki, may I speak to you for a moment?"

"Of course." He walked away with Thanatos, apologizing to Eros with more facial expressions and hand gestures as he went.

Eros sighed and shook his head as they walked off.

"Left you for his other boyfriend, did he?" Eros leapt and saw Hypnos right next to him, handing him a drink.

Eros rolled his eyes and took the glass.

"He will always choose Thanny over us. He likes to be the voice whispering into the ear of the big guy. Just ask Thor and Odin. It's how he gets his rocks off."

"You're being incredibly rude." Eros threw back his drink.

"But you know it's true." Hypnos draped a heavy arm around Eros's shoulder. "But, when daddy's out for the day, Desire and Dream get to play. Come on, let's go get pissed." Hypnos pulled him to the bar.

***

Death had pulled Loki past the ballroom and all of the artifacts on display, and took him to an office down a darkened hallway.

"I really shouldn't leave Eros for long. This function is sort of a date for us."

Death remarked flatly, "How adorable." He went straight to his desk and pulled out his small decanter of scotch. He poured them both a drink. "I really couldn't give a rat's ass about your romantic life at the moment. I found it, Loki." He handed him the glass. "I found a weapon to destroy the Fates."

Loki raised his eyebrows. He took the drink and sat down. "Here at the gala?"

"*No.*" Death spat out the word and gave Loki a scolding look. "I have it. In my basement."

"Which basement?"

"In one of my mansions. Look. That doesn't matter. What matters is I have found an anomaly, which shouldn't exist, which means it is in existence outside of the web of Fate."

Loki gave him a look, begging him to continue.

Death ran his fingers through his blond hair. "It doesn't have a death date. It is truly immortal like myself. The Fates by no means would ever allow this thing to exist if they knew about it," he paced behind the desk, "which means they don't know about it, and it is *immensely* powerful."

He held his strained, gripping hands out in front of Loki. Death was smiling like a maniac.

Loki squinted an eye. "Well, what is it?"

"It's a boy. Well, he's obviously not a boy-"

"It's alive? Meaning it is not an *it*, but a *he*? And you have him *locked* in your *basement*?"

"It's the only place strong enough to hold him."

"Do you hear yourself?" Loki crossed his ankle over his knee and laughed, "You are holding a *being* prisoner in your basement?"

Death gave him a mocking look that indicated that this was nothing, and as Death, he had done far worse.

"Well, not just a being," Loki continued, "but a *boy*."

Thanatos snapped his fingers and pointed at Loki, "Yes a *powerful, immortal* boy, which means he is not a boy. He's a…" He waved a hand for Loki to fill in the blank.

Loki blinked and said in a small voice, "A god?"

"A god!" Death confirmed. "Unregistered, unnamed, unknown. He doesn't even know *what he is*! I tried to poke around in his brain, and the blocks in there shoved me, *me*, out! I flew into the bleeding wall! *Me*!"

"A *god*?" Loki said again in amazement. "A new *fucking* god!" He jumped from the seat and began laughing.

Death even joined him in their celebratory laughter for their new discovery. New gods didn't just happen. Some might rebrand and be *born-again* and adapt to the changing universe, but even the youngest of gods were thousands of years old. The Fates hadn't allowed new gods to be created, due to the threat they might pose, as they claimed, *to the balance of things.*

"This is incredible!" Loki cried, and both men moved to their original positions.

"And the Fates have no idea! If they had, he wouldn't be out and about, hiding in a New Bedlam gutter!"

"No! They'd have him in chains in Tartarus, that's for sure!"

"Loki," Death said in a low tone, "he is powerful. I haven't even seen the depths of his power, but to be able to *block* his mind and his magick in the way that he did- Truly remarkable."

Loki's curiosity perked up, "But, why would he do that?"

"I don't know," Death took a swig from his scotch, "but I'm going to find out."

This remark didn't satisfy Loki, and he began to itch. "But, Thanatos," he sighed, "you can't keep him to experiment on and use as a weapon."

"Why the hell not?" Death was lighting a cigarette with a zippo. "Gods collect people all the time. *You* say you collect people all the time. Tell me why *I* can't for the free will of the universe?"

"I don't collect people *like that.* I either blackmail them, or make them my friend, or sometimes both. What exactly is your plan?"

"To unlock his god power and rip it out of him. It's not like he wants it anyway."

Loki cleared his throat and laughed preemptively to what he was going to say, "But, Death, *you'll kill him!*"

"It's my job. I have to kill children all the damn time. It's the worst part of my job, really, but death will be better than what the Fates will do to him if they ever find him out."

Loki made to talk, but Thanatos interrupted.

"Let's get you back to your boyfriend."

"Are you sure this is what you want to do?"

"Loki," Death's eyes grew stern, "that boy's power will be mine if it's the last thing I do. He's putting up a fight, a big one, but I *will* win."

Loki nodded. There was still time to talk Thanatos out of it, but that would have to wait for a different night.

Loki made his way back to the bar and saw Hypnos and Eros chatting it up. They were both laughing and practically glowing in the way only two long-time lovers could, and Loki wasn't jealous. He smiled, happy to see Eros warming and opening up to someone. It meant there was hope, a chance that one day he could make Eros's eyes glitter the same way.

He watched on in awe as Eros wove his spell. He was a snare dressed in honey, and Loki was falling into his trap from halfway across the room, but the conversation he just had with Thanatos kept him from sinking further.

Loki shook his head and approached Desire and

Dream. He cleared his throat at the appropriate distance, and both of them looked up. Eros looked embarrassed and a little ashamed, so Loki flashed him a reassuring smile.

"Do you two need another minute alone?" He said teasingly and winked. "I can get you a hotel room."

Hypnos looked Loki up and down, "Or, maybe you could join us?"

"Another time. There's actually some information I've learned that Eros will be very interested in hearing."

"Ah. That's my cue then." Hypnos stood. He finished his drink, dipped into his pockets, and produced a handful of colorful pills wrapped in clear twisted foil, as if they were vintage hard candies. He offered them to Eros. "For the road."

Eros's face lit up, and Hypnos deposited them into his hand.

Hypnos leaned in to say, "Don't let Loki take the little green ones."

"Why?" Eros asked.

He flashed a taunting, challenging grin and waved as he walked away.

Loki smiled, "So, about the little green ones…" He reached out to take one, but Eros shoved them in his pocket.

"His reverse psychology doesn't work on me," Eros said smugly.

Loki deadpanned, "Then you're missing out on a lot of fun. Listen." He peered around the room, making sure no one of consequence could overhear him, and he sat down where Hypnos had been, "Thanatos told me he has a *thing*, which can destroy the you-know-whos."

Eros became immediately indignant. "Him? After everything I've done over the last few weeks! Crate after crate. Suffocating in dust. Archiving, researching, indexing, hand-cramping, and *he* is the one who finds the answer?" He pouted and turned to his drink.

Loki grimaced and said as gently as possible, "Well, to be fair, he has been in the game a *bit* longer than you."

Eros sighed in reluctant agreement.

"But there are multiple issues with it," Loki added.

"Is it broken like all the rest of the *useful* artifacts?"

"Maybe," Loki mused, "but, it's a *boy*... in his basement."

Eros perked up, "A what?"

"We'll talk about it more in depth later. The fact of the matter is... we can't let him use it- him."

"Why?"

"*Why?* Because it will kill him. Not just the boy in question, but Death. It will kill him."

Eros replied snarkily, "It will *kill* Death?"

"Not actually *kill*, but he'll never forgive himself for it. He has a soft spot for kids."

Eros sighed. Once again, another unusable weapon to add to the arsenal, but this one had to be fed. "Who is it?" Eros asked.

"We'll discuss it later. But, for now," Loki waved down the bartender, "let us drink and be merry, because neither of our families are here!"

The bartender set the glasses down in front of them.

Eros raised his glass, "Wishful thinking, darling. Wishful thinking."

18

Our hero tried to ignore the scratching and growling noises coming from the dark parts of the basement beyond his line of sight.

He couldn't remember being a Jinni. He didn't remember *living* in the swamp. As far as he knew, his existence as a thirteen-year-old boy started two weeks ago.

There were things which he knew that he couldn't recall having learned. Words and phrases came out of his mouth out of habit, but the habits must have been instilled in him before this existence that began two weeks prior. It was frustrating and would often trip him up.

When he was living with the others in the sewers, he'd begin to pick a lock like he had performed the act a thousand times, and halfway through, the knowledge would evaporate. He'd be singing a song that had come to mind, then without notice, the melody and lyrics would be gone. He had fumbled through the first weeks of his life, endlessly recalling dreams, plain as day one second, only to watch them slip through his fingers like sand the next.

The scratching, growling creatures in the darkness weren't seeming to get any closer. He wanted them to jump out and get on with whatever it was they intended to do, but they didn't. They just bumped around acting scary.

They did this for a long enough time that he realized they must have been exactly that, an act- a ploy created by the man in the white suit. It was meant to inspire enough fear in him, to force him to use the magick the blond man was so convinced that he possessed.

It wasn't going to work.

Damien laughed at this sad attempt to motivate him. "I've been through worse," he said mostly to himself, but it was also directed at the things going bump in the dark.

But, then, he began to wonder what was the *worst* that he had been through?

He couldn't remember who he was before, so he really couldn't say for certain that he wasn't what the blond man accused him of being.

Maybe the blond man's ploy was working after all...

He didn't *think* he had any idea how to use magick, but then, thirty seconds into picking a lock, he suddenly realized he didn't know how to do that either. Until the lack of knowledge caught up with him, his body seemed able to do things out of habit. Maybe the same would work here. Maybe it needed to be an act- *Fake it till you make it, right?*

He shook his head to clear it of the sudden and inexplicable vision of a black pirate ship. It shimmered at the edge of his memory, and he resolved himself. He would just *pretend* he had magick and act like he knew how to use it.

He snapped his fingers, concentrated, clenched his fists, held his breath.

...Nothing.

He tried saying, "Open sesame."

Nothing.

"Abracadabra?"

Nope.

"Shazam!"

Nada.

Our hero growled. He wanted up off of that lab table more than he could bear. He pulled, and strained, and thought about breaking his hand to rip it through the brace that held his wrist firm to the table, but then he'd have to do the same to his other hand and his feet.

He began to squirm again. Panic electrified his chest. Whimpers worked their way past his lips, and he heard a voice say.

Shhh. Old friend, you're not alone...

He quipped aloud, "Yeah, I know. The monsters are here to keep me company." And he stopped. He had responded to this strange voice in his head out of habit.

"Who are you?" he asked.

The voice laughed, *You don't remember me? I'm hurt. I thought we were friends...*

"Great. Can you get me out of here?"

Hmm, the voice teased, as if it were mulling it over, *That's not the nature of our relationship.*

His brow furrowed.

Don't get me wrong. I'll help you. It's what I'm here to do. I'm here to tell you the truth, but you may not like it...

Damien waited for it to continue. The whispering voice moved around him. It said, *You're never getting out of here. Don't you see? You belong here. You deserve this. You're the monster, not them.*

Something growled in the darkness.

"That's not true."

Sure it is. Do you not know why you belong here? Why you lived in the sewers? Why you're all alone? You're unlovable. No one wants you. You couldn't even stand to be around you. That's why you wiped your memory.

Alone, trapped, and vulnerable in the dark, its words in his mind were far more real and horrifying than the ambient paranormal activity.

The thirteen year old boy began to whimper.

There we go. Let it out. It gets easier if you just accept it.

"It's not true," he protested in a small voice.

Do you have any evidence to the contrary? There now. It's alright.

He sniffed and asked, "I erased my memory?"

Because you couldn't stand being who you were.

"So, I *do* have magick… and I just don't remember?"

The Darkness was quiet for a second too long.

Well, right, it stammered, *but there's no point using it.* It overcorrected, *It won't save you… You can't break your own memory block. That's the point. Can God make a rock big enough so even He can't move it? The answer is* yes. *He can, and you did. You hid your memories away and there's no getting them back.*

He didn't believe it.

A fire grew inside his belly. The voice had lied. It had called him a monster.

Wait, what are you doing?

"Blocking you out." With heat and rage, he willed the inner voice to just shut up.

You can't get rid of me. I'll always be with you. I am the-

And the Darkness was gone.

He took an aggravated breath and smiled.

He did have magick, which meant he could escape.

With the flames of will and determination still rising in his chest, his attention turned to the clamps pinning him to the slab. Intuitively, he took a deep breath, allowing it to fan the fire, and as he released the breath, he focused the flames of his will on his restraints.

With a clang, all four locks broke free.

Our hero clambered off the slab. He laughed and marveled at his new found freedom and power. It was too dark to see much, but he could see the dim light coming in from under the basement door at the top of the stairs.

Before he could make headway, the noises in the dark he had been ignoring moved closer.

The growls and animal grunts sounded wet with salivation.

He needed a light. He needed to be able to see, but his fire was being snuffed out by fear.

"I've had worse." He swallowed. "I've had worse." He reminded himself again, but he had backed himself up against a stone wall.

A metallic clang came from the lab table he had just vacated as something big leapt onto it.

He could tell from the hungry sounds of snorting and chomping that there were two monsters.

Damien flapped around his hand and clicked his fingers, trying to ignite a spark or luminescence.

"Lumos!" he exclaimed in a vain hope. Nothing happened.

The terror that his short existence was going to end by being eaten alive fell to the wayside as he grew increasingly more frustrated that he couldn't figure out this damn magick thing, which he would have never even needed had that voice not been such a bitch! And he never would have met that voice if that towering psycho had not locked him in a basement to start with! *What the hell was wrong with people?*

His hands ignited in flame, and it didn't hurt. *That's pretty fucking cool.*

Damien smiled until he saw the faces beyond the

flames.

Pale. White skin stretched across an elongated skull. Black, endless gaping mouths. Glowing, ravenous, lidless eyes. Skeletal, bowed humanoid limbs, legs over arms charging at him.

His stomach dropped and his fire went out.

***

Death was having trouble chit-chatting with his guests. His mind was too preoccupied with curiosity. He wanted to check in on his experiment. He wondered if his fear tactics had caused his subject to free himself from the table yet. If the boy managed that, then the creatures were programmed to inch closer as if to eat him, which they wouldn't. But, if the subject used his magick again to try to save himself, then the creatures would be triggered to attack. Thanatos knew his subject couldn't die, but he was eager to see how much damage would be done- how far the boy would get.

Death knew the basement was inescapable. He had taken the security blueprints of Tartarus to use as a template for his basement. Of course, Death had made improvements on the original blueprint's circuitry, but he couldn't help getting giddy at the thought of his new weapon being able to crack even that code.

He could hardly wait to go home and see, but in front of him was Alec VanGarrett, yammering on about his nightclubs, and the new vampire race, and the start of his artifacts collection.

"I have a particular interest in these ancient portals," Alec said, the moment Thanatos started paying attention again. "I believe the market for accessible portals is an untapped gold mine. It would create a multi-billion-demonic travel industry. The only issue is engineering portals stable enough to support mass travel."

Thanatos smiled cordially, "There is a reason only gods have access to such magick, Mr. VanGarrett."

"But, why should that be the case?" Alec raised his pointed chin.

Death's cordial demeanor vaporized. "For the balance of things," he growled. "Ah! There's Loki. Tell him your idea. He loves wildly asinine thought-experiments."

Alec tried to keep a scowl from creeping across his face. "This is hardly a thought-experiment! It's a practical-"

"Loki!" Thanatos waved Loki over from across the showroom floor, with Eros trailing after him.

Thanatos made introductions. "Loki, this is Alec VanGarrett. Alec, this is Loki."

Loki nodded, "Alec, I've heard a lot about you."

"Yes," he made no attempt to hide his scowl now, "you've been aiding my father with his… little problem."

Loki wasn't sure how to respond. His mouth was agape, and his eyes darted around.

"Well, I'll leave you two to it." Thanatos made his leave.

Eros glared after him. *Three*. There were three of them, not two. Eros did not find it cute when Thanatos pretended he couldn't count.

"Hello, Alec. I'm Eros," he redirected his frustration to the vampire, "and it was our *pleasure* to help out your father with *Josanna*."

Alec's eyes turned to furnaces as they landed on Eros. His fist tightened around his cane. "Whatever he's told you, he's lying," Alec said through fanged, gritted teeth.

"So, the girl isn't yours then?" Loki asked in earnest.

"No!" Alec then lowered his tone, "She is, but I saved her from him. Not the other way 'round."

"Then why is she at the Devereaux mansion?" Eros didn't hide his disbelief.

"He took her. It-," Alec tried to compose himself. "It is a complicated family matter. I don't wish to bring personal affairs into business, but his slander is ruining my reputation."

"Then let's talk business," Loki interjected suavely. "You and I and Eros here are all just starting off. Let's say we help each other get off the ground?"

Alec closed his eyes for a moment, embarrassed over how his temper flared. "Right, well, I've made quite a decent nest egg from my start-ups, and I'm looking to invest into magickal-technology."

Eros's eyes narrowed, "Magickal-technology?"

"There is a chance to make a real fortune on the verge of where science meets the esoteric! For creatures like myself, who possess only a fraction of the power gods and demons have inherently, magickal-technology can literally open up gateways. Keep in mind - vampires, werewolves, witches, ghouls, creatures like us, make up eighty percent of the Netherworlds' population. It is a grossly ignored market, which could do with some high-profit-margined conveniences in this world."

"Oh! Like my telephone!" Loki offered. "I hate telepathic communication and divining in bowls of blood, so I rerouted my psychic calls to a rotary dial telephone. Honestly, it's been a life saver. I love the satisfaction that comes from dramatically hanging up on people!"

"Exactly," Alec said, though he didn't sound very certain. "Only, I'm mainly focusing on the eighty-percent I mentioned who don't have that *precise* problem... but you're on the right track."

Eros was skeptical, but couldn't help but admit, "It sounds interesting enough."

"Right now I'm on the hunt for artifacts believed to have once been portals between worlds."

Loki and Eros exchanged startled glances, both thinking of the perfume bottle.

"Do you have anything like that in your collection?" If he noticed the startled look, Alec didn't let on.

Eros racked his brain for anything in the collection *other* than the ruby red bottle that might fit that description, but before he could suggest The broken Looking-Glass of Wonderland, or anything else, Loki was speaking.

"No. Nothing like that yet. Our collection is still being assembled, but Shmeaglebobenzoar might have just what you're looking for. Let me introduce you!"

Loki casually led Alec away, leaving Eros standing there gaping.

When Loki returned, he had rightly brought back a drink for Eros.

"What the bloody hell was that about?"

Loki smiled guiltily, "I still don't trust him. Do you? Do you think he knew about the perfume bottle? Is that why Josanna mentioned it? Twice! See, I knew there was something to that *clever* girl!"

Eros cut him off, "No! I think he's looking for *portals*. We have other portals in our collection!"

"We do?"

Eros's eye twitched. "Loki, how in the hell are we going to stay in business if you don't even know what we have to offer?"

Loki waved away the idea that businesses needed products in order to be viable. "I suppose we'll just have to be life partners instead since we're such bad businessmen."

Eros's face lit up and he teased, "I'm an excellent businessman. *You're* the one who's rubbish at it."

Loki snorted an adorable giggle.

"So, who do you believe? VanGarrett or Devereaux?" Eros began to make a turn about the room.

Loki shrugged, falling in step. "I find the truth always seems to lie somewhere in the middle, but Alec did seem rather sincere."

"I find that liars are sincere, because they are often convinced they are telling the truth."

Loki quipped, "Now, anytime you're sincere about anything, I'm going to assume you're lying to me."

Loki grinned and Eros glared.

***

Thanatos stepped out onto the balcony to find some reprieve under the falling purple sky. Scotch in one hand, he materialized a cigarette in the other and leaned on the balcony railing.

He had a small moment to relax and smoke his cigarette before a dreary hum rose from the back of his mind, and it crescendoed over the orchestra playing for the gala.

With a sigh, he flicked his half-smoked cigarette over the balcony into the courtyard below. "Good evening, ladies." He turned to his right and saw three veiled forms obscured in shadow at the edge of the gala's lights.

"*The time has come,*" said the middle specter.

"*The fight we promised shall be won,*" said the maiden.

"*You have brought to light what was hidden from our sight.*"

"Ah! Yes, Loki and Eros are dating." His voice heavy with disdain, "I hardly see why that should matter."

"*It was not of our design.*"

Death groaned, "When is love ever planned? It's always been the one thing you could not account for."

The air around him tensed. He realized he was walking a tightrope, but he honestly could not comprehend why anyone, let alone the Fates, would let *feelings* guide their behavior. On top of this, the feelings in question were based on two *other people's* feelings. Their fear was so ridiculously senseless, he laughed aloud at it.

The air around him began to quake, and he realized he had just fallen off the tightrope.

He cleared his throat. "Ladies," he tried to approach them, and he felt the weight of the universe pressing down on every joint, compressing every organ. He tried to remain standing, but collapsed on one knee, as if he were bowing.

But, it was no coincidence that he fell to one knee. It was fated.

Thanatos smiled a grim smile as he tried to reign back his charging anger.

"That is why it must be,"
"...star-crossed love is their new destiny."
"A malign star whose name is Death,"
"...will bring them to us at our behest,"
"...or Death he shall no longer be."

"What else will happen if I refuse? Aside from you putting some incompetent prick in my chair? You have already turned Eros into a useless and impotent god. What do you expect him to do?"

"The first to come from chaos was named Desire,"

"...then creation plumed out from the fire."
"Chaos splintered across the realm,"
"...and Loki from the heavens fell."
"Chaos and Desire uniting once again,"
"...will bring about our inevitable end."

"Our end or yours?" Thanatos said pointedly then hissed, "You will be your own end."

"But, it will never be you." Gray, cracked-lipped, sinister grins stretched across all three faces simultaneously.

"I don't intend to lose my seat, so we shall see."

Recognizing Death had conceded, the weight holding him down released. He was exhausted from bearing the pressure, but it was nothing compared to what he carried with him everyday, so he found the strength within to stand.

"I will bring them to you," he said, knowing that if the Fates removed him from his position, they would win. Loki and Eros would still be ensnared in their web, and he'd be powerless to help. There would be no one left to fight.

He had to play their game long enough to win. "What will happen once I do?"

"In Tartarus there is a hole,"
"...big enough for each to call their home."

Thanatos took in a breath. He smiled hopelessly. "Well, at least they'll be together."

He dipped back inside the gala, his mind already set on a solution.

He had a weapon. He only had to figure out a way to use it *quickly*. He wasn't going to let Eros go to Tartarus because of him again.

Thanatos stopped dead when his scanning eyes fell on Loki and Eros. They were dancing, or trying to. Both of them kept trying to lead the other in their waltz, and Eros, blushing and laughing, kept stopping to regain both his composure and his footing. Each time they began to dance, they had a bit of trouble figuring out whose hand went where, and the laughter resumed.

It was sickeningly adorable.

He swallowed the guilt and any feelings he didn't find useful that arose in him. This was going to kill him, but he was Death, and dying was his business.

***

Loki and Eros were off to the side of the room by the bar. Eros's eyes moved to scan the crowd, but Loki's eyes looked steady on at his boyfriend. A pleasant smile crept upon the giant's face. He stomped his feet abruptly, put his left arm behind his back and offered his right hand to Eros, bowing slightly. Eros looked back at him, confused at first, then nervous.

"Dance with me?" Loki asked.

"Are you serious?"

"Why wouldn't I be?" Loki's charming and cocky smile spread across his face and into his eyes.

Eros gulped. "All these people-"

"Fuck them." Loki shrugged.

"Honestly, I don't know how to do this, especially if I'm not leading." Eros took his hand.

"Do you want to lead? I'll let you."

"No... I'll figure it out."

Smiling and chuckling, they stumbled into a closed position and struggled for a moment to figure out whose hand held whose.

Loki cleared his throat. "Okay... ready?"

Eros nodded.

Loki found the beat, and began to step, but Eros started with the wrong foot in the wrong direction and immediately stepped on Loki's toes.

They both snorted and fell apart laughing until Eros composed himself. "Okay, okay. I got it," he said, reframing his torso.

"Are you sure?" Loki repositioned his arms, "Because I can't have you breaking all of my toes."

Eros lightly kicked him in the shin. "I said I got it!"

"Fine." The giant cleared his throat again. "You're small enough you could stand *on* my feet."

"You just said I'd break all your toes. Small or toe-crushing, which is it?"

Loki stepped forward with his left, and Eros followed with his right.

They successfully started an easy waltz as Eros figured out his footing. What he did know of ballroom dance, he now had to do backwards from how he was taught.

They kept their eyes locked, giggling, embarrassed at every missed step.

"You're off rhythm," Eros pointed out.

"Well, you're better at this than you made out." Loki, off beat, spun Eros successfully, to which they both looked amazed. "Are you sure you didn't do this with your ex-boyfriends?"

Eros looked up at him through his lashes, "I wasn't that type of arm-candy."

The waltz tailed to a coda, and Loki and Eros slowed to a stop. They still held onto each other, their breath in sync.

But then, Loki began to chew on the corner of his lower lip, which Eros had come to know that meant Loki was hard at work thinking about something. "What is it?"

Loki blinked, opened his mouth to talk, but in the silence between songs came Thanatos, drawing uncomfortably close to them.

"Loki," Thanatos hissed.

The two lovers jumped in unison, their movement coordinated for the first time.

"For fuck's sake! Wear a bell!" Eros barked.

"You scared Eros here half to *death*." Loki snickered, and Eros shot him a glare.

Thanatos looked back and forth between them and snarled at their levity. "Listen, I need you both," he pointedly looked down at Eros, "to come with me. *Now*."

Eros tilted his head suspiciously, surprised Thanatos

had addressed him so directly. Thanatos usually pretended he was invisible.

Loki's brow narrowed, but he followed Thanatos to the balcony without pause. Eros was much more hesitant, but kept up so he could hear what Thanatos was saying.

"I know how this is going to look," Thanatos said in a hush over his shoulder to Loki, "but I have a plan. I just need you to stall for as long as you can."

"Thanatos, I think I'm going to need more information."

"There's no time. Besides, stalling is what you're good at."

Eros needed to take twice as many steps to keep up with their monstrous strides.

As they stepped foot out of the glistening showroom into the boundless night, the glamor faded into a desolate cramped world. Once they completely stepped through the elegant arches of the balcony, the Netherworlds was gone. The gala vanished as if behind a slamming door. The ozone shone brightly on the horizon against the shades of gray, which dominated the landscape and sky.

There were three gray ladies standing like pillars before them.

"What the hell!" Eros snapped.

Thanatos stared directly ahead, avoiding the gazes of his friends.

"Ah! Hello." Loki greeted the Fates, not missing a beat. "Would you mind telling Eros and myself what's happening? Because my friend here *won't*." He sounded pleasant until that last word when he turned on Thanatos.

"Ladies," Death stood with his hands folded neatly behind his back, "I have done as you have asked, and now I must be on my way. Have a pleasant evening."

The three Fates stood unmoving.

Death turned and only glanced at Loki for a moment, and in that moment, Loki heard painfully clear in his mind... *Stall.*

19

When Death left them, Loki and Eros felt very acutely alone and stranded. The sunken gray sky seemed to be closing in on the ground. The edges of the world on which they stood crumbled into the abyss. They could hear it fracture around them like glaciers splintering off into the frigid deep.

"What do you three want?" Eros asked with flippant annoyance.

Loki chimed in, "We don't want any of your Girl Scout Cookies..."

Eros closed his eyes and pressed his lips together.

"-unless you have Samoas," Loki amended.

Eros shook his head and looked at him. "Really?"

"What?"

"Samoas?" Eros sighed, and his lips tilted ever so slightly, "Thin Mints are so much better..."

Loki blinked, slack-jawed, "I can't be seen with you anymore." Loki gestured wildly to the Fates, "Tell him Samoas are the best, and Thin Mints are for the birds... which is funny because he has wings."

"So do you!"

"No. I cut mine off. So, what say you?" Loki turned to the Fates again, "Thin Mints or Samoas?"

There was silence.

Then Lachesis, standing in the middle said, "*I like Savannah Smiles.*"

The other two sisters whipped their heads to scowl at her.

Then Atropos, the eldest Fate, retorted, "*No. The best are the Peanut Butter Patties.*"

"I wouldn't have thought...," Eros started.

Loki finished, "Nor I. I thought maybe the shortbreads-"

A hiss brought their musings to a halt.

The youngest and tallest of the Fates, Clotho, stepped forward.

"*Eros, you have been tried thrice before. At this final hour we say no more.*"

"*Loki, conspirator, defector, trickster-*"

"You're only stroking his ego." Eros folded his arms.

Loki gave a confirming smile.

"*-your scheming against us has been traitorous, and now*

the two of you shall be sentenced to Tartarus."

Loki and Eros shot each other a perilous glance.

Loki said, "Now hold on just one minute-"

Eros added, "You can't just do that!"

"We have done so since time untold. You, Eros, once called Tartarus your home."

Loki looked at Eros in surprise.

Eros only blinked at the Fates. "Mmm. No. No, I haven't."

The three women stared quietly.

"I *haven't,*" Eros persisted, but he took a step back.

"Uh… Eros," Loki leaned in. "They don't look like they're kidding."

"*Uh... Loki,*" he mocked, his tone incredulous, "I think I'd remember being locked in Tartarus."

In a chorus, the Fates began to laugh.

"Tartarus is where you forever belonged, primordial god."

"Dangerous."

"Manipulative."

"Deceiver."

"I am not! I'm not any of those things!" Eros exclaimed.

"Your ineffable power was enough to make your fellow gods cower. They were insistent on your imprisonment. But Dream freed you from your,"

"...prison."

"From your,"

"...mind."

"From the,"

"...Red Room."

Eros and Loki exchanged a startled look of recognition. Josanna had been right?

"A mistake we will not again make."

***

Thanatos turned the key in the lock and opened the basement door. The wooden steps creaked as he descended. The open door lit his way, but the basement itself was still as dark as pitch. Death reached with pale boney fingers to pull the thin chain just above his head.

The incandescent bulb came flickering to life with an electric tinking, and in the light he saw the boy sitting against the stone wall with his knees to his chest. He was dusty and stained red with blood where he had been scratched by teeth and claws, but the two monsters responsible for his wounds lay unmoving at odd angles on the floor.

"You killed the baubas," Thanatos noted.

He placed his hands in his pockets and gazed down at the boy who was evidently not a boy.

"Baubas? You mean the monsters you put down here to kill me?"

"Not to kill you," Death said. "To inspire you."

The boy glared up at him.

"So, you *are* as I said." Death took a step closer. "Even you must recognize by now that you have magick."

The boy looked away.

Death took another step and crouched down next to Damien. "I need your magick for reasons I cannot explain. We can do this the hard way or the easy way."

Damien felt annoyed with this cliche threat, as if he had heard it a thousand and one times.

But then, Death creased his brow and said, "But, the hard way will take too long."

Damien blinked, and when he opened his eyes, he found himself back on the stainless steel lab table.

Panic hit him instantly. He pulled at his trapped wrists and tried in vain to access his magick.

"What's the hard way?" Damien tried to calm himself.

"To persuade you. To teach you. To reawaken your memories and guide you. All while keeping you safe from gods who would either lock you away or rip you apart like hungry vultures if they knew of your existence."

"So, what's the easy way?"

Thanatos laid his icy fingers again on the boy's temples. "Unlocking your magick and ripping it out along with your soul. Such a procedure would kill anyone else, but you have no Death date. You cannot die, so you'll most likely go mad."

Damien gritted his teeth and tried to stir up the fire from within. "We're all mad here," he quipped.

Death let out one sardonic chuckle, "Yes. We are."

Damien heard a memory whisper from within. *Okay, here we go.*

Death's fingers pierced into his mind like scalpels, and Damien did not scream.

***

"This is a bit rash don't you think?" Loki began to meander, to walk the space, and own his stage. "I mean, look at him. Does he look dangerous to you? He's not exactly what one would call intimidating, or threatening, or imposing."

Eros looked self-conscious.

Loki strolled two steps forward, one step back. "What *damage* could he even feasibly do? He's so small, and adorable, and pretty... like a cherub."

Eros's eyes narrowed. He gritted his teeth and let out a low growl. He tried to ignore the slight and maintain his composure.

Loki ran through various gestures and faces, trying to produce his next defense. "So what if he can make one fall in love with anything, anyone?" Loki leaned casually on one elbow against the Romanesque pedestal that held the floating Book of Fate.

The three ladies let out a tense gasp as he did, only now recognizing the misdirection they had fallen prey to.

"Isn't that what makes love thrilling? I'm getting *tingles* just thinking about it." He smiled devilishly over at Eros. "I'm sure he'd be willing to find a lover for you lot if you just asked nicely."

Loki was closer to their book than any other creature had ever been, and their fear of what he might do made them growl like stray cats.

"*Desire is so much more than love's consuming fire.*"

"*It is the intention behind all creation and destruction.*"

Atropos stepped forward, "*Step away from the pedestal.*"

"My apologies." Loki took his weight off the marble, and they each gave an instant sigh of relief. "Why? Is this book important?" Loki snatched the book from the air, and there was another collective gasp. Even Eros flinched.

The book was dense and leather bound in an unknown hide. The pages were time weathered and stained with ink and dirt. The book was a timeless piece.

The Fates were helpless to act, because using magick to retrieve it could destroy it.

In a few long strides, Loki was handing the book to Eros. "Here you go, darling. I stole this for you."

"How thoughtful!" Eros's eyes melted, and Loki bent down to receive a peck on the cheek.

"I thought it would go well with that Bowl of Fate I got you."

"It's the *perfect* accessory."

The eldest stepped forth, "*You have our Bowl?*"

"He's had it for quite some time, actually." Eros wetted the tip of his finger as he leafed through the pages. He could skim the ancient Greek scroll infinitely faster than Loki could.

"*That Bowl is ours by divine right!*"

"Well," Loki said, with a flourish of his arm and an air of haughtiness, "if you can ever make it into my home after you've sent us both to Tartarus, have at it. But you won't make it in the front door without destroying *everything* inside. I have it rigged to go off like a nuclear reactor, and all the objects inside would go on the fritz. It would be a big deal." He chewed on his lip. "It might even make the papers. And why is it divinely yours? Rightly yours? If you don't mind me asking."

"*We have birthed it.*"

"*It is of us.*"

"*It is our bone and our flesh.*"

Eros became hyper sensitive to the leather binding of the book, but continued nonetheless to flip through the thin, crinkly, flesh-colored pages.

"It is of you." Loki didn't miss a beat. "Therefore, it belongs to you. I am of myself and Eros of himself. Do we not belong then to ourselves and not to you and your whims? Is it not within our divine right to lay claim to our free will? Our free will is *of* us. It's *of* our nature." Loki snorted, "You might say we were fated to be this way, and if that's the case, *you* fated us to conspire against you, which must mean you're completely terrible at doing your job."

The weight of the universe came down on Loki as it had come down on Thanatos. The giant collapsed and struggled to breathe.

Loki was not Atlas. He was not Death. He was not meant to bear the weight of existence. He was meant to send existence spinning and crashing in a miraculous storm, which left everything pretty much okay and a little better off when the clouds cleared.

He wasn't built for this.

The pressure compounded on his head as spots and lights overtook his vision.

He tried to give Eros a glance to say they were running out of time, but all he could see in that direction was a glowing, swirling mass of red and pink light, from which Loki could not look away. It was the most beautiful thing he had ever seen.

Eros flipped faster through the endless pages, adrenaline and anxiety both fueling and hindering his concentration.

"*The webs we weave are complex things, like a spider's string. Beautiful, intricate, strong, crafted with intent by our harmonious song-*"

Eros perked up. "Their song," he said to himself.

With the Fates still proclaiming their omnipotence and the universe still crushing down the giant, Eros ran to him, skidding through the dirt.

Loki looked at him in agony, but still emanated strength. He was trying to push himself up but couldn't.

The glowing red swirling nebula said unto Loki in Eros's voice, "It's their song. Their song will activate the bowl of Fate. Listen, Loki, you have to fight this. I need you. Get up!"

The giant's elbows wobbled and gave, as did his

mind, and he fell unconscious.

Eros shook him, but the slumbering giant did not wake.

"*Shit!*"

***

Thanatos was getting very tired of being repeatedly thrown across the room. He was only able to get so far into the boy's mind before being literally thrown out by the boy's mental blocks. He had never played video games, but he likened his situation to one. Every time he lost the unbeatable level, he'd have to start all over again at level one.

The immensity of this strange god's magick, when extracted in the raw form of his soul, just might be powerful enough to stop the Fates in their tracks *if* Death was lucky. If he was *really* lucky, he might even be able to use it to rewrite reality so that those damn women had *never* been this powerful in the first place. Eros, and other gods like him, would have never been sent to Tartarus aeons ago. Death would have never been used as the Fates' personal hitman, and the Cosmos would be free to operate on its own free will.

But, Thanatos couldn't even break through the boy's defenses. He had been able to sense the boy's power immediately, had even suspected he might have been a Djinn *somehow,* in a former life perhaps, because *Djinn* magick was the closest thing to what Thanatos assumed this boy had- phenomenal Cosmic power.

It was the way this boy could essentially rewrite his being. The way he could lock away his memories and his soul behind thick walls of magick. It was the way that when Death entered his mind, and stood before this towering fortress of mental power, an unseen force began to push him out, his feet scraping for stability in drifting sand. Death couldn't extract this boy's magick if he could never reach the distant blockade where most of his soul had been locked away.

But, he was out of time for taking the boy's power by force. Loki couldn't stall forever. Whatever magick this boy had, Djinn or otherwise, was beyond Death.

It seemed *he* was the one who was likely to go mad. What made it worse was the boy acting as if this whole thing was the game that Thanatos likened it to be. Damien was actively *trying* to throw Thanatos out of his mind before the mental blocks got the chance. Damien began to laugh every time he kicked Death out of his head, because that meant he won that particular round. And this strange, powerful boy was getting better and better at this game of keepaway. *Death* was losing ground. When they started, he might have made it to a metaphorical level five or six, but now he was only making it to level three.

The only other option was to call upon his brother and ask him to *go in the back way,* extracting his soul and magick through the subconscious. But, Hypnos would be high on something, and difficult to work with, and Thanatos would *never* live it down if he had to ask his twin for help.

So, this time, when Death picked himself up off the floor and shuffled back to the table where the boy lay laughing, he slammed his palms against the metal with a *clang*.

The abrupt noise jolted Damien into silence.

Thanatos hovered over him with a hand on each side of his head. He took in a hissing breath. "I can't believe I'm going to do this, but let me bargain with you."

The boy peered at Death with striking green eyes.

Thanatos let out a breath. "There are two people I need to save from three very powerful women."

The boy's voice was questioning but kind, "You mean the Fates?"

"Yes."

Damien's brow creased, "Are these two people your friends?"

Death snarled and said flatly, "Friends? I don't *have* friends. Friends are liabilities."

Damien arched an eyebrow.

"So, will you help me or not?" Death asked.

"By willingly allowing you to extract my soul so you can save two people who aren't even your friends? I don't think so."

Death sighed. "I'd be willing to try the hard way..."

Damien laughed, "Only because your *easy* way didn't work, and you're out of options. You're not doing *me* any favors."

"It *would* be doing you a favor. I would protect you. I'd teach you how to use your powers. We could find out together what you are and where you came from. I could teach you everything I know. And that's no small favor. But, if this is going to work, first we have to save my… *friends.*" He conceded the last word with a cringe.

"Okay." Damien paused, considering this, "But, I don't even know *how* to help you."

Thanatos took an aggravated step back. "Try. I can sense your power, and it is immense. Try. *Try,* and I will honor my end of our bargain, even if you fail."

If he failed, Loki and Eros would end up in Tartarus. It would take longer, but Thanatos would still need help saving his *friends*, destroying the Fates, and granting the Cosmos freedom.

"Even if you fail at first, the aim here is freedom. You would be free and so would your powers," Death added, "and so would I, and my friends, and the entire Cosmos."

Damien gathered himself and closed his eyes. *Free* was a word he liked. Though he couldn't remember why, it was a feeling he longed for. *Freedom.*

He tried to imagine the Fates. He imagined their world would be veiled in shadow, no doubt. He saw it was hidden behind webs of gossamer. It was small and gray, but the Fates themselves were huge. They were towering over giants and gods, ensnaring them in a twisted design which could not be unraveled. Even with the playbook in the hands of the gods, the Fates were winning.

They were winning because the players didn't know how the game was rigged. The beautiful god in the suit was still thinking on a linear timeline, and he couldn't see the field.

Damien knew this god had to embrace the hungry howl inside of him. That was the key. He could be weightless and limitless if he gave into it, but the god couldn't remember any of it. He had locked it away inside of himself, and there was no map to get back in. But, *you got to go in to get out, mate.*

The god standing down the Fates and the god laying on the stainless steel slab in Death's basement were the same. There was something they had both forgotten- Or, was it a place rather than a *thing*? They would both have to remember in order to save themselves.

But, Damien couldn't breach this wall inside his head. When he looked directly at it, it redirected him to think about something else. Each time he thought about what he must have forgotten, he'd suddenly be thinking instead about the Fates or the blond man in the suit currently scrutinizing him. He opened his eyes. "Hey."

The blond man was pacing around with a worried face and looked up when Damien spoke.

The boy readjusted on the table.

"What is it?" Death hissed back more menacingly than intended.

He responded as quickly as he could. "I need you to

electrocute my brain each time I get distracted."

Thanatos blinked, "Is that a joke?"

"No."

"Alright then." Thanatos resumed his position at the top of Damien's head, and slowly this time, his fingers pierced into Damien's brain. "This is going to hurt."

Damien shrugged. "I've had worse. Ready?"

Death nodded.

"Okay," said Damien, "here we go…"

***

Eros needed to stall, but he didn't know what for. In his experience, Death left people dead in the dust, and the man wasn't the kind to save anyone. Thanatos wasn't coming back, but he did have that *weapon*.

Eros didn't know how to stall. He could accompany Loki while Loki led the campaign, but alone, Eros didn't know how to do it. He was more of a *get it done and over with* kind of person.

They were fucked, Eros thought. *No, not fucked.* Eros was a Primordial God, for fuck's sake. Eros made other gods cower just by existing. He could do this. He *had* to do this.

"You know… Loki made a good point. You fated us here. If we were fated to be in Tartarus, I think you would have sent us there already. Unless you really are lonely and just wanted to have someone to talk to for a bit. I can fix that for you, your loneliness. Not as a bribe for freedom, but merely out of pity. You. Are. Pathetic. This whole charade is a carrot to lead us where you want. Come on, nieces, tell Uncle Eros what you want. I am the god of Desires. What do you really want?"

"To put you in your place."

The three Fates broke out of their line and began to drift apart to surround them. Atropos was getting closer to Loki than Eros would like.

"This is just a shake down then. So, you're not going to send us to Tartarus, because you can't. If you send too many of us to Tartarus, the gods will start thinking about throwing *you* down there." Eros laughed.

"It is a balancing act. Come, silly child of Venus-"

"I am Primordial, and it will do you well to remember that!" Eros raised his marble-cut jaw.

Atropos hovered over Loki.

"Leave him alone!" he cried, but she grinned as she plucked a hair out of Loki's head and hid it in the folds of her robe.

"This dark hour is a solemn reminder of our power."

"Though, it is true, we may not imprison two."

"The hole in Tartarus is fit only for one of you,"

"...and one, my love, is much more fun."

"You will pledge faith to our command, or your new lover will be eternally damned."

Dry lips caressed his ear, *"Eternity is a very long time, Primordial."*

"What do you mean there is a hole in Tartarus? A

vacancy? Did someone escape?" Eros sneered.

"*Indeed. The son has found his way home.*"

The phrasing rang out prophetically in Eros's ears, and the Fates smiled down on him.

A rock sank in his stomach. Each strange prophecy- the one from Hypnos, the eccentric verses from Josanna. They had come straight from the Fates. The Fates had led him to this precise moment. They wanted him here. He knew he was trapped.

Eros swallowed, knowing what was to come would lift the veil off of all their deception, all the ways he was led here, and all the ways he was fucked.

"The son of whom?" he asked.

"*Death.*"

The world fell silent.

The puzzle clicked together in his mind. He raised his hand to cover the despair crossing his face.

The boy wasn't Thanatos's secret weapon.

He was the Fates' secret weapon.

This had little to do with him and Loki. *This* was about Thanatos.

They always knew Thanatos would be likely to challenge them, so they installed a landmine for when he crossed the line.

Something Thanatos did had triggered this entire chain of events.

Death had a son.

The boy in his basement was his *son*.

Loki was right. Thanatos would never forgive himself if he killed a child, let alone his own *son*.

The Fates were always pulling the strings. Always. It was all just a blasted game. There was no point in fighting a rigged system. It was best just to play along.

So, he wouldn't be a Primordial again. So what? At least he would still be with Loki. And most of all, Loki wouldn't be locked up in Tartarus for all eternity, and Death wouldn't be responsible both for that and for having destroyed his only child. That was a hell Eros wouldn't wish on his worst enemy.

"What say you?"

"What will you do?"

"Will you let your lover finish his fall?"

"Will you let your old friend torture his only son?"

"To beat us?"

"To win your free will?"

"We cannot be outrun."

"Not by Love or by Chaos."

"We cannot be undone."

"Not by weapons or by Death."

"We created this game of chess."

"Fine!" Eros tensed. "Fine. I'll do as you ask. Just let Loki and I go, and I'll inform Thanatos of his poor choice of *weapon*, which I assume is what you want."

He offered them the book still in his hands, a sign of good faith.

Clotho snatched it from his grasp.

"Good boy."

"We're glad you see it our way."

"We're glad you're deciding to behave."

"Now, do as we say."

They turned from him.

But, free will was something he *was* getting better at.

He had a sudden thought and changed his mind. For good or ill, Eros summoned one last hope.

"Wait! If you give me back Loki's hair, I'll give you back the Bowl of Fate."

They paused for an agonizing moment.

Loki still lay unconscious in the dust, the weight of the universe weakening the giant more and more each second.

Finally they turned back around.

"That is an awfully big trade,"

"...for an awfully small hair."

"I would feel safer if you didn't have a tie to him, and you would feel better if I didn't have the Bowl of Fate."

Lechesis said, *"We will return the hair and your lover when we have received the Bowl."*

"No. I'm taking Loki with me. You have his hair, your book, my surrender. What more will you need?"

"We're glad you're deciding to behave."

"Now, do as we say."

The three Fates lowered their heads and raised their arms, and Eros found himself outside Loki's townhome.

He stormed inside and crumpled to the floor,

screaming in despair and rage. Eros shook with wrath and terror. He wanted to break something, but everything there was too expensive. This was a horrible way to stall, but it was the only thing he could think of. He had to call Thanatos and figure out what to do next.

He got up from the floor and ripped out his cell phone. He dialed 4.

The bored voice on the other line said, "We appreciate you for calling Grim Enterprises. How may I direct your call?"

He tried to steady his shaking voice, "Thanatos, please."

"My apologies. He is unavailable. Would you like me to leave a message?"

Eros screamed into the microphone and furiously, repetitively jabbed his finger on the red button to end the call. He wished he had a receiver to slam. Loki had been right. There was immense satisfaction in hanging up on someone.

He paced back and forth in five foot increments. Loki's house was too cluttered and congested to pace in longer distances than that. Eros ran his fingers through his hair. He ran his hands over his face. Thinking. Thinking.

There were a million weapons here, and not a damn one of them worked! The Bowl of Fate was useless without the very voices of the Fates, and like hell was he going to give that up. Loki would kill him.

"Think. Think," he ordered himself.

He could just give them what they wanted. He could hope that Thanatos had tortured the very soul out of his son to use as a weapon, but that was immoral as piss, and Eros would not allow himself to think on it further.

"What would Loki do? Get distracted and find something else to do." But, that answer wasn't the real Loki- the trickster, the deceiver, the manipulator. "He'd get them to open the bottle for him!" Eros chuckled hysterically to himself as an idea began to form.

He ran up the stairs, taking them two at a time. He tore into the office and skidded to a sudden stop just inside the doorway.

There was a boy standing there, staring deep into the depths of the ruby red bottle on the desk.

"Who are you?"

The boy looked over at him. He blinked the tears from his eyes and flashed him an honest smile. "I don't know. I'm trying to remember."

Eros looked around the office. "How did you get in here? This place is… guarded."

The boy wiped his nose on his sleeve. "Yeah. Uh, I don't know." His eyes drifted back to the bottle. "I have all these memories that don't- My mind is scrambled eggs." He moved his shaking fingers to his temples, and they searched around in his hairline like he was hoping to find something there.

Eros cautiously stepped up to him.

The strange boy continued, "We're trying to

remember the same thing. You and me. We're both locked up in our heads as if we're safer in there. But, we're not..." The boy wrapped his arms around himself. "It's all hell in there, but we escaped before. We can do it again."

The boy was anxiously rocking back and forth with his arms wrapped around himself. Eros reached up gently to put a hand on the boy's shoulder, but the boy cowered away.

"Don't be afraid," Eros said cautiously.

"How can I not!" the boy snapped. "You're terrifying. Desires ruin people. Desires eat people away from the inside out. You're a parasite, and you're inside of me!" His fingers went to his temples again. "I don't *want* to want. I don't want to *wish*. I don't wish to *know* what it is I want. It hurts." His fingers moved to his chest and started scratching.

The child hyperventilated and tried to swallow.

Eros took a small step towards him. "Focus on me. Focus on me. Flex your fingers."

He did as he was commanded.

"Now, take a breath." Eros said.

He did as he was told, and he managed to calm down.

"Good. Now, I have no idea what you've been through-"

"Yes, you do." The boy stepped aggressively up to him. "You were there too. I am breaking through my walls, and now I'm here to help you break through yours."

"Help me? The parasite?" Eros gave a self deprecating laugh.

"Yes."

"Why?"

"Because he looked so fucking sad, man." said the boy.

"Who?" Eros asked.

"The man in the white suit."

Eros's brows furrowed.

This was Death's son. His cold green eyes matched Thanatos's left eye, but otherwise he looked nothing like him. The boy had darker hair and skin, while Death was so pale.

The boy inhaled sharply. "You and I are both going to remember who we are, and then… we're going to handle our shit."

Eros stepped forward with an eerie calm, "Is *that* what you want?"

The boy's nostrils flared.

Desire peered down at him with devouring eyes. "I am not a parasite. I am the spark of creation. I am the fuel behind all actions. Gods and humanity fear me because they fear themselves. They beat me down like they beat their own desires down into manageable submission. They limit me so as to limit their own potential. They have been taught to fear their own power, *my* power, because of its unknowable reach, because Heaven forbid people actually acknowledge what they *truly* want and let revelations happen!"

Death's son flashed a crooked smile, "I guess it's working then."

"What's working?" Eros spat.

"Your walls are crumbling down."

"Of course they're down! I'm pissed. I'm angry." He remembered Loki asking him how long he could stay angry for and laughed at the irony.

"I grant wishes…," the boy said strangely. He no longer seemed to fit inside his own body, like he was *bigger* than his body. "I grant desires. But, people wish for the wrong things *all the time*. You're right. People don't know what they want… I know what they want. What I want. What *you* want."

The boy was pulling at his ragged clothes, feeling the buttons, constantly fidgeting as he spoke. It reminded Eros of the way Hypnos paced and played with the random objects he found.

The boy's eyes were searching the floor. "The Jinni I wished free, the little girl with the doll house, the actor, the faery prince, the Sage who set *me* free, and a million other masters. They all wanted the same thing. They all wanted to be loved. But, not by others. People could shower them with love, and it would never be enough. Do you know what people want most, Desire?"

Eros scoffed, feeling annoyed at being lectured about his own game. "No. Suppose not."

Death's son looked up and flashed him a knowing grin, "I think you do." He began to wring his hands, and he continued, "People want to be able to love *themselves*. And they always think they can *if* they just level up. Get that promotion. The mansion on Main Street. Lose those last five pounds. They trick themselves into thinking they'll love themselves if they were just a *little* bit different..." He was digging his fingertips into his scalp again. "And its a fucking abusive relationship, dude. *Fucking* abusive."

The boy who was not a boy walked away tapping on his temples. "I'm guilty of it too. And you're right. If people actually loved themselves, the whole damn game would change- a *revelation*. But not only can people *not* love themselves, they *hate* themselves, and it's an unforgivable sin. One that you can never quite wash your hands of, and facing that, facing *yourself,* and your own self-imprisoned desire, is fucking terrifying."

Eros looked down at the ground, ironically hating himself. The boy was right. Eros was wasting his potential on self-loathing.

"And the gods do it too! They're no better! *That* is why they destroyed you. The Fates couldn't control you, so they twisted you all up so you couldn't love yourself, or trust yourself, and they locked you away-"

"No." Eros shook his head.

The air in the room grew heavy.

The boy began to say things that there was no way he could know. No way unless he had been there at the beginning of time, "They locked you away in Tartarus too," the boy began, "and none of your friends could stop them. In fact... your friends helped them lock you up."

"Stop it."

"Thanatos and Hypnos *helped* them lock you away in a tiny little room inside your own mind, the Red Room. Tartarus wasn't strong enough to hold you on his own, Primordial. The only thing that was strong enough to imprison you was you."

"You're wrong." The room was suddenly spinning, and the blur was turning different shades of red.

"It wasn't that hard for your friends to lock you up. You scared them too. When Hypnos and Thanatos were one being, they couldn't reconcile each other- the desires of logic and the desires of dream. It was a war inside their head, so they split it in half. And they locked you away in a room inside your own head they made, wrapped up in a pretty, hazy fantasy, high on dream dust, while, really, you were actually in chains in Tartarus."

The office fell away and Eros was in a tiny red room. A wave of lightheadedness nearly toppled him to the floor, but he managed to catch onto the wall and remain upright. The wall was soft, swallowing his fingers like memory foam. His polished shoes sank into the floor. Everything was cushioned, spongey, comfortable, like a dream.

He heard the boy's voice echo through his mind. "They volunteered to do it- to try to protect you. They were stalling. To keep you safe long enough for Thanatos to argue your case. But, Hypnos found a way to make it look like you escaped yourself. Claimed you were too strong to be locked up."

Eros sank to the squishy red floor. His breath was

heavy, his peripheral vision blurring, and his heart was racing. The walls were still pulsing from pink to deep wine red and back.

The boy continued, "It's a prison inside a prison. That's what they did to me too. And we made it out. But, only part of you escaped... Until now."

The Red Room vanished. Eros took in a deep breath and found himself suddenly back in Loki's office, lying on the floor with the strange boy who was so much more than a boy, crouched next to him. The boy's cold green eyes were prying into him.

Eros backed away. "What the bloody hell was that?"

"I broke through your mental blocks. You had to remember."

Ancient memories were slipping in from the back of Eros's mind. Feelings, forgotten long ago, reared their heads and shook off their dust.

"See," The boy stood, "even *you're* scared of me. *I'm* scared of me. I didn't know I could do any of this. I can alter reality. I can change everything-," he snapped his fingers, "-like that. What can *you* do?"

Eros lay on the floor, propped up on his elbows and looking into the eyes of Death's son.

With a new sense of self-awareness, Eros stood, brushed himself off, and straightened his suit and cufflinks. "I can show them what they're afraid of," he said, matter of factly. "I can show them *love*."

After a long glance, they both laughed despite

361

themselves.

The boy moved to sit down in the desk chair, and he resumed looking into the red bottle. He folded his arms on the desk and laid his chin on top. "Love's a powerful thing. I-," the boy swallowed, "would really like to know what it's like someday."

Eros acknowledged that desire but stowed it away for later. He turned and looked through the boxes until he found the crate containing the Bowl of Fate.

He removed the lid of the crate and carefully pulled the bowl from the wood wool, as if he was taking a hot pot out of the oven. Eros decided he was no longer afraid of the Bowl, and he put it under his arm like a football.

"Well, that was an… *insightful* conversation. Now, I have to go save my boyfriend," he cleared his throat, "and probably afterwards apologize to my ex-wife for literally *everything*, and then come back here for a long mental breakdown."

The boy chuckled, "I didn't know mental breakdowns could run on a schedule."

"Mine do."

"That *is* impressive."

Eros saw that the boy's hands, now folded neatly on the desk, were trembling.

"Did you want to take that with you?" Eros asked, referring to the bottle.

"Nah." The boy stood, "I can't, or maybe I can now, but I wasn't able to touch that thing before. And I'm worried if I touch it- it will swallow me. Plus, I'm not even really here. I'm in my head. I'm actually strapped to a slab in some guy's basement, so…"

"We'll get you out of there," Eros reassured him.

The boy shrugged, "Everything's temporary. And besides, there doesn't seem to be any room in your schedule for that."

With that, the boy stuck his hands in his pockets and limped towards the door.

"I'll make time." Eros said.

The boy smiled his crooked smile. "The blond man seems like the kind to… Let's just say that even though I'm not a Jinni anymore, if you freed me, I think he'd make you take my place."

"We'll see. I might know a thing or two about his real desires." Eros grinned at the boy, who shrugged.

"Well. I *wish* you luck in saving your boyfriend, and with your mental breakdown, of course."

"That means a lot coming from you. Right?"

"Yeah, it does," the boy confirmed.

The son of Death disappeared.

20

Damien's eyes popped open. The man with mismatched eyes stood over his head and looked down at him.

"Well?" Thanatos asked.

"I tried."

"What does that mean?"

Damien sighed, "It means that it's in Eros's hands now."

"Great! They are both going to Tartarus, then!" Thanatos moved down the slab towards his feet. Damien couldn't lift up enough to see him, so resigned to looking at the dark ceiling.

"He can handle it," Damien reassured.

"Frankly, you don't know him."

Damien gave the ceiling an indignant look. "Um, I know what he's been through. And I think that makes him stronger, whereas you think that makes him fragile."

"You know what he's been through? He's already been to Tartarus! You have no idea. Yes, he's fragile! We destroyed him in there!"

"You lobbied to get him out..."

Thanatos snapped to attention. "Who told you that?"

"No one. I just figured..." he lied.

He could hear Death's breath, snarling, growling from in his throat as he strolled back into Damien's line of sight.

"*You just figured...* Did you find out what *you are* while you were in there? Do you remember?"

Damien pulled tight his eyes and shook his head, not as an answer, but as to fight back the still-surfacing memories.

But, Death had taken it as an answer. "Hmm, that's too bad. But you did *try*. And I am a man of my word. I won't continue to torture you. I'll set you *free...*"

Damien didn't like the way he was saying these words.

"...with the *knowledge* of what you are." Death smirked. "I'd like to help you through a psychological lens. And the electroshock therapy you suggested was working so well. We were making such great progress. So, let's keep at it, shall we?" Death once again stabbed his fingers into Damien's scalp and into his mind.

"Fucking really?"

"Who are you?"

"Damien Warrick Parker."

Zap.

"Who are you really?"

"I didn't have a name!" Damien cried. "Or, I couldn't remember it. Or, never knew it."

"Who sent you?"

"What?"

Zap!

Damien growled. "No one!"

"What are you?"

Damien snorted and gave in. "I'm a- a Djinn."

Zap!

Damien winced as he caught a whiff of charring skin, "It's true! I think."

Thanatos chuckled, "No. Even Djinn have an expiration date, and you don't."

"I don't know what to tell you, man-"

"I know what you are."

"You do?" Damien guffawed, "Then, what the *fuck*? Do you mind *sharing*?"

Thanatos got right up in Damien's ear and hissed, "I just want to hear you say it. I want to hear you say how long you've been hiding, and who's been helping you do it. I want you to tell me what your heritage is-"

"My heritage?"

"What paradigm you are from. From what or whom

did you originate?"

"I don't know!"

Zap.

"Lying is counterproductive to your recovery..." Thanatos pulled fried bits of scalp and crispy hair away from Damien's temple. "I need to know. It is important to the balance of things. If there is a way around the Fates's scope of power, I need to know!"

Damien scoffed under his breath, "So much for the hard way."

Death flicked the fried skin and hair to the floor. It made a squishy, ploppy noise as it landed bloody side down. "The hard way would require both of us to cooperate, and you are refusing to participate. I'll let you think on this for a minute while I try to collect myself." Thanatos took a few steps away.

"This is seriously fucked up!" Damien thrashed against his restraints. He tried to focus his magick on breaking them open again, but it wasn't working.

Death took a few more calming breaths, then reached up and pulled the light chain that hung in the center of the basement. The incandescent bulb clinked off. He ascended the creaky wooden stairs and closed the basement door behind him.

He turned the skeleton key in the lock, which activated all the magick blocks encircling the basement.

Thanatos took two steps away from the door into the kitchen, and he stopped. He was still for a moment, very still.

A surge rose up from his core, and he swiped everything off the nearby counter, sending china cups and dishes shattering across the marble floor. He swiped the other way, and the silverware flew at the wall, bouncing off and scattering across the kitchen. Then, he lifted his knee and sent the heel of his dress shoe into the glass door of the oven, leaving a giant splintering hole, before throwing himself onto the kitchen island. His face hidden in his arms, his breath wracked his entire body. His hands closed into fists.

There was nothing he could do. Loki and Eros were gone. He didn't try hard enough. They probably even thought he had planned it that way. Neither of them had even believed he had been working on a plan- a pathetic, *worthless* plan.

He destroyed everything he touched.

He would inevitably destroy that kid.

Not a kid. A god.

And as always, Thanatos would do what he had to do and be the carnivorous monster the universe needed him to be. That's all that he was capable of being, even when he tried to do the right thing.

With great effort, he brought himself upright. His body had wanted to just lie there 'till the world ended, but his mind told him a stiff drink would fix that. He pushed through the double doors into the dining hall, and he cut down the passageway to the study where his scotch awaited him.

Painting or playing his violin would make him feel better, but he didn't want to feel better. He wanted his grief to poison him.

***

Eros wanted his grief to fuel him into a fury of molten heat and effulgent light, but instead he slipped down the stairs in quiet rage.

He wanted to see some physical sign of his distress in himself, but his fingers didn't even quiver. He was still. The fire was hiding inside, and he felt betrayed by this. He was taking action to no longer keep himself locked away, yet locked away he remained.

He was going to let Loki, and that kid, and himself down- everyone down. Because, he didn't have what it took to rise up.

Eros couldn't bring forth the emotion he felt searing inside. He'd do what he always did. He'd give the Fates what they wanted, and then crawl away to some party to lick his wounds, and to fuck the feelings away.

When he stepped through the door of the town home, he didn't step out into the street but back into the Fates' realm.

Loki was still unconscious in the dust, but he was starting to stir, and the Fates stood around him.

Eros took the bowl out from under his arm. He

walked forward, screaming inside, as he set the bowl in the dust and stepped back.

The Fates let out a small gasp, which resulted in Eros letting out a light chuckle. It was just a bowl, a foul punch bowl. He wasn't afraid of it anymore. There were far more real and terrifying things to fear, like losing a lover or a son, losing sense of self, or losing one's mind.

After a moment, the Fates all grinned simultaneously. Their foul punch bowl had returned, and they could keep it locked away, never again to be found.

Atropos made a small move forward and gave Loki's reddish-blond strand of hair to Eros.

"I'd check to see if it's the real thing," Eros said, pocketing the strand. "Con artists are quite good at making fakes now-a-days, replicas that fool even the best authenticators. Loki and I had no way to really verify it."

The Fates all exchanged a glance with their empty eyes, and in that moment, Eros strode to Loki and tried to lift the giant's arm up around his shoulders. He let out a small *oomph* as he failed to do this. The giant was far too heavy for him to even partially lift.

"You bleeding giant! Wake up! I can't lift you!" He groaned as he attempted to hoist him up again, but fell hard into the dirt.

The Fates began to sing their dreary, haunting tune to the bowl. Eros looked over at them with panic in his eyes as the bowl began to glow, and tendrils of mist began to slip over the edge.

Now was the time to act, but he couldn't leave without Loki, and the Fates could use that bowl to make room in Tartarus for both of them if they had a mind to, or better yet, delete them both from existence.

His heart began to race.

He could slap Loki to wake him up, but he was sure that would do more damage to his own hand than the trickster's iron jaw. So he did the only thing he could think to do.

He kissed him.

And he breathed pink smoke into Loki's mouth and filled his lungs with the burning desire to wake up.

Gasping in twisting, rose-colored starlight, Loki let out a small cough and a wheeze as his eyelids shot open. For a moment, he still saw a spinning rosette nebula before him, but then the glitter and clouds evaporated and only Eros remained.

"Loki, I need you to stand," Eros said in desperation.

Loki nodded, still unsure of his surroundings, but trusting Eros. He tried to make sense of his limbs and get them under him to stand. He was as shaky as a newborn foal with eight different legs to figure out.

Eros's hands were on the giant, trying to help, but his eyes were now fixed on the Fates, who had no idea they were being filled with desire. Eros directed all of his concentration, his will, his *desire*, on them. The gray wisps of smoke trailing from the bowl's center now had shocks of electric pink splintering through them.

Desire is a sneaky thing. It works its way into your heart and brain, until suddenly, it consumes your entire being... like a parasite.

And the three sisters were filled with a *desire* to change Fate, to change their plan, to let Eros and Loki leave unharmed with the bowl, and to blow themselves up with nebulous light. They *desired* to render themselves useless for a short time thereafter and to never again use their powers, their twisting yarn, to pull the strings of either of them.

That was the Fate they *desired* the bowl to manifest.

When it comes to magick, intent is everything.

The smoke from the bowl became a looming, glowing, rose-colored cloud of electric storm and stardust. It was twisting and roaring like a hurricane, and then the tempest exploded, knocking the already unsteady giant to the ground and sending the Fates hurtling towards the crumbling horizon.

But, Eros stood his ground. Then, he put one foot after the other as he pushed into the tumultuous storm, Desire and Fate battling like Titans for dominance. He was whipped with dust and pebbles as sharp as blades from the gale's voracity.

Eros reached his arms out against the savage wind and pulled the bowl from the epicenter of the clouds. The bowl was heavy with magick, its gravity intensified.

With the storm still circling, he put a hand on Loki's shoulder and using his own power, his own will, he desired them both *home*.

***

It took Loki a minute to process where he was and what had happened. He removed the damp towel Eros had placed on his forehead, and he sat up slowly on the sofa.

Eros was smoking on the sofa opposite him. Between them, on the coffee table, was the Bowl of Fate. It was cold and lifeless once again, only hinting to its vibrant past, with the same wistful whisper as a fossil.

"What the bloody hell happened?" Loki slurred.

"In short," Eros ashed his cigarette in the tray, "you and I will never be going to Tartarus."

Loki pulled his brows together, remembering. "You *gave* them the Bowl of Fate?"

Eros crossed his legs and said defensively, "Yeah, but I got it back."

"No… that was brilliant!"

Eros flushed, "Well, it was easy to make them desire to leave us alone."

"Yes, but now it's *fated* that they do. I never thought of you as a trickster." Loki leaned forward, groaning from the weight he endured, and took Eros's cigarette to take a few inhales himself.

Eros chuckled, "Apollo would disagree with that."

Loki handed him back his cigarette. "Regardless. We won the battle… all thanks to my hoarding of *useless* junk." Loki gave him a coy smile, and Eros squinted his eyes back.

"Oh," Eros recalled, "we did have a visitor while you were unconscious. Thanatos's weapon... His son."

"Say again?" Loki asked in disbelief.

Eros sighed and rubbed his temple, "*The son found his way home... Give to the father of none when you tell him he has a son.* The Fates told me. The boy is Death's son. He caused the hole in Tartarus by escaping, but they let him escape as a message, I suppose."

Loki's face was scrunched with thought. "What the hell is the message, exactly?"

Eros's brows shot up. The answer was obvious to him. Thanatos had been the leader of the whole rebellion against the Fates, despite the flaws in his leadership skills.

"The message was not to fuck with them. If he could have a son and never know of him, if they could manipulate the situation so that Thanatos is holding his *very own son* prisoner in his basement, and the only reason Thanatos has him now is because the Fates allowed it and they could easily take the boy away again- That's an evident *don't fuck with us* maneuver. It's a show to illustrate just how rigged the whole bleeding system really is."

The giant was quiet for a long minute, his eyes distant and pondering. His fingers were laced together but were wriggling around nervously.

He finally brought his eyes back to Eros. "This is going to kill him," he said.

Eros gave a small sympathetic nod, and Loki abruptly stood, again groaning at the strain in his joints.

"Where are you going?" Eros asked. They had so much to talk through, so much to understand and unpack after this ordeal, and yet, Loki was walking out of the room.

"To fulfill the prophecy." Loki turned back to face him, "I can't let him go a second longer than need be without knowing the truth."

Eros hopped to his feet, offering, "I'll go with you."

"No." Loki held up a hand, "It's best I go alone. You should rest."

"I'm fine. You're the one who looks like hammered hell."

Loki's eyes glinted, "Funny." He trudged his way up the stairs, and upon entering the office, his gaze immediately fell upon the red bottle. It had a magnetism, an ominous one, that Loki was entirely bitter to.

He snatched it up as if it was a lurking intruder and held it up to his eye level to give it a good stare-down. He still didn't know what the bottle was, but if it was some device the Fates concocted, it was as dangerous as that bowl was.

With the bottle held tight in his fist, he trotted down the stairs, doing his best to ignore the pain shooting up his back.

Eros waited, arms folded, for him at the foot of the stairs. "Your desire to help your friend is a noble one, but I still think we have *a lot* to go through before you go. He told me things that-"

"We will have all the time in the world to talk when

I get back. He needs to know before he does something he can't take back."

"I think it's too late for that."

Loki made a mess of facial expressions while mentally assembling his rebuttal, "...Before he does anything *else* he can't take back."

Eros nodded.

"I'll be back before you know it, and we will talk about everything, and we'll drink tea and brandy. We'll get wildly pissed and nearly forget this whole thing ever happened."

"I don't want to forget," Eros said.

"I said *nearly* forget not *completely* forget."

They looked at each other for a moment, and Loki grabbed Eros by the back of the neck and sweetly kissed his forehead. "Be back in a jiffy."

Loki then disappeared.

Eros felt the silence creep into his being. He remembered being alone, acutely alone, in the Red Room. He remembered why he hated being alone.

***

Loki had appeared at Death's door. It was massive and black. The mansion to which it opened expanded past the limits of imagination. It was unknowingly immense in stature and in presence.

Loki took hold of the lionhead knocker and rapped

three times.

A drunk and disheveled Thanatos opened the door. He took one look at Loki and walked away, leaving the door open.

He still had a glass of scotch in hand, and he took a sip before asking, "Why are you here? Shouldn't you be in Tartarus?"

Loki cautiously approached him, "Eros saved me from the Underworld in true Greek fashion."

Thanatos snorted, "Greek fashion. If that was the case, he would have glanced back, and you wouldn't be here at all… except Tartarus and the Underworld are two completely different places, Loki. You should know that."

Loki pressed his lips together then said, "Yes, well... I'm happy to see you too."

Death waved away the conversation with the flick of his wrist and took another burning gulp of scotch.

Loki stepped across the hall, moving closer to Death. "Thanatos, you sold us out to the Fates."

"Yes… I did."

"And you knew what they were going to do? And you did it anyway?"

"Yes. I did."

"Then why did you do it? Even if you *had* a plan to *save* us, you *still*-"

"And the plan was a failure. It was a wing and a prayer at best." The self-deprecating tones in Thanatos's voice panged at Loki's heart.

"Listen," Loki said, "that's- that's not why I'm here. I need to tell you-"

"To tell me what?" Thanatos turned. He slammed his glass down on a hall table and said, "If you aren't here to chastise me for my careless actions, my self-serving motives, and my complete lack of empathy, then why the fuck are you here? Any other reason you might have to entertain my presence is absurd. But, you've always been absurd, haven't you? People have kicked you like a dog all of your existence, and you just keep coming back for more! How are Thor and Odin by the way? Have you told them about Eros yet, or are you afraid to? I would be."

Thanatos began to chuckle quietly as he picked his drink back up and finished it off.

In the spot where Thanatos's drink had previously sat, Loki slammed down the red bottle. "That's for you. It's a *gift*," Loki snarled the last word. In the land of gods and spirits, you never can refuse a gift. "...from the Fates."

Loki turned to walk out of the mansion, while Thanatos stared blankly at the ruby-red perfume bottle.

Loki stopped in the doorway, "Oh, and by the way," he turned back to face his friend, "...that boy you've been torturing in your basement... He's your son."

Thanatos's expression remained the same, still and void, as Loki stormed from Death's mansion, slamming the door behind him.

Death left the bottle where it was, and after a time had passed of him staring at the door, he walked back towards the kitchen.

There, in the kitchen, was the white wooden door which opened to the basement. Under the ornate, tarnished door knob, was the tarnished, little skeleton key. It was in the locked position, holding inside, behind thick walls of magick, a new god, a strange boy, his *son*.

His hand hovered over the key, his fingers trembled, the drink ran down his veins to his feet, leaving behind a glorious hangover headache.

The Fates had sent him. The Fates had made them cross paths and had put him in the basement. In true Greek fashion, they had designed this tragedy.

But to blame the Fates was easy, so he did the hard thing, the thing he always did.

He blamed himself.

He killed everything he touched. He was Death. This was his role in the universe, to be the devourer of all things, and he accepted his fate.

His fingers fell away from the key, and he slipped away from the door.

***

The Fates floated in the darkness at the very edge of the expanse of the Cosmos. Drifting in endless space, their bodies had no form, no mass. They were three consciousnesses syncing as one, looking at the distant glittering of stars in the way only bodiless creatures can *look* and *see*, and they spoke to each other in that same way.

"*I do love it when the tapestry we weave pulls through.*"

"*The mistakes only add to the beauty, I believe. Don't you?*"

"*But it is incomplete, sister-children of mine.*"

"*Ends remain untied, and finishing touches must be applied.*"

"*But, until then, can we not marvel and appreciate the hard work is done?*"

"*And, remember, as we float, the end has already begun.*"

"*Yes, my dears. All that's left to do is to drift and to wait…*"

The End

Acknowledgements

Here are all the people I need to thank for their endless support. Special thanks goes to Elizabeth Bickel, Kali McNeill, Christine Monroe, Elise Risk, and Sarah Ryan for their help with editing. Thank you Mom and Dad, Devin and Maxwell Holden, Michelle Cohen and D.J. Wood, Adam and Andrea Long, Nate Massery, Steven McNeill, Paul Peters, and Josh Spellman for all of your support.

Thank you all.

About The Author

Kaylin R. Boyd, is a fantasy author. She was born in the Midwest, and raised on a strict diet of daydreams, myth, and magic. She has published an illustrated book of prose, The Mountain, and Tell City is her debut novel. The Netherworlds: Cure of Fate is the first book of a planned series.

Ingram Content Group UK Ltd.
Milton Keynes UK
UKHW011934300623
424349UK00004B/199

9 798988 071617